Lies

Warrior Stone Book 3

R B Harkess

Published by Metaphoric Media,
Broxbourne, UK
www.metaphoric-media.co.uk

ISBN 978-1976047978

For my Mum, who is good at finding
speling mistaks

1

When I die.

Hand written, in bold capitals, on the envelope.

Claire Stone, Year 10 student and Underland Warrior, stared at the hateful thing. It lay on her father's desk, slightly askew. Her cheek tickled and she absently brushed aside the tear before it could drop onto the paper.

She had to look inside, but it felt so wrong. This wasn't for her, it was for her mother. Nor was her father dead. Both her parents were in hospital, locked in magical sleep. Her face scrunched up again and more tears came. There hadn't been a choice. It had been the only thing she could do, for their protection and hers.

She gently poked the envelope with a finger, straightening it. It had been two days since Stuart brought her home. The battle with the Morph Lord had hurt her in ways she didn't yet understand, and she had been unable to summon or control enough magic to jump herself out of Underland. A tiny smile crept through the tears. Stuart - boyfriend, fellow Warrior, traitor, and brother in arms - had remembered her house well enough to jump them back without help.

And he was due at the house to take her back to the hospital in... She looked up at the pocket watch that hung from a stand in the centre of the desk, a prize or a present. Her dad was oddly proud of it. It had stopped, and a cold sickness weighed her down. There were so many stories of watches stopping when their owner died.

The door-bell rang and she flinched. When she opened the front door, Stuart held out a crash helmet.

"Ready?"

Claire shook her head and opened the door wider. Stuart took the hint and stepped inside. "What's up?" he asked, then raised his eyebrows when she closed the door. Claire said nothing, and jerked her head to say he should follow as she trekked back to the tiny, messy room her father used as his man-cave. Claire pointed at the desk. Stuart leaned forward to look.

"Oh."

"Should I open it?"

"And you're asking me because...?"

Claire held out her hand for him to shake, and saw his face fall. Not much, but enough to notice. He reached out his hand and took hers, and they both twitched at the faint tingle of magic, heavily suppressed in their own world — the Real — but still there.

"Because you have to be honest with me," she replied. Tolks wove the spell between them weeks ago. Stuart had betrayed her, but claimed he hadn't known how far things would go before he made the agreement. When he offered to help, part of her wanted to rip out his throat and part desperately wanted his calm strength. The spell kept him honest, but she still couldn't find it in her to fully trust him. Yet. It pained her to see that realisation on his face.

"Yes, you should open it. There may be stuff in there you don't want to see, but things are still happening around you that need sorting. Have you told his work yet?"

Claire shook her head. Stuart lifted the envelope and handed it to her. For an angry instant she resented him for touching it, and making her touch it. She slipped a finger under the loose edge of the flap and tore it open

My Darling Alice
    I know you know, but I have to say it because if you are reading

this I probably can't say it again. I love you, and I love Claire, more than I love life itself and I shall miss you both for eternity.

My will is in the bottom drawer of my desk, where the files live. In the same envelope is a memory stick with all my accounts and passwords on it. Its encrypted, and the password is the name of the hotel we went to on that weekend your parents thought you were sleeping over at Helen's. You may need to get Claire to help you with that.

A snuffly chuckle burst out of Claire, and she scrubbed her sleeve under her nose. So true. Her mother was a determined and extravagant technophobe. The next paragraph gave details of who to contact at his work, then went onto more personal thoughts that Claire didn't feel comfortable reading. She took out her phone, copied the email address of her father's boss, then put the letter back into the envelope.

"Hard?" asked Stuart. Claire nodded and wiped her nose again, this time on a tissue. "You still want to go to the hospital?"

Claire nodded. "I need to send an email first."

Stuart followed her up to her bedroom. "Cleaner not come in this week?"

Claire winced and wished she had asked him to wait downstairs. Her mattress was on the floor, slashed and eviscerated. Stuffing from pillows and her quilt covered the room like snow and her most of her clothes had been ripped from drawers and closets and thrown around the room.

"Have you had a buglary?"

Claire smiled, loving the way his accent twisted the occasional word. "No. My parents did this, I think. Well, the Morphs inside them, anyway. They must have been looking for something."

The computer desk was on its side, but the laptop looked undamaged and booted when she prodded the appropriate button.

Surprisingly, the wifi and broadband were still up too. She opened an app to send an email to her father's boss.

"You know you can't stay here, don't you?"

Claire swivelled round in her chair and glared at Stuart, who had perched on the base of her ruined bed.

"Why not?"

"Come on, Claire. I know you're all independent and look after yourself. You wouldn't be a Warrior if you couldn't. But the system will catch up with you if you try to go it alone here. There must be some family you can call?"

"I'll be fine."

"Trust me, you do not want the social sticking their noses in."

Claire fumed, knowing he was right but hating the thought of bringing somebody else into the mess that was her life right now.

"How, Stuart? How do I explain I've put my parents in to a magically induced sleep because monsters from another world infested them and tried to capture me because I messed up their Overlord's plan to take over yet another world? Social services? I'm more worried about being sectioned. How much good would I be to them on some loony ward pumped so full of stay-calm and don't-care that I can't take myself to the toilet." She was shouting now, but couldn't stop herself. In fact, it felt good.

Stuart took two long steps then sank to his knees next to her and put his hands firmly on her shoulders. "Precisely, and if the sosh get you, that could be exactly what happens. There must be someone in your family you trust? Or you can work around?"

Stuart's hands were warm and strong on her shoulders, and part of her wished he would lean closer and wrap his arms around her. Nobody had held her, hugged her, for days. But she had things to do, and Stuart earned himself an instant credit for lifting his hands as soon as she tensed her shoulders. She turned back to the keyboard and finished the email, but in the back of her mind Stuart's last words whispered to her over and over, making her feel ugly and soiled. Who in her family could she most easily manipulate?

2

"Do you not want me to hang around for company?" Stuart's eyes darted around the hospital room and he shifted his weight between his feet.

Claire shook her head and settled in the only chair, next to her mother's bed. "I'm going to have enough fun explaining what I can to Nana. Throwing a boyfriend into the mix so soon would probably overload her."

They had already visited her father. He was down to a single drip in his arm and a monitor on his finger. The tube up his nose made Claire feel sick every time she saw it. Other than that, he looked well; his skin wasn't sallow and his lips were pink and not pinched.

Her mother was much the same, except for the dressing on her wrist. Claire couldn't look at it. It was she who had smashed her mother's arm against the car door, trying to pull free of her, and even though it wasn't her mother controlling her body at the time, Claire's gut still twisted with guilt when she saw it.

"Is this woman a nun or something?"

Claire managed a smile she didn't really feel. "You never met my mum, did you? She's a bit, well, scatty. It runs in her side of the family, so Nana's not much better."

"Ah, so it's going to overcome you in a few years, and you'll turn into a cat lady?"

Claire snorted. "Right. Anyway, she said she'd get here about now, so..."

"So you want me to bugger off? I'm just a taxi to you, aren't I?" But he was grinning as he picked up the spare helmet he had loaned her. "Do you want me to come by later?"

Claire shook her head. "I'll text you, or something. Might be a day or two. Need to find out how things are going to work out."

"There's that thing with the Council tomorrow. Can you jump in on your own?"

Claire framed her thoughts around the jump, that subtle twist of reality with a dash of magic that would turn her out of this world and into Underland. Red hot needles stabbed into the backs of her eyes.

Stuart must have seen the pain on her face and winced. "I'm guessing that's a no. Call me. We can sort something. I don't think Tolks wants you to miss it."

Claire nodded, and before she could lean away Stuart bent down and kissed her cheek. "Be careful."

Claire frowned at him for stealing the kiss, but then the corner of her mouth hitched up. He gave her a wide grin before striding out of the ward like he was seven feet tall.

Shaking her head, Claire turned back to her mother and took her good hand. Knowing that something else was living in her mother's body tormented her, but she couldn't convince her heart that the person lying in front of her wasn't the same one who had given birth to her and looked after her for fifteen years. She felt her teeth grind as her jaw clenched. She would find a way to undo this, no matter what the Council said. If it could be done, it could be undone.

A small hand touched her lightly on the shoulder. Claire flinched and her head twisted around, expecting a nurse to ask her to move out of the way, but she saw a dandelion explosion of white hair. Then, not quite sure how she got there, she was standing in front of Nana May, holding on to her as if she was drowning, feeling arms and bags wrapping around her as she rained tears and sobs onto the little woman's shoulder.

"Perhaps I should put these down before we fall over and break something?" said Nana May. Her voice was soft and light and carried a permanent hint of uncertainty. Claire took a reluctant step back. Nana May was a couple of inches shorter than her, slight of build, and had no discernible dress sense, as proven by the purple herringbone coat and the teal green jogging bottoms and sweat shirt. She placed a carrier bag on the end of the bed, then let her oversize canvas handbag - more the size of a sack - slide off her shoulder to join it. Claire stole a chair from beside another bed and put it close to her own. Nana May started digging out bags of grapes and apples, and looked helplessly around for somewhere to put them. Claire took her hand and pulled her gently to the seat.

"You know she's asleep, don't you?"

"Well, I know what you told me on the phone, but that didn't seem to make much sense, so I brought something anyway. Is there a doctor to speak to?"

Claire turned her head, looking for a nurse, but the ward seemed deserted. There were only four beds in the room, and only one more of those had an occupant.

"I could maybe find one, but I don't think they can tell you more than I already know." Claire tried to keep her face from showing that she knew a damned sight more than the doctors, and that if she told Nana May what was really going on, she would never believe her. "There was a car accident. Mum and Dad were asleep when the ambulance got there. Not a coma, or anything. Just asleep."

"Well that doesn't seem right. When did all this happen?"

"About ten days ago."

"Ten days? And nobody thought to call me? What about your father's parents? Have you told them?"

"They're dead, Nana May. You went to his mum's funeral three years ago, before we got the new house?"

Nana May frowned then shrugged. "If you say so, dear. Didn't he have a brother?"

Claire kept her face straight. She didn't like her uncle much, and trusted him less. Since their mother had died, every time he

14

and her father met they seemed to argue, and from what Claire had heard money was always at the bottom of the row.

"I haven't told him yet. I don't think they get on. Look, I'm sorry I didn't tell you sooner. They were just asleep. I thought they would wake up in a day or so."

Nana May patted her hand. "That's all right, Claire. I'm here now."

They took a cab back to Claire's home. While she gathered her things, she kept Nana May away from the wreck of her room by sending her searching for water stopcocks and gas valves, arguing that with nobody living there for a while it would be safer to shut the house down. Claire kept it down to two bags; one bag of clothes, and one of necessities such as laptops, e-reader, hairdryer, and a folder containing maps and documentation she had collected from Underland. They called another cab to leave.

Her grandmother's house was tiny, at least by Claire's standards. A two-up-two-down mid-terraced cottage in a slightly tatty but still civilised estate in North London. As she stood at the doorway to what was obviously Nana May's hobby room, Claire wondered how they would find space for her bags, let alone a bed. She folded her long Warrior's coat into a bundle then put it and the rest of her world under a table bearing a sewing machine and an embroidery frame from which a partly stitched cat stared back at her through one eye.

"What a beautiful pendant," Nana May exclaimed as Claire turned around. "May I see it?"

It took Claire a moment to realise her nan had caught a glimpse of her Kevlar. The amulet protected her from attack, physical or magical, while she was in Underland. It was so much a part of her now that Claire rarely thought of it.

She fought down an instinctive reluctance. From the start, they drummed into her that nothing from Underland got back to The

15

Real. Even though everybody made an exception for their Kevlar, it seemed wrong to let her grandmother touch it. Unable to think of a good reason to say no, she lifted the leather cord over her neck and placed the amulet in her grandmother's outstretched palm.

Nana May ran her thumb softly over the copper windings around the outer armature, tracing around and around, then lifted the pendant closer to her face. Propping her glasses on her forehead, she squinted at the ruby gem in the centre. "What an astonishing stone. You could swear there was something glittering inside. Where on earth did you get it?"

"Accessories R Us," Claire lied, and resisted the urge to snatch the Kevlar back.

"We used to get such lovely things when I was a girl. There were so many hand-made things back in the days of flower power." She handed the Kevlar back to Claire, eyes dreamy and focused on a different time and place. She turned to go back down the stairs, but then looked over her shoulder. "Of course, a lot of it was crap, too."

Underkin. On the two top tables were Sitharii and, surprisingly, Angels. The Angels were so like humans Claire found them were creepy, but the Sitharii - Underland's bureaucrats - were tall, thin and angular, with skin that looked deathly grey and an attitude to match. On either side sat representatives of the Hrund, blocky people renowned for strength and calmness, and the Grenlix.

Tolks and Jack were already sitting on the bench, and Claire couldn't shake the feeling they were all on trial. Tolks, also a Grenlik, was a good friend. Rarely over a metre and a half tall, Grenlix were one of the races who could make magic work in Underland. Anybody could use a magically powered device, so long as it had Grenlik-engineered controls, but Grenlix could manipulate magic directly. Claire was not an expert on Grenlik body language but she knew the basics, and the two Grenlix at the table were acting like a divorced couple arguing over maintenance.

Jack's exact status was uncertain. Once a friend, then wrongly promoted to boyfriend, it was debatable now if there was anything left between him and Clare.

"Is it appropriate that these humans appear armed?"

The room fell silent and all turned to look at the Angel representative. Rather than embarrassment, the Angel seemed to relish the attention and leaned back in his chair. Claire and Stuart came to a halt behind the bench. Tolks didn't move, but Jack flicked a look over his shoulder. The Sitharii with the most paperwork shuffled it noisily.

"Please sit, Junior Observer Stone."

"Beg pardon?" said Claire, calmly, but Stuart didn't seem in the mood for politics.

"That's Warrior Stone to you," Stuart rumbled. Claire put her hand on his arm to shut him up, and felt it tremble with anger.

"But the recorded rank—"

"Was a setup by Aslnaff, who this Warrior saved your sorry arses from when he tried to sell you out the Beneath." Claire spoke for herself this time, and tried not to wince at her mangled grammar.

The Sitharii was rapping his knuckled on the table. "We will have order."

"The Grenlik council supports the statements by Warriors Grey and Stone. Miss Stone's correct rank should read "Warrior"."

Claire looked at the Grenlik table, surprised until she recognised the councillor as being the one who had helped her look after Tolks when the Morph Lord injured him. She nodded an acknowledgement, but noted that the other Grenlik scowled.

"As do the Hrund."

Now that was a surprise. The Hrund rarely came down on anybody's side. The Sitharii chairperson pinched his lips into a sour moue.

"The point is acceded. For the time being, Miss Stone is returned to the status of Warrior. Now, if we can get down to the business of this meeting?"

"Which is?" Claire asked.

"Obviously, the recent unpleasantness in the office of former Administrator Aslnaff."

Claire flipped her long coat aside and sat on the bench. "No."

The Sitharii spluttered while the other members of the council muttered amongst themselves. It was the Angel who raised his voice over the hubbub.

"You brought forces to bear against the Morph Lord that we do not understand."

"And because of what Aslnaff was doing, my mother and father have been taken over by Morphs. Not simply infected, but actually taken over."

"Nobody in Underland asked you to involve yourself in this matter."

"If Warrior Stone had not had the presence of mind to get involved, you would all currently be under the dominion of a

Morph Lord," shouted Tolks, jumping to his feet.

"This is plainly a bulk magic situation and thus comes under the Sitharii."

"Objection! This is unknown magic and must be investigated by the Grenlik academy before it is assigned—"

"The Coalition of Angel Domains cannot support any unilateral investigation—"

Claire watched the meeting dissolve into bickering and her heart fell. How stupid was she? She had only saved their pathetic world for them. Expecting a thank you at the very least, or better still some serious help sorting out her parents, was obviously naive and optimistic. She stood up, and had already taken the first step to walk out of the room when anger lit up her mind. She turned back. This was not how it was going to be. Drawing in a little magic, she clapped her hands.

The resulting crack made everybody in the room flinch. Claire marched forward until she was in the midst of the tables, then turned in a half circle, glaring at each member in turn.

"This is how it works. The Morphs hurt my parents, and it's your fault. You either decide to help me find a way to fix them, or I walk. If you want any help from me, you must help me first. It's as simple as that." She looked around the table again.

"You owe me."

Her exit was less dramatic than she had hoped. As she swept towards the doors there was nobody to open them for her, and because they opened inwards she had to stop and fiddle with them. She wasn't trying to be a diva, but during the meeting she realised the only way to get anything out of these people was to make sure she had something that they wanted. And to make it abundantly clear it was her they had to negotiate with.

Grudgingly, they had agreed to help her find a way to bring back her parents, and she agreed to work with them to discover what the hell it was she had used to defeat the Morph Lord - but only when she had seen them acting in good faith.

Now she strode along the corridor and back towards the stairs. The doors bumped closed behind her and several sets of footsteps hurried to catch up. She strode on, the heels of her boots thudding against the marble floor. She wasn't ready to talk.

As Claire took the first step down the stairs her knee gave way. Her balance tipped forward, her body twisting around and away from the handrail. There was nothing for her to grab, and nothing in her future but pain.

The air thickened before her, soft and insubstantial, but enough to slow her down. A hand grabbed her coat and she saw Stuart holding her with one hand and the rail with the other. Behind him Tolks held his hands as though he was cupping something in them. Stressed stitches creaked as the seams of her coat tightened under her arms, and everything stopped.

"Watch where you're going, girl." Stuart growled, the strain on his face letting her know he was not comfortable with her weight on his arm. She shuffled to her feet and touched his hand to tell him he could let go.

"You may not be so recovered from your battle as you think," suggested Tolks, his skin looking greyer than normal.

"I'm OK," said Claire, brushing down her coat. "I just—" She just what? She discreetly put her weight on the treacherous knee, but it was solid and strong. "Suppose I must have tripped."

Had she stumbled, or had there been a delicate shove in the back of her knee? She pushed the thought aside. There had been nobody near her but her friends. She was being paranoid.

They stopped at a squash stand on the south bank. Stuart took a sip from the creamy drink, sighed happily, then broke the silence.

"Cheesus, girl, but you're impressive." He slurped his squash again. "And scary, too. Never would have been able to face down the Council with that much style. I get gobby."

"Indeed," said Tolks. "The game you played was one of considerable risk, but executed most skilfully. Was it your intention that events played out as they did, or did you extemporise as opportunity arose?"

Claire had never learned to accept compliments, and felt blood heat her cheeks. "Both. But I thought if the Council wouldn't help, then we could go to your people independently. I'm really not interested in the SFU or the Council any more. I don't owe them anything."

She turned to Jack, who had not spoken a word. He still wore a dressing on his head and his left arm in a sling from where a Morph threw him across the room during the battle in Aslnaff's office. "Thank you for coming."

He shrugged, then winced. "It was important." His eyes dropped away from her face and he stared at the floor. "I don't know if I can do it again, though."

Tears pricked in the corners of Claire's eyes. Their brief relationship had never been real, at least not to her, and now she heard in his voice that Jack had finally accepted the situation too.

It would have been nice to stay friends, but today was the day it ended. She stepped forward and, very carefully, put her arms around him and shared a last hug. When she let go he gave an encompassing wave then walked off along the embankment. Ten steps later he disappeared.

"I'd best be going too," said Claire. "I get tired quick."

"Want me to jump you home?" Stuart asked.

Claire didn't answer immediately, but reached out to touch the magic that would twist space and time to get her back to where she had started from. The spell she had used in the meeting hadn't hurt, but jumping was different. It was so commonplace, it barely counted as magic at all. She braced against the pain, but though her brain felt tender, it was manageable. "No, I'll try it myself. Can you remember the room?"

Stuart nodded. Jumping was all about having a firm image in the mind of where you were going. It wasn't possible to jump somewhere you hadn't been, except by accident. Besides, he had to come with her, or Nana May would wonder where he had gone.

Claire gave Tolks a brief hug, stepped back, and jumped out before he could complain.

The toilet flushed and Claire realised she had made a huge mistake. Still off balance from the jump, she stumbled to the doorway. She hadn't heard Nana May come up stairs while she and Stuart had been chatting, and now he wasn't here and they were wearing different clothes. As her mind struggled to invent a feasible lie, Stuart jumped in behind her at the moment the toilet door opened.

"Well, don't you look different." Nana May pulled up short in the doorway, looking surprised and confused.

"What do you think?" said Claire as soon as her nana appeared. "Costumes, for a science fiction convention." She held her breath as the surprise on Nana May's face turned to curiosity. "We've been working on them for a couple of months." A swirl of air on the back of her neck told her Stuart was standing behind her.

"Characters from a cartoon," he added, and Claire wished he would keep his mouth shut. What if Nana asked which cartoon?

"Well, it's very clever. I like your gun."

Claire winced inwardly. Things were going from bad to worse. She had forgotten she still carried a weapon, and that her goggles hung around her neck.

"May I see it?" Her grandmother was holding out her hand. Reluctantly, Claire unclipped it from the holster and handed it over, grip first.

"My, it's heavy for a toy, isn't it," said Nana May, looking first at the left side, then the pointy end, then the right. "Still, it does make it feel real." She held it a moment longer, tracing lines with a finger until she touched the charge indicator, then she handed it back. "I think it's nice you can find things to distract you. Your mum and dad wouldn't want you moping about all the time." She squeezed past them on the narrow landing and went downstairs.

"What was all that about?" Stuart muttered in her ear.

Claire shrugged. She was happy she had been able to pass things off with such a tiny lie. Everything in her life was lies, and she hated the person they were making her become. Still, there was something about the encounter that wasn't right.

She waited until Stuart jumped back in to stow his gear, then began to change out of her uniform. As she took off her coat something stiff poked into her arm and she remembered the letter she had stuffed into a pocket. She drew it out, dropped her coat onto the air bed, then sat on the chair at her grandmother's work table and smoothed the envelope flat. The flap was tucked in not glued or sealed. She flicked it open and took out the single page within.

"Warrior Stone,

It has come to our attention that you are, or may be, currently engaged in manipulating levels of magical energy for which you have no training. Whilst we acknowledge and admire your demonstrated abilities to date, we would like to offer you any assistance we may. Please call on us at any time, office hours.

Ostrenalia"

And at the top of the page was an address, and a crest Claire took several moments to recognise. Her mouth made a wide "O". The Guild of Industrial Magic, the exclusive domain of the Sitharii women who managed all the bulk transfer of magical energy, had just approached her. She folded the letter, tucked it and the envelope into one of her bags, and finished changing while she tried to decide if the offer was a good thing, or a trap.

into a wall underneath a stone staircase, which Claire found odd. A whisper of magic from Ostrenalia tickled Claire's skin and the door swung open. It was two inches thick, steel, and studded along the edge with inch-wide bolts. Behind, a flight of stone steps led beneath the house.

"Containment," Ostrenalia explained. "These are laboratories, and we wouldn't want anything blowing the street up." She gave a tinkling laugh, as if it was some in-joke she had shared with an outsider. Claire nodded, trying not to frown, and followed the Sitharii down the stairs.

At the bottom, a narrow hall went on for about thirty paces, with two doors on each side. Along the ceiling, crystals formed a mesh that glittered like metal. Oddly, the doors opened out of the rooms, not into them. Ostrenalia pointed up. "Do you like our safety net?"

"Very pretty, but what—?"

"If there is loss of containment too severe for the rooms to handle, the door will blow open and release the energy into this space, where it is absorbed by the crystals. Once there, it can be dissipated harmlessly back into the background field."

Claire nodded, listening but busy making her own experiment as she reached out into surprisingly rich magical field. Perhaps more was leaking out here than Ostrenalia wanted to admit. The Sitharii gestured to the door on the right, closest to them. "Please."

Claire stepped into the room, expecting similarities to Tolks' workshop. It looked more like a library, or a study. Bookshelves around the walls, an elegant light fitting and matching wall sconces, comfortable, deep-piled carpet, and a roll-front writing desk. A meter-long crystal dominated one side of the room, supported by a beautiful wrought iron frame. Ostrenalia hurried past her to the desk, where she flipped a book closed. Claire got an impression of hand written script, and guessed it was a day book or diary.

"Isn't it beautiful," said Ostrenalia gazing at the crystal.

"Like the ones in Ealing, but a much more sensible size." Those were twenty feel tall and a hundred yards long, and sitting on top of one as a recharged flooded into it was not an experience she wanted to repeat.

"You have seen inside the western storage unit? When?"

Claire bit her tongue and called herself every kind of idiot. "I'm probably already in enough trouble for mentioning I went there."

Ostrenalia chuckled. "You may be right, Miss Stone. What a warehouse of surprises you are. Can you feel the crystal? Be careful. Do not attempt to pass beyond the surface. Not yet."

Claire opened her mind to the magic and gasped. The aura radiating from the crystal was as different from the background field as kitchen ice was to a glacier. "I see the aura."

"Good. What colour is it?"

"It's... it's every colour. It keeps shifting, up and down the spectrum. It's like a kaleidoscope" The aura mesmerised her, pulling at her with feathery grips of steel. Claire fought to hold herself back though every thread of her ached to sink into the magical field.

"Come away from it, now, Miss Stone. Close your mind to it. I understand it is difficult, but..."

Claire shook her head and turned away, moving her eyes to Ostrenalia. The Sitharii looked shocked, only for a moment, then her face arranged itself back into passive benevolence.

"You are very capable, Miss Stone. I admit we had our doubts, and wondered if you were in fact a conduit through which others would act. Others, even some of my weaker sisters, have needed assistance to turn away from a Source. I think we may be able to teach each other a great deal."

Claire looked at the clock on the wall. More time had passed than she could account for. She must have been looking into the crystal for a while. She needed to get on with her day. "I don't mean to be rude, but——"

"The world moves on. Of course, Miss Stone. Before you go, I have a gift for you." Ostrenalia turned to her desk and opened a small drawer. From it she took a crystal. As far as Claire could see it was identical to the one Ostrenalia wore at her neck. She dangled it in the air, holding it by a golden ring looped through a setting at one end of the crystal. Claire held her hand out, and felt an unexpected weight as the gem dropped into her palm.

"These serve a similar purpose for us as your personal protection amulet. One may use them as a place to safely contain minor... shall we say "accidents"? I would like you to have this one. If you feel we can be of help to you, please come back and I will be happy to show you how to use it."

6

Claire let herself back into Tolks' shop, secured all the bolts, then made her way across to the workshop door. She tapped politely before entering.

The workshop had space for six to work at high benches. Four of the positions were empty, only the outlines of tools on pegboards showing what they had once been. Claire had her own bench, right next to Tolks' and close to the small stove that never went out.

"You timing is fortuitous," said Tolks, never one for idle greetings.

"Why?"

"Do you feel up to meeting with some of the Grenlik Academy? I have been passed a message that they would be pleased to see you at any time you find convenient."

Claire hitched herself onto her stool. So many offers so close together. "I wasn't expecting anything so soon. Are they for real?"

"If you mean are they genuine in their interest in helping you with your dilemma, I would have to say I expect the level of commitment will vary, but on the whole, yes. I suspect that some pressure has been applied."

"Because they want whatever I used?"

"Exactly." Tolks considered his next words carefully. "Of course, I do not need to say that it may be wise not to discuss your ability for a time."

"With who?"

"Anybody."

"Oh." Claire shuffled on her stool. She was staring at the teeth of a gift horse. Somebody wanted to talk to her about her parents, and she was wasting time. "Why not. Let's go."

Tolks raised a hand and stopped her sliding from her stool. "I believe we can travel in some comfort, if you will allow me a moment." He reached into a pocket and pulled out an Underland phone, into which he spoke for a few seconds. Claire could read Grenlik better than she spoke it, but Tolks muttered and she only caught a few words. "Transport has been arranged and should be with us within the half hour, giving us time for..." and he waved his beloved coffee pot.

Claire had never been in a carriage in Underland. She rode the Underground, and the occasional omnibus, but most of the time she walked. The Grenlik-sized vehicle that arrived was typical of Underland. It looked like a miniature stage coach for Shetland ponies to pull, but rather than hayburners at the front, a donkey engine provided motive power. The operator sat on a saddle above the engine and controlled it by means of a lever and a tiller. It brought to mind a rotavator her father had rented in a misguided attempt to turn a corner of their garden into a vegetable patch for her mother.

The coach rocked alarmingly from side to side as they climbed inside. Everything was built to Grenlik scale. Claire's head was too close to the roof, and her buttocks too low to the ground so her knees stuck up in the air. As soon as they began to move, she wished she had decided to walk. The carriage bounced erratically on its springs, and she found herself battling between claustrophobia and nausea.

"Which Hive are we going to?"

"None," Tolks answered. "The Academy is not located in a dwelling place. Nobody wanted to offer a home to an institute studying experimental magic." Claire could see their point. "The Academy is to the north."

Claire looked out the window and tried to relate where they were to the Real, but there was nothing she recognised. The traffic got sparser, as did the number of buildings, then they were passing through a huge iron gate and into a walled estate.

The coach stopped and Claire climbed gratefully out. The building was three storeys tall and austere. Most structures in Underland copied classic gothic Victorian twiddles and decorations, but here there was nothing but functional stone. "How far down does it go?"

"This is not a hive, child. Nobody lives here. Why would it be sunk into the earth?"

"I thought — never mind."

Every Grenlik structure Claire had visited had been a Hive, buried deep into the earth for the comfort of its inhabitants. Even the floors above ground looked like tunnels. Tolks could hardly blame her for not knowing this was an exception.

The double doors swung open as they reached them and an official bowed them in to the mausoleum. Claire trudged through dimly lit corridors and up stairs until her legs began to ache and she was considering telling them she was going to sit in the next room they passed and the meeting could come to her. The fight with the Morph Lord, and with Aslnaff, had been as much physical as magical, and she still tired easily.

A final door opened and they were in a cosy, comfortable room with a half-dozen chairs and a small table holding drinks and light refreshments. Claire breathed a sigh of relief. Each step deeper into the building had made her think more she was heading towards another stuffy inquisition.

The three Grenlix already in the room rose when Claire entered.

"Good day, Warrior Stone. It is a pleasure to finally and properly introduce myself to you. I am Grenlik Nagrath. May I present Grenlik Trunz and Yashik, my fellow Chancellors of this establishment."

So now she had a name. Nagrath had helped her with Tolks

after the great battle, and had sat with her while she recovered. He had also been the one Tolks had called to during the fight, to tell him that Claire was *Krezik Zha*, a term she still did not understand.

"You presume much, Nagrath, to share names which are not yours to give." Trunz dropped ungraciously into his chair.

Nagrath motioned that everybody should sit. "Trunz, surely you do not argue that the lady must prove herself? After all that has happened?"

"Which I was not there to witness. And are we to support this absurd claim that she is *Krezik Zha*?"

"She used magic as recently as yesterday. I bear witness," said Nagrath. His voice was calm, but there was a subtle challenge in his tone. "Grenlik Tolks, can you substantiate your claim?"

Tolks shifted in his seat, which made Claire glance at him. He looked nervous. Tolks never looked nervous.

"I sensed a potential in the Warrior not long after I met her. I did her a service, and in return dissembled that I needed her help with some research. I undertook to educate her in some basic meditation techniques and, through them, was able to confirm that she was able to touch the magical field."

Yashik leant forward. "And what led you to believe that you should make yourself responsible for this, rather than referring it to the academy?"

"I feared ridicule, Chancellor. There are some who would mock without definitive proof." Tolks flicked a glance a Trunz. "I have already been blighted by such."

"I still see no evidence of any—"

Claire created a ball of fire on the tip of her forefinger and flicked it at Trunz. An instant before it struck his face, she recalled it and set it to orbiting gently above their heads. Trunz sputtered indignantly, but she could see amused sparkles in the eyes of the other two chancellors.

"Is there any specific test you would like me to do?" said Claire, sweet as poisoned honey.

"A human able to do tricks does not make her *Krezik Zha*, and I will have no truck with superstitions and ghost stories that give other Underkin the chance to mock us," Trunz swatted at the fireball as it flew past him. Claire let it disperse in a shower of glitter.

"Shall we put that claim aside for the moment," suggested Nagrath. "I see no reason it should influence our investigation into the plight of this young lady's parents."

"Indeed," said Yashik. "We can continue with our discussion of other matters in due course. Perhaps if the Warrior could tell us what she knows of the situation?"

"I was warned not to interfere, not to poke my nose into things like those evil goggle. I ignored the warning, and Morphs infected my mum and dad." Claire forced herself to keep her voice level, her face dispassionate. "At first, they didn't care about anything, then they started to do anything they pleased, or to spite each other."

Trunz scowled. "This is not news. The effects of Morph infection in humans has been widely reported. It has been of no interest to us. As to the—" there was a pointed paused, then "— Warrior's assumption it was triggered by her meddling in affairs she should not, that is not for us to speculate."

"That meddling saved Underland from invasion—" Tolks' tone was angry and he leaned so far forward in his chair he was almost standing. Nagrath waved his hand and Tolks fell silent, but Claire could feel his anger as he settled back in his seat.

"It didn't end there," she continued. "They started deliberately trying to annoy each other. That makes no sense for something that supposed to be a dumb infection."

"I am still waiting to hear evidence, rather than supposition." Trunz turned his head away, looking upwards. Claire thought he was trying to look superior, but though it just made him look an idiot.

"They came to my school, talked to the Head, and convinced her that I had been skipping meds for some fake emotional condition."

All three chancellors leaned forward with sharp eyes.

"The Morphs took direct control of their bodies; could speak through them?" Yashik sounded astonished.

"If we can believe this—" Trunz began, but Yashik snapped a finger at him and the chancellor shrank back.

"Show the Warrior some respect."

Trunz stared at Yashik, expression confused, mouth open as if to argue. Their eyes locked for a moment, then Trunz looked away, green flushing his cheeks. Claire cursed the wheels within wheels of the Grenlik psyche, and tried not to let the side story they were acting out distract her.

"They were convincing enough to get school to let them take her out of class. If either of them were touching me I couldn't feel Underland to jump out, and they made sure I was never out of contact. They said they were taking me for questioning, but didn't say who by. One of them managed to drive my father's car." She hesitated. 'Drive' might be a bit generous. The Morph had been suicidal, but it had understood the principles. Again, she decided to keep things simple. "I managed to use a spell to distract him long enough to make him crash. Then I used another spell to put them to sleep until I could figure out what to do.

"This is not possible," Trunz complained. He flicked a guilty glance at Yashik, but then his expression firmed into something akin to belligerence. "Are we really going to waste any more time on this fantasy? There is no magical field density in the Real. It would be impossible for our foe to act in this way, or for this human to perform the feats she claims."

"Again, let us hear the complete story and then discuss it?"

Yashik suggested. Claire could see Trunz was reluctant to concede, but he gave in — which suggested that in some way Yashik outranked him. Claire filed the nugget away under "potentially useful" and carried on with her story.

Tolks fidgeted, then sat straight. "I acquired an Atrilyne. She took it to the Real, detonated it, and made use of the residual magic in the ambient field to perform the spell."

"You detonated a magic bomb in the Real?" Trunz's tone was hushed, barely a whisper, and both Nagrath and Yashik flinched back in their chairs, shocked. Tolks cleared his throat.

"I should have let them capture me and take me off for interrogation, and who knows what else?"

"There was no risk of injury to any except the Morphs, and the magic would quickly dissipate before it could be detected or misused." Tolks added. "The collateral damage to Real technology was localised and acceptable."

"And how much of this did you know in advance?" Trunz roared. "Never have I heard of such reckless, irresponsible, illegal use of—"

Claire pulled the same trick she had used in the Council meeting and produced a clap of explosive volume.

"Thank you, Warrior," said Nagrath. "Perhaps we could—"

"I will have no truck with these actions and I demand that there is an investigation into—" Trunz raised his voice to a near shout. Nagrath held up his hand. Trunz scowled but shut up.

"I agree that there should be further discussions, but not here and now. This conversation is to find out what happened to the Warrior's parents, and whether there is anything we can do to restore them."

"Of course not," snapped Trunz, and Claire's heart stopped. "There has never been any research into the infection of humans, and frankly I find the whole story of possession unlikely in the extreme."

"You speak in haste," Yashik argued. "There is research we can begin, others with whom to consult, records in which to research."

"You know as well as I do the time would be wasted."

"I know we told this young woman we would try," snapped Nagrath, "and I know that the Council is expecting us to do exactly that. Will you report back to them that we simply dismissed her? For I shan't."

Yashik rose to his feet. "Grenlix, we are required by both honour and duty to consider this situation to the best of our abilities." Her turned to face Claire. "I thank you, Warrior, for your clear and concise description of events. We will discuss them with our various colleges and report back to you in no more than one week with our progress and findings. Is this acceptable to you?"

Claire rose and bowed. "It is. Thank you, Grenlik Chancellor."

"Then let us begin." Yashik collected Trunz with a look, and they swept from the room. Nagrath waited for a moment, head cocked to one side as thought he was listening, then scowled.

"Tolks, you blithering idiot. What were you thinking?"

7

Tolks flinched. Claire knew her mouth was hanging open but could do little about it.

"I'm sorry, Master, but there was little else we could do at the time."

"I mean talking about it, not doing it. Sometimes I wonder if you listened to a word I said. Trunz will use that against you, Grenlik. Be on your guard." Nagrath sat down, and waved the others back into their chairs. "Apologies, Warrior Stone." Claire made a 'no worries' gesture with her hand and concentrated on trying not to look like an idiot. "I think we owe you an explanation."

"Ya think?" Claire muttered.

"There is an oral tradition in Grenlik lore, as well as a written one. Passed down from Master to student for generation after generation, it speaks of a time more than two millennia past. Grenlix were a proud people then, respected for their wisdom and their great mastery of all things magical. All sought their counsel, from each of the three realms. I'm not suggesting that everybody was hopping from world to world, but those that needed to know were aware of the existence of the other worlds, and how to travel between them. For us, it was a golden age." Nagrath looked up at the ceiling, eyes distant.

"Ah, what a place this world must have been then. Our teachings speak of clear skies, sparkling rivers, and cities that rose gracefully into the sky in slender spires. Until those who we now call Morphs began to infiltrate Underland."

Claire, watching Nagrath's face, saw deep sadness flicker across it and suddenly his words were not dry history. He believed what he was saying, deeply.

"It began much as things are now, except at first we had no way to detect them. They settled among us, taking our forms, infiltrating our society, building their strength until they were ready to attack us, striking from our very heart like a worm in an apple."

"What did they want?"

"You. Or more accurately, access to the Real. What they harvest from your people we simply don't understand. It may be a foodstuff, it may be more desirable than the finest luxury. We never found out. At the same time as they struck at our heart, they stole our knowledge. The combined might of the Grenlix, the Sitharii Magi, and the strongest from the Real fought them back, driving them into their own world, all the time searching for a way to keep them there.

"They discovered the principle of the *Krezik Chet Knar*. For many long years we struggled to make it work, and all the time the Demons struck at us from beneath. We held many back, but enough got through to the Real to begin inflicting major losses within the magical community.

"When we finally understood how to make the *Krezik Chet Knar* work, it was almost too late. There was no magic powerful enough in the world to energise it. Singly and in groups our Loremasters had let the foul device suck the life from their bodies, but still it failed us. We needed a different type of energy, a force we had theorised must exist, but had never managed to tap.

"The Morphs launched a final attack, wiping out the Sitharii Magi. In desperation, the last of the Grenlix and Medrin — the one human savant still working with them — threw all they had left at the *Krezik Chet Knar*. It drank everything and mocked them for more. At the last moment, a new energy appeared, and it came only from Medrin. The *Krezik Chet Knar* lived."

Nagrath sighed and rose from his chair, then walked across to a sideboard and poured two glasses of green fluid. He sipped from one and handed the other to Tolks. "I offer no insult. You would not find this palatable." He took his seat and drew a deep breath. Tolks took up the story.

"The effort, it is said, ruined us. Two generations of Grenlik Loremasters lost their lives, and in the Real all had passed bar Medrin. We were weak, and enemies we had not known we had betrayed us. Angel's raided our institutions. They stole what they thought they could use, and destroyed what they didn't understand. Quickly, our world fell back into a darkened age."

"The last act of Medrin was to disable the device that controlled the *Krezik Chet Knar*, scattering the parts so that none could interfere with what had been done."

"Did he go home then?" Claire asked.

"No. According to our lore, he lived amongst us for some time, still wise and learned but never again able to practise magic until he passed."

Claire nodded. There was much to take in, much to process. She looked at the table, found a carafe of water, and sniffed it cautiously before pouring it into a glass. Glancing at Tolks, and at Nagrath, she could tell there was more to come. "So why are you telling me this?"

"Do you not see the similarities? Medrin used energies far beyond anything we had been able to manipulate, and we have recovered a fraction of our skill since the Intervention. He had an understanding of the *Krezik Chet Knar* that surpassed our own, even though we constructed it. He could touch the Interstitial Magic."

"I still don't get it," said Claire, although she had a sneaking idea where Tolks was going and didn't really like it.

"He was the *Krezik Zha*."

"And you think I might be the next one?" When Morphs had attacked her in Aslnaff's office, Claire heard Tolks shout the word to Nagrath, but had been too busy to think about it.

"Perhaps," said Nagrath. "Some few of us have tried to keep

the old teachings alive through the millennia. Our brothers grant us little respect. We are, apparently, anachronistic fools who dwell in the past. Other Underkin dismiss our history and mock us, calling us little people with grand ideas above our natural station. There are those among us, like Trunz, who would stamp out the old ways. They claim it gives others the opportunity to mock us."

"And yet it is us they turn to when things start to go wrong, us they turn to when they wish to steal some updated technology rather than developing our own, us they turn to—"

Claire had never heard Tolks so angry. Nagrath raised his hand and her tutor cut off in mid word.

"Gently, gently. It is true, but let us not forget that in doing so they have allowed us to make progress in areas we would never have been able to experiment, and have given us ample opportunities to... well, in the field of information gathering."

"So why did you make those terrible new goggles?" Claire's own fury started to boil. Goggles were the main tool of all Observers and Warriors, letting the wearer detect and track passing Morphs. Administrator Aslnaff, trying to wipe out the human presence in Underland, had ordered new goggles, designed to interfere with the memories of whoever wore them. It had almost worked. Nagrath looked profoundly embarrassed.

"Most distressing. We acknowledge that the goggles were Grenlik made — who else could manufacture them? — but we have yet to find out who fulfilled the commission."

Claire struggled to put her anger on hold. She still didn't trust the Grenlix as a whole, not any longer, but right now she needed them to help with her parents. That was more important.

"So, what if I am this *Krezik Zha?*"

"For one, it may help with your parents. If you are the *Krezik Zha*, you control the *Krezik Chet Knar*, and that gives you a strong negotiating position."

"Why?"

"Because you would control the barriers between the worlds"

8

The words seemed to suck all the sound from the room, and the Grenlix looked expectantly at her. Claire flicked her eyes from one to the other. Were they expecting her to faint or something? Was it supposed to impress her? *Was* she impressed? She guessed she ought to be, but somehow it felt like just another scoop of weird dropped on top of the weirdest place she had ever been. And if it brought her a step closer to fixing her mum and dad, then she was all for it. "So how do we find out?"

Nagrath frowned. "We are not sure."

"If we complete the device…" Tolks was unusually diffident. Claire knew he was talking about the odd cube he had given her to use as a meditation aide, and that she had been helping him find missing parts for. Everything started to go wrong when Claire had accidentally woken it.

"It was messing around with that damned thing that caused all this," she muttered.

"In truth, it was your meddling with it rather than following the instruct—"

Again, Nagrath cut Tolks off. "I see no purpose in assigning blame. We are not even sure that this device is the controller of the *Krezik Chet Knar*."

"But you said it was broken up."

"Indeed, it was. As soon as my ancestors suspected that the walls between the worlds were breaking down, they determined to reassemble it. The work has taken some four hundred years."

"So this is a bad thing?" Claire asked.

Tolks nodded. "If the barriers between the worlds were as they should be, the Morphs could not so easily steal through to our world, nor to yours. The average density of the magical field is declining every year, and is less than half what we believe it to have been when Medrin sealed the worlds. As we drain more and more in the cities an increasing number of dead-spots are appearing, even though we import energy from outside the city. When the Morphs started to break through four hundred years ago, we were helpless against them, until the first child fell through from your world and we realised you were more sensitive to them."

Claire digested this, trying to shake off a feeling that she wasn't getting the whole story. "But we don't have the last shard. It's buried somewhere in Mt. Primrose. We'll never get it out of there." She was happy to get the subject away from the whole *Krezik Zha* thing, if temporarily. The white magic was hers, and she didn't really want to share it. Not yet, anyway.

"The Angels will be required to co-operate with us," said Nagrath. "The Council has already decreed it so."

Riiiight, thought Claire. The Angels she had encountered would do exactly what they wanted to do, and would tie the Council in knots if they didn't want to play.

"Want me to see if it's still there?"

Nagrath's eye-ridges flicked outwards in surprise. Tolks looked smug. "Do you require a map."

Claire nodded. She could use the locating spell like a radar, but she wasn't sure exactly which direction pointed to Mt Primrose. Nagrath rang a bell, muttered to an aide who poked her head around the door, and in short order an A4 map of UnderLondon lay on the floor. Claire sat next to it, squatting on the floor, and held it in her mind as she wove the skeins of magic into the pattern of the spell.

She flicked the detector out, and flinched. At the same instant Nagrath and Tolks both gasped. The spell hurt, like someone had thumped the back of her head. The spell had way more energy behind it than she gave it. A spark of deepest blue immediately shone in her mind, and a moment later Tolks began to curse.

Claire readied herself to let the spell collapse, but as she did so she caught another flicker of blue from the corner of her mental eye. The spell unravelled and she looked up.

Tolks was patting at the carpet with the tablecloth, mopping water from the scorched remains of the map. "Mark the map, girl," he said when he saw her looking at him, "not incinerate it."

"Did you see where it started?" she asked.

"Close enough to Mt Primrose to say it is still there."

"Why can I still smell smoke?"

"That happens when you set fire to paper," Tolks snapped, but Claire was on her feet and looking around the room. What she smelt was not paper burning, but wood.

"There!" she cried, and pointed to a thread of grey rising from the floor. Nagrath rushed across, snatching the water carafe as he passed. A black spot on the floorboard let off a thin tendril of smoke, until Nagrath carefully tipped the carafe and a drop of water hissed on the floorboard.

"An ember?" suggested Tolks.

Nagrath shook his head. "A flake of paper could not char timber."

Tolks turned his face up to his master's. "A second trace? But where?"

Nagrath looked speculatively at Claire. "Do you know?"

Claire shook her head. "I caught a glimmer as the spell was unravelling."

"Then we have a possible line, but no confirmed distance." Nagrath looked disappointed. "Could you do the spell again?"

"I can always ask for more water," said Tolks.

"Maybe," Claire tried to sound enthusiastic. "The last one sort of hurt."

"Then another time," said Nagrath. "In fact, forgive us for taking so much of your time, and wearying you. It is all too easy to forget you have experienced great trauma recently, and still need time to recover. Are you able to make your own transition to the Real, or should we arrange assistance?"

"I should be OK. I jumped in."

"Then we can continue this discussion in the near future."

Nagrath gave her a polite bow, which Claire returned. She was glad of the break, even though Nagrath was dismissing her. She wrapped space around her and jumped out — and a donkey kicked her in the side of the head.

Bright lines rippled across Claire's vision as she arrived in her new room, and she crashed into the door before sliding untidily to the floor. A moment later footsteps thumped up the stairs and Claire had just enough time to roll onto her airbed before, after a perfunctory knock, the door swung open.

"Where have you been?" Nana May's a face wore the curious parental blend of anger and concern. Claire, confused, didn't answer. Her head was still hurting after the jump. "You shouldn't disappear like that. And then to sneak back in and slam your door? Well."

Sick realisation crept through Claire's thoughts and she glanced at the clock beside her bed. It made no sense. She checked her watch. Same time. Damn it, she had missed the snap-back. She hadn't arrived at the same instant she left; she had slipped two hours. And she was still wearing her Warrior uniform.

"I — uh," she scrabbled for an explanation. "I'm really sorry. I have a migraine hovering over me and I wanted to walk it off. I didn't think I should bother you."

"Wearing that? I know fashion today is accepting of the unusual, but..." Nana May ran out of steam. "I suppose it isn't a whacky as Goth, but..." again her words trailed off, but this time her eyes locked on the Kevlar amulet. Claire fought back an urge to cover it with her hand. Nana May spoke again, but her words were slow, as though they weren't quite hers. "We'll say no more, but try to be more mindful… of the time?"

Claire held her breath. Nana May blinked, then returned to the moment. She gave Claire a bright smile as if nothing had happened, and pattered back down the stairs.

9

A mid-morning text from Stuart told her she had an invite to a parley with the Angels that afternoon and asked her if she needed help getting in. Claire's head was clearer after a night's sleep and the thought of jumping back into Underland no longer had the attraction of putting her hand into fire, so she told him to sod off. A smiley and two "x's softened the text.

As she dressed in her uniform, Claire wondered if it might be an idea to take it back to Underland. Before everything had kicked off in Aslnaff's office, she had changed in the locker room like all the other SFU operatives. She had no idea how things were after the fight. She hadn't stood a duty shift, or spoken to anybody but Stuart, and wasn't sure she wanted to. What if they all blamed her? They would have skeleton crews in most posts, and everybody would be working their asses off trying to cover the load. She decided to talk to Stuart later. For now, her parents came first.

She took her weapon from her bag and looked it over with a Warrior's habitual motion. Hers was an older model, a Mk 18 she had inherited from a very good friend when the Special Facilities Unit had tried to demote her. Tolks had tested it and pronounced it safe, and that was good enough for her. She clipped it into its holster and took a moment before she confronted the surprise invitation.

Everybody wanted a piece of her. The invitation to this meeting was a mystery, but she wasn't going to pass up the opportunity to look inside an Angel nest. The text gave a time and a location. Claire figured out the closest place she knew to that point and jumped in. Five minutes after she arrived, out of breath, at the rendezvous, a steam cab wheezed to a stop at the side of the road. The door opened, and Nagrath's head emerged.

"Come along, Warrior Stone. No time to waste."

Claire climbed in and squeezed herself into a corner. Normally, there would have been room for four, but the presence of a Hrund complicated things. Opposite her sat Nagrath and a Sitharii she didn't recognise. She nodded politely to him, and in return got a frosty glare and a slight inclination of the chin before the Sitharii went back to idly brushing at the ludicrously tall top-hat in his lap.

The cab pulled away into traffic, but soon turned off the road again. There was a brief pause, a heavy creak, and a change in the light matched a sudden increase in the noise the cab was making. Claire peered through the window. They were in a tunnel.

It made sense. Mount Primrose was a fake mountain in the middle of Under-London. She had heard it was only there because of heavy duty magical supports that the Angels paid absurd amounts to keep fed with energy. She just hoped she didn't have to climb to the top.

The cab stopped and they climbed out. Claire tried not to gawp. The doors they were standing before looked stolen from an ancient church, all heavy metal bracing and studs. A liveried Angel, who still managed to look at them as though they were street sweepers, waved them grandly inside.

There were pillars everywhere, and ceiling decorations exploded from the top of each of them. Grand crystal fixtures glittered from the ceiling, and fire-bowls stood along the walls. They sounded like a typewriter as they clattered along the tiled hall.

At the end an elevator door opened for them, the grille rattling noisily to the side as the operator hauled on the handle. The doorman muttered, waved them all into the lift and, with a worrying clunk, the cage rose up into the body of the mountain.

There was no pattern to the floors; some were separated by a half metre of rock, and for others they passed through solid mountain for minutes before exploding out into a new level.

Claire counted twenty-eight floors before the elevator shuddered to a halt. Another functionary in uniform escorted them to a meeting room and Claire's heart sank. All she was doing was going from meeting to meeting. Nobody was doing anything. How much more of this would she have to put up with? The Hrund and the Sitharii stood apart from each other, and even farther from Claire and Nagrath. She used the partial privacy to whisper a question.

"What are they doing here?"

"Making sure everybody abides by the agreement and sticks to the rules," Nagrath replied, but the rest of his words drowned in a bustle of activity from the other end of the room. A door opened, two Angels in wedding suits marched in, and behind them sauntered a male who looked like a Grand Master in the Masons, or a parody of one. He moved with a deliberate arrogance, and his jacket jangled from all the medals and decorations pinned to and draped over it. The hair on the back of her neck bristled; not with fear, but with anger.

One of the grooms cleared his throat. "Presenting Grand Multifex Humbard, Prince of Mount Primrose, Protector of the first and third mysteries, beloved of his people. Those who have business with the Multifex, drawn near and be respectful."

Claire glanced back at those who had entered with her. The Sitharii and the Hrund were stony-faced, impassive. Nagrath wore a benevolent smile. She did what she could to keep her increasing hostility off her face. This Humbard was like Aslnaff; he wound people up for fun.

"We thank the Grand Multifex for his most valuable time and would ask his assistance, in line with the recent Council statement of mutual co-operation regarding the unfortunate situation of Warr—"

"The point, Grenlik," drawled Humbard.

Claire peeked from the corner of her eye and saw Nagrath straighten his back and shoulders. The Angel was getting to him, too. "Ah, of course. We believe that part of an artefact we have an interest in may be under the protection of yourselves. My young friend here can—"

"No need." The Multifex snapped his fingers and held out his hand. One of the grooms behind him reached forward and placed a ring box in his palm. "I anticipated that you would still be obsessing over that absurd myth. Here is the artefact."

Nagrath tapped Claire lightly on the arm. With the lightest touch and the least effort she could manage, she threw out the detector spell she had used the day before. The pain in her head was no more than a scratch, and in her sight alone a blue glimmer outlined the ring-box. She gave the slightest of nods.

"We thank you for your gracious co-operation, Rank. May my young associate...?"

Humbard nodded, bored, and Claire looked anywhere but at his face as she walked the six steps between them. She sensed he was wrong, and she wanted to give him no opportunity to meet her eyes and get inside her head. Her hands itched to pull her goggles over her eyes so she could get a better look at his aura, but she knew she couldn't get away with it, even with her reputation for being unimpressed by authority. Instead she reached out, plucked the ring-box from his hand like it lay in a bed of nettles, and bowed politely before backing towards her seat.

Nagrath was already standing, as were the two observers. "Our business here is done, so if we may take our leave?" The old Grenlik waited for a condescending wave of an imperious hand before bowing deeply and walking backwards to the rear of the room.

Claire's back prickled until the door closed behind them.

"Exactly what is your problem?" Stuart threw his hands in the air.

"Didn't he do exactly what he was supposed to?"

Stuart sat on Nana May's sewing chair, while Claire sat cross-legged on the air-bed. She had picked up an emery board to run across her nails, but had spent the past five minutes turning it over and over in her fingers as she told Stuart what had happened. Now she flicked it at him.

"He's an Angel, stupid. When has an Angel ever done what they're supposed to? We walk in there, he snaps his fingers before we've even finished asking for it, then hands it over with no more than a snide comment as payback."

"Can I see it?"

"What?"

"This shard thing."

Claire shook her head. "As soon as we finished Nagrath hustled me back to Tolks' shop and we put it in the safe."

Stuart frowned. "Now that is odd. If it needs locking away, wouldn't it be better in this academy place?"

"Unless Tolks is a secret agent," said Claire, ducking her head and looking out the tops of her eyes. Stuart threw the emery board back at her.

"You've been doing too much magic. It's affecting your brain."

Claire's thoughts froze, and it must have shown on her face.

"What's wrong? What did I say?"

Claire had been worrying about exactly that. It hurt each time she worked a spell. The level of pain varied, hurting more if the spell was new, of she used more power. Stuff that had already hurt her no longer did, like a scar had formed, but the trend was obvious and there weren't any options. She had to stay strong. She had to be able to do whatever she needed to do. Stuart knelt on the floor beside the bed, as close as he could get to her, and put his hand on her knee.

"Are you OK?"

Claire shrugged, suddenly miserable. "I don't know, and I have

58

to be. Oh Stu, what if I've broken something? What if I can't help them?" She lifted her eyes to his, aware there were tear-tracks down her cheeks but not caring. Stuart chuckled, then laughed. Claire untangled a leg and kicked at him.

"Stop it. You're horrible."

Stuart grabbed the foot before it hit him anywhere important. "I'm sorry. It's just... well, you're Warrior Stone. You make Evie Jones look like a wuss, and here you are mithering that you—"

The pillow caught him squarely in the face and the rest of his sermon forgotten as they struggled for control of the squidgy weapon. When Nana May called up the stairs to 'see if everything was all right" they both giggled like kids. Claire had Stuart pinned against the wall, kneeling next to him, facing him, and suddenly it was a moment. She could feel his breath on her cheek, and his cologne was powerful in her nose. Her face was so close to his she could count his eyelashes, long and thick and gently curved. She leaned forward a little more, until her lips could brush against his. "Thank you," she whispered, barely moving.

"For what," he answered, and she was sure she felt their lips touch again, soft as angel wings.

"For believing in me."

He smiled, and his hand gently caressed her back then pulled her closer.

10

Still in her pyjamas, Claire heard her jaw click as she yawned. She had found a note on the kitchen worktop. Nana May was out for the morning, half of which Claire's extensive lie-in had already consumed.

Stuart had stayed until nine, then Claire kicked him out before Nana May could start making pointed noises. Besides, he was travelling on his bike, and she worried about him riding in the dark.

The one kiss had lasted a sweet eternity, or a few minutes depending on your time frame. Then there had been a lot of holding hands and not really that much conversation, for which Claire had been grateful. His presence was such a comfort, and she didn't want to spoil it by chewing over her problems. She needed the down-time.

She yawned again and stared at the toaster, placing her hand above it to see if the thing actually worked. Her night had not been restful. When she had slept, nightmares plagued her. Either her parents were dying because they had been asleep too long, or the monsters inside them were waking up and eating their minds. When she lay awake, all she could think of was the shard, hidden in Tolks safe.

The toaster popped, making her jump, and she burnt her fingers as she picked the bread out. A quick smear of fake butter and a bite. Was the shard the last one? And if it was, what was the other trace she had picked up? Even if it wasn't, might it give her some level of control, some new ability she could use? And why was Tolks so reluctant for her to attach it to the cube?

Suddenly she was properly awake, annoyed and suspicious. She threw the half-eaten toast in the bin and stomped up to her room.

It was time she and Tolks had a chat.

The shop was emptier than usual when she jumped in, and it took Claire a moment to realise there was no light leaking around the workshop door. A chill ran up her spine as the dusty room became darker and the shadows took on depth and substance. Claire pursed her lips, annoyed at herself for letting it get to her, and marched up to the workshop door.

The stove in the corner was on, but the dull glow from its vents reached no more than a few centimetres into the near darkness. Claire reached out, turned the knob to brighten the lights, and the room filled with a soft pink glow. She let out a breath she didn't realise she had been holding when there was no huddled shape of Tolks slumped in a corner.

The other door in the workshop opened into the private area of Tolk's dwelling. Claire opened it, yelled "Tolks!" and cocked her head to listen for a reply. Nothing, just the whistle of air in her nose. She closed the door softly and went to her bench. Tolks was out.

It took one hand to count the number of times this had happened before. When it did, she usually left and returned later. Today, though, his absence poked at her like a personal insult, even though she knew she was being silly. Yes, it had been more than a month since she had hospitalised her parents, and she burned to move things on. Yes, someone in the Grenlik community had worked with Aslnaff to cut out the memories of all the humans a few months ago, and she was finding it difficult to trust them.

Tolks was a Grenlik, but Tolks was Tolks. How could she be feeling this way about him?

Her eyes fell on the safe. The brooding lump of metal crouched in the corner next to the stove, its door all that separated her from the mysterious cube and the new shard from the Angels. Tolks had taught her how to meditate using the cube. Even if she couldn't actually do anything today, it would help settle her mind if she could spend even a few minutes meditating with it.

She slid off her stool and knelt in front of the safe. To the side of the handle was the wheel of a combination lock, and below it a large keyhole. That they had decided to put the cube and the shard in this safe, rather than taking it to the academy, must mean the safe was meaner than it looked.

Claire wove a spell that detected magical traps and laced it through the fingers of her right hand. Cautiously, keeping the spell as tenuous and delicate as she could, and making very sure not to touch the safe, she ran her hand around and across the door.

The handle had a trap, as did the dial of the combination lock, but with magic so unsophisticated it made Claire suspicious. There were no alarms, nothing to tell Tolks that someone was tampering with the safe. Expecting something to blow up in her face at any moment, Claire began to unpick the protective spells.

Half an hour later she shuffled back from the safe and wiped a sheen of moisture from her top lip. She had done it. Her last sweep with the detector showed no coherent magical energy in or around the safe. It had been too easy, at least so far, and asked the question even louder why they had stored such important stuff here?

Then another question occurred to her. What was she doing, and where was she going? She knew her excuse that she wanted to meditate was a lie — damn it, now she was lying to herself too. Was she a bored puppy chewing on a shoe? A trick that she could reveal proudly to her master when he came home? Or was she trying to show him this wasn't a safe place?

Claire worked her tongue around a mouth gone unexpectedly dry. Or was she doing this for a reason she couldn't admit to herself, at least not yet.

Picking locks was one of the first tricks Tolks had taught her. Modern Underland mistrusted Grenlix, and had a reputation for petty crime and dishonesty. They exceled at magics of deception, of theft and concealment. So why had Tolks, and Nagrath, locked everything away in a place he had to know she could open? And so she was back to trap or invitation.

The spell for picking locks stuck out the end of her forefinger like a key, and she slid it into the keyhole in the safe. Part of her was still expecting magical booby-traps. Tolks had once used one to throw her across the room in a training exercise. If there was anything here she hadn't noticed, and she didn't expect it to be so gentle.

Inside the lock, the delicacy of the mechanism didn't match the size of the keyhole. The key was a trick; it didn't just turn and slide past a few levers. There were locks within locks, five of them; complex interlinked gearing, mechanical puzzles that were more machine than lock, and it wasn't going to work to solve each one in turn. Claire had to solve all the locks and apply them simultaneously. It was like trying to play chess in her head.

When the bolt finally slid back it took her by surprise; she thought she had two more levels to untangle. She looked up at the clock above the stove and winced. She had been knelt there for an hour. She shifted her weight, trying to get up, and found both her legs had gone numb.

Ten minutes of agonising pins and needles later Claire took a bottle of water from her workbench and drank deeply. Her eyes wandered back to the safe. There was only the combination lock to beat, now. It's good practice, she told herself. I'm sharpening my skills. Or that would be what she told Tolks if he interrupted her.

She took a dust sheet from one of the other benches and folded it into a cushion before kneeling in front of the safe again. The lock-pick spell had dissolved from her fingertip when she had stopped concentrating on it, so she wove a new one — placing the tip of the pick against the middle of the dial and pushing it inside.

Her finger ached, and the resistance was as if she was trying to push through clay.

As the probe sank deeper into the door an image of the combination mechanism built up in her mind. It looked ordinary enough; there were no bits hanging off the side as though they didn't belong there.

Claire turned the dial with her left hand and watched the way the wheels worked, the little tabs turning notches back and forth. Being able to see what was going on inside made the lock childishly easy to defeat, but Claire stopped as the last notch was about to drop into place.

How could this not be a trap? And yet, she had checked over and over. Her attention wavered and the spell wobbled. If she lost it now, she would have to start again, and the ache she had felt when she pushed the probe into the lock was now a steady throb. She concentrated, twisted the wheel the last tiny arc and the fence-bar dropped into place. One last turn and the cam released the handle.

Claire flinched back, expecting a nasty surprise, but the safe remained inert. Pulling her sleeve down over her hand she pulled open the door and saw the silk wrapped shape of the cube. Next to it sat the ring-box holding the shard they had collected from the Angel Humbard. Claire took them both to her workbench and removed their wrappings.

The cube looked different. The first time she had seen it, it had been a featureless gunmetal grey composite of sliding blocks that almost made a full cube. Now the cube was perfect, flawless, though the colour was the same. The shard, this time in the shape of a wafer-thin hexagon, had the same hue and lustre. Claire cleared her mind, feeling each slow breath as the air brushed softly through her nose. When she could sense the cube in her thoughts, she reached out and lightly touched it with her mind.

Inside, the cube was a three-dimensional maze of microscopic gears and magical circuitry, all dead and motionless. Blocks of mechanism could move around within the structure like a sliding tile game, but apart from one brief and glorious moment, the cube was, and always had been, inert.

Claire allowed her thoughts to brush across the cube at the most superficial level; she wasn't trying to meditate, yet, and she wasn't trying to repair it. Not today. Still, there was a difference, deep, deep down in the heart of the mechanism. It called to her, compelling her to investigate. She pulled her mind away. Another time. She had more important work to do

Without coming out of her trance, Claire lifted the new shard from the workbench and dropped it gently onto the top of the cube. Nothing happened. Claire tapped it with a finger. Still nothing. The previous shards had sunk into the cube without help, instantly becoming lost in the shifting modules and complex workings. Claire focused her thoughts, moving around inside until she was directly beneath the new shard. She could sense its presence against the outer edge of the cube, equally that the device had no intention of letting it in. If she gave it a little nudge, a tap? She let her thoughts slip from the cube and into the shard.

Steel-hard walls of cold, dark magic slammed shut around her mind.

11

Claire could still feel her body, but faintly, like a pencil sketch, and someone was scrubbing away at the lines with an eraser. Sensations from her toes and fingers faded away, but not like simple numbness; she was being disconnected from her body one cell at a time.

Claire battered at the walls of her prison. She could still feel background magic but, like her body, it was a shadow of what it should have been. Even so, she began to gather in what she could reach as it seemed a fair bet she was going to need it. She checked around the virtual perimeter of her cage again. It felt smaller, but that could be because she was more familiar with it second time around. She focused down, digging at the wall with a magical gimlet, trying to prise off a thread she could use to unravel the spell, or at least disrupt it enough to understand its structure. The surface of the spell was obdurate and dense. Whoever had put it together knew what they were doing and they had expended a great deal of energy on it.

Claire let her concentration expand out from the tiny point she had narrowed it down to — and bumped her head, figuratively, on the walls of the spell. It was half the size it had been. Claire took an inventory; she had lost contact with her hands and feet. The absence, whatever it was, had eaten away more of her body.

Until she figured out what was going on, Claire had to stop things getting any worse, and the most pressing problem was the shrinking cage. The background field was getting thinner and thinner, but she gathered up what she could and wove it into three rods of magic, as strong as steel. She rammed them against the walls of the prison and held her virtual breath.

First one, then all three of the rods began to bend. Claire

scrabbled for more magic to brace them, but gave up as soon as she started. There wasn't enough. One after the other, her rods snapped and disappeared in sparkling showers of discoherent magic.

The cage snapped suddenly smaller as the braces disappeared, as if catching up for lost time. This wasn't tight, or a little claustrophobic; whatever this prison was made of, it was crushing her mind. Mild irritation transformed into tendrils of fear. Claire pushed them aside, but their taste lingered, sour and cloying.

She knew she couldn't jump out. She didn't really need to touch magic to jump, but she did need a body. Hers was now erased to the shoulders and hips. There was one thing she could do, one way she could think of to fight back. She reached deep into her soul, searching for the white magic.

There was nothing there. The tendrils of fear turned into tentacles, thick and slimy, wrapping themselves around her mind, trying to paralyse her will. She reached out again, angry that the magic wasn't there when she needed it, demanding it show itself to her.

And then there was a thread, a tiny whisker poking through a crack in the wall of the world. She reached out, grabbed it, and pulled. White magic flowed into her like a breath of cool air on a sultry day. She wove a sphere of protection around herself and drove it outwards to shatter the trap she had fallen into. Immovable force met irresistible object. The walls of her cage were no longer closing in on her, but neither was she able to push them back.

She didn't understand. Nothing had been able to withstand white magic when she had let it loose, and yet here the harder she pushed the more the cage resisted. Energy was flooding in to her, but had nowhere to go, and it was hurting her. On a different level, she knew if she shut off the white magic the cage would instantly collapse to nothing, and take her mind with it.

Claire now battled on two fronts; one trying to balance the pressure from the cage, the other trying to hold back the rising tide of white magic. If she failed, one or the other was going to kill her.

Time became pointless. What was happening had no connection to reality; it could have been happening for an instant, or Claire could have been locked in the struggle for centuries. All she knew was that she was getting tired, and that she was losing control. The white magic burned her mind like furnace flames. The more it hurt her, the more her control weakened. Each instant became a torment, until Claire was screaming inside her mind. All that was left of her body was her head and her heart, and even that faltered, stumbling in its rhythm, darts of phantom pain shooting across her all but erased chest.

And Claire finally accepted that this was her end. She had dug herself a hole so deep there was no way to climb out, not even with the white magic. Her heart begged her to let go, to end the pain, but her mind clung stubbornly on, holding onto the fire of the white magic, refusing to surrender.

12

A clang, louder than the doors of all the hells slamming shut at the same time, reverberated through Claire's mind. She screamed, covering imaginary ears with hands she no longer had. In an instant the cage ceased to exist. The white magic exploded outwards, wild, uncontrolled, like the birth of a universe, pulling Claire with it. Her mind expanded, first marvelling at the microscopic dot the prison had compressed her into, then in growing fear as she thinned out on the magical wind. The white magic was going to do the opposite to her; the cage had tried to crush her, but the white magic was going to disperse her through whatever multiverse it acted across.

Claire struggled to hold herself together, and at the same time to control the wild magic. Apart from what it was doing to her, this much energy released into the local field would be like a bomb going off. She noticed an eddy in the magical stream, a pocket of resistance, of stillness, and the memory of Ostrenalia's crystal burst into her mind.

Instinctively, Claire felt for the crystal, feeling its structure, pouring the wild white magic into its multidimensional interstices. It burned her, ripping away everything that had healed over in past weeks and exposing her to such agony she couldn't draw breath to scream. What control she had grew ragged, then failed completely. A kaleidoscopic burst of colour ripped through her thoughts, and Claire found herself in her own body again.

She opened her eyes, slitting them against the overwhelmingly bright light, and saw Tolks, grey skin flushed with green and face thunderous, standing next to the now closed safe. Her workbench was empty, apart from a silk cloth. Claire covered her face with her hands.

"Treachery!" Tolks hissed. "Impetuous treachery. It cannot be borne. I can have no more to do with you. Get out."

Claire stood, or tried to. Her knees were not, apparently, connecting the upper and lower parts of her legs, and if she hadn't been able to grab the edge of the workbench she would have fallen. As soon as she was stable, Claire tried to jump out. Pain stabbed into the backs of her eyes and she gasped. "I— I may need a moment."

"Then take one away from here."

Claire stared. He really meant it. She pulled herself up to her full height, trying to wrap herself in whatever dignity she had left, and made her way to the door that led to the shop. Twice her hand reached out to a workbench to steady her, but she opened the door and got through it without stumbling. Tolks didn't follow. She reached into her pocket and pulled out her communicator, praying someone she knew would be in Underland. She pressed the call button and spoke Stuart's name as clearly as she could, then focused on working her way across the disused shop while the call connected.

"Claire?"

A single sob. "I'm sort of in trouble. Can you come get me?"

"Where are you?"

"I'll be outside Tolks shop."

"Outside?"

"Long story. I can't jump, Stu."

"Again?"

"Same long story. Please. I'm scared."

"Five minutes, maybe ten." And the communicator went dead.

Where was he that he could be there so quickly? None of the observer posts were in this part of London; there were never any Morph incursions around here. And yet it would take him more like half an hour to get from anywhere he should be.

Claire put it aside. She wanted to stay in the shop. She was in no state to be out on the street. Even with a fully charged Kevlar, there were some Underkin who might have a go at her if she looked weak. Any yet, what if Tolks came out and there was another scene?

She was at the door now. There were six bolts to deal with, and Tolks would be out soon to lock them all again. She didn't have much choice, but she took her time opening the door, knowing the Grenlik was listening for her to leave. It opened with a soft creak and she looked out into the murky yellow light of Underland. The street was busy — or, at least, sufficiently crowded that she was instantly uncomfortable. Going outside was a terrible, vulnerable step to take.

The door at the back of the shop rattled. She looked over her shoulder, hoping he was coming to apologise, or at least listen to reason, but he wasn't there. He was letting her know it was time she left. Claire stepped out onto the street and closed the door behind her.

It felt like every Grenlik on the street stopped what they were doing to look at her. Tolks' establishment, like most Grenlik shops, was in the side of a Hive; a hulking monolithic slab of a building that housed thousands, with dozens of shops built into arches in the outside walls. She walked away, but in two steps realised that moving would make it more difficult for Stuart to find her.

Her head swam. She had no option but to wait, alone and obvious. She tried to make herself more imposing, pulling her goggles over her eyes and staring at every Grenlix who stared at her. She lounged against the wall and tracked them as they moved past her, trying to appear as though she was looking for something. She was; Stuart walking along the street towards her.

A movement in the air and a minute whisper of magic warned her that someone was jumping in close to her. Two objects, obviously, couldn't occupy the same space, so the incoming body pushed aside anything already there. Claire moved too slowly and an incoming jump pushed her aside. She fell to one knee, grazing her hand on the bricks of the hive, and looked up in astonishment to see it was Stuart who had jumped in so close to her. He crouched down beside her.

"What the hell?"

"Just get me out of here."

"To where? I've no snap-back." Answering her plea for help, Stuart had sacrificed the twist in time that allowed him to return to the real at the same instant he had left.

Claire's thoughts scattered in confusion. "What time is it?"

"A little after one."

She had been in Underland for three hours. There was no way of knowing if Nana May had come home, and Stuart couldn't take her back in time to when she left. She realised she didn't care. "Take me back to the house. I want to go home."

They jumped, and appeared in an alley between two blocks of terraces. Claire could see a bike, presumably Stuart's, parked at the end, and two curious boys giving it the once-over. They were looking right at them, eyes wide as saucers. "Piss off," yelled Stuart, and the boys disappeared. "Don't worry," he muttered. "Who'd believe them."

Claire had no keys. Hammering on the door, frustratingly, showed Nana May wasn't home. Claire wanted to get inside and lie down. Her head was thumping and her vision greying at the edges. She was dimly aware of Stuart propping her against the wall next to the door then running off. A moment later the front door opened and he let her in.

"How...?" she mumbled as she helped her up the stairs.

"You really want me to tell you how well I remember your bedroom?"

Claire knew she ought to find that funny, but had no strength. She collapsed onto her bed, drifting away as soon as she landed, vaguely aware of someone turning her back and forth to get her coat off, then tugging at her feet.

Some time later a shaken shoulder woke her enough to take the two pills and water forced on her, and then, at another time, her eyes crept open to see Stuart sitting on the floor next to her bed, reading one of her books. The room was gloomy and he had a book-light clipped to the top. It made him look like he had a blue aura. He saw her, and reached out to touch her hand. She felt it, and was sure he spoke, but she drifted away again. Knowing he was still there made her feel warm, and the pain in her head somehow reduced.

He shook her shoulder again. The room was darker now, illuminated only by the soft glow of a table lamp. A door rattled downstairs and she felt Stuart's breath on her ear. "I have to go now." Soft lips touched her brow, then the air stirred as he jumped out. Claire stretched, and gathered together what wits she could to make up a convincing story for her grandmother.

13

The promise of chicken and mushroom soup dragged Claire from her bed. She had woken earlier long enough to tell Nana May she had another migraine, but the smell of the soup, with a subtle hint of warm bread, was now irresistible. She changed into her PJs, wincing whenever she moved her head too quickly, and took the stairs at a cautious pace and with a hand clamped firmly onto the bannister. Nana waved her into the tiny lounge where a voluminous pink comforter, complete with sewn-in sleeves, was waiting for her. Her grandmother appeared a few moments later with the promised food balanced on a lap tray. Claire swooped on the soup like she hadn't eaten in a week while Nana May watched some senseless game show on the TV.

"Thanks, Nana," said Claire, looking up. "I really needed this." Her grandmother waved a hand dismissively, concentrating on her show, but Claire's gaze locked for a moment. She squinted, blinked, and then looked down at her soup again. A trick of the light, or an aftereffect of the headache. But for a moment, it had looked like Nana May had the same blue aura as the booklight had given Stuart.

There was a text waiting for her in the morning — two, in fact, and both from Stuart. The first one was an "are you ok" timestamped an hour after she had gone back to bed. The second was this morning, a few minutes ago.

"U wont blve this. Not 1 lttr for u. 3. Meet me in town. Lib @ 11? xx"

Claire didn't speak txt very well and took a moment to decode it. She messaged him back, and got ready.

The buses were perversely efficient and she arrived twenty

minutes early. She found an empty bench in the atrium and dug out her e-reader. People passing too close by were a minor distraction, but Claire's head lifted like a hound for no reason she could... there, across the atrium, by the information desk. A girl, younger than her, and with a distinct hint of blue in the air around her.

Claire's heart hammered. What was going on? She looked around, but nobody else was glowing. She turned back to the help desk, but the girl had gone. Claire jumped to her feet, then onto the bench, scanning across the crowd for a sight of her. She had to ask her—

"Are you that desperate to see me?"

Stuart looked up at her — only slightly — his lips smiling but creases of worry around his eyes. Claire blinked, moved her head from side to side, trying to get a view of him that wasn't backlit by the glass front of the atrium. The sunlight outside was making it difficult to see if—

"Are you right?" The smile disappeared. Claire hopped down from the bench and gave him her broadest smile.

"I'm just dandy. So what's so important you have to drag me away from my sickbed?"

The library had a small coffee shop on the lower level. They found a table at the back and Stuart bought Claire a hot chocolate. When they settled and he checked that nobody was paying them undue attention, he pulled three envelopes from his jacket and lay them on the table in front of her.

"What do they say?" she asked, earning herself a scathing look. She turned them over and saw all three sealed with blobs of wax. One seal she recognised — the SFU were her old employers, and organised the human-run Morph detection and control unit. Another seal was that of the Grenlik Research Academy, large and imposing. The last seal was a plain blob of wax.

"You don't have to open them now," said Stuart, but his eyes burned with curiosity. He sipped at what would inevitably be a double shot skinny latte with a fist full of sugar and tried to look bored. Claire put two letters down, and slipped her thumb beneath the flap of the messages from the SFU.

"Don't tell me they fired you again?"

"Not exactly," said Claire, then she groaned. "They want me to come back to full duty as a Warrior."

Stuart grunted. "No surprise. It's not good down there. Few runners, and not enough Observers to run all the OPs. Averaging one Warrior to four Observation Posts."

"Why didn't you tell me it was so bad?"

"Didn't want to worry you."

"How many strikes?"

"Four to six."

"A week!"

"A night."

Claire sat back in her chair, shocked, and stared at the letter. Any human that stopped going to Underland would forget about it. The process took four to six weeks. Worse, Aslnaff had issued booby-trapped goggles to everybody, with magic built into them that accelerated the process down to days. Claire thought they had discovered it in time, that they could save most of them, or at least wake their memories up again. It seemed she was wrong. She looked up at Stuart, and noticed a tired slump to his shoulders she had missed because she wasn't looking for it. And then she saw the aura. She stifled a squeak by covering her mouth.

"So?"

Claire couldn't answer, and Stuart frowned.

"Are you coming back or not? I don't think it would make much difference operationally, but it might help morale to know we have another Warrior. And who she is."

Claire snorted and stared into her drink. "I'm hardly Little Miss Popular." Claire had been fast-tracked, entered the system as a Warrior, bypassing years of training and experience.

"Don't underrate yourself," said Stuart. His voice was unexpectedly serious, and she glanced up to see the same in his eyes.

"I guess. If I can stop self-harming my brain."

"Are you going to tell me what happened yesterday?"

Claire picked up the envelope from the Grenlik academy and tapped it against her other hand. "Let me read this first. It might change how the story ends." She slid her thumb under the flap and the seal broke with a crack. A brief tingle of magic disentangled itself from the paper once it had decided she was the real her. Inside was a single sheet of paper. It was headed with the same imposing crest as the seal and the message was hand written in Grenlik script.

"Greetings, Warrior Stone

"Whilst I cannot say I agree with your impetuous actions regarding certain equipment on the premises of a Grenlik of our mutual acquaintance, I wholly disagree with said Grenlik's comments and reaction. To this end, I invite you most cordially to discuss the situation at the Academy, at your earliest convenience. Forewarning would be appreciated, but may not, it is understood, be possible. If you are comfortable providing for your own arrival, please present yourself at the main door, otherwise transport will be provided.

With greatest respect."

There was no signature, but she didn't expect one. Grenlix didn't hand their name around like humans did, and rarely mentioned it if the other person knew who they were talking to. The author of the letter was Nagrath, the "Grenlik of mutual acquaintance" had to be Tolks. Claire still hadn't got her head around Tolks having a boss, or calling anybody Master, but it seemed he had stepped over a line. That had never been her intention. The fault was hers.

Her eyes flicked up from the letter and glimpsed Stuart, eyebrows raised, waiting for an answer. Before she could decide on anything, she had to know if she could get around on her own again. Being a burden on others was happening too often. Gingerly, she opened her mind to the thought of jumping, made the tentative connection to Underland. Nothing in her mind exploded, and no virtual mules kicked her in the head. Still, there was no substitute for the real thing. She rose to her feet, and held out a hand to stop Stuart doing the same. "I'll be back in two minutes."

The ladies' toilet was around the corner from the cafe, and thankfully a stall was free. Claire slipped inside and locked the door. Bracing herself, and scrunching her eyes up against the anticipated pain, she jumped in.

It was weird to be standing in front of her locker. It had been a while, and she saw a fine patina of dust on the combination lock. She instantly jumped back to the toilet.

On the way back to her table, Claire saw the girl who had passed her in the lobby. There was no aura around her now, but Claire changed her route so that she could walk right next to her. As she passed, the girl looked up, eyes open wide, then winked.

"Can I help you?"

Claire cheeks tingled, but she smiled. "Sorry, thought you were someone else."

"No problem. Good hunting."

There was no doubt. It wasn't a smell, exactly, but whatever it was worked the same way. Claire could sense that the girl had been in Underland, and recently too. And she must have stunk of it. That was what the girl had meant. There was only one reason a human would be in Underland, and that was hunting Morphs.

"Did it work?" Stuart asked, then when she nodded asked "Who was the girl?"

Claire looked away. "One of us. I smelt it on her as I passed."

"Do I know her?" Stuart twisted in his seat to get a better view and Claire kicked him in the shin.

"No window shopping."

"Professional interest. So, do you think you can stand duty?"

Claire nodded. "Probably. I have to sort this business out with Tolks first though."

"I'll get them to assign you an OP for evening shift tomorrow. Now, what the hell did you do to piss the Grenlix off?"

Claire told him. His face went stony, harder and less expressive the farther she got into the story. By the time she finished, he was glaring at her and she felt she had got on the wrong side of a teacher.

"Jeez, woman. You have no concept of personal safety, do you?"

"It was fine the last time I did it. Nothing happened. The cube absorbed the shard. No drama. I wanted to see what difference it made, in case I could use to help my parents."

Stuart's face softened a little. "I know, but you are meddling in stuff you don't understand."

"It's stuff nobody understands," Claire interrupted, her voice low but angry. "And nobody gives a toss that while they noodle over it my parents are lying in hospital."

Stuart held up his hands. "I'm just saying you aren't going to be much use to them if you get yourself killed. I have to go, sort out your duty shift tomorrow. Will you be OK getting home?"

She nodded stiffly, then forced herself to relax and smiled up at him. He leant forward and kissed her firmly on the lips. She reached up with her hand and laid it on his cheek before he pulled away, and then he was gone.

14

Claire jumped in mid-morning the next day. She had no idea how long the meeting with the Nagrath would take, but her shift didn't start until 10pm. She was still waiting to find out where.

As soon a she appeared in the courtyard, one of the huge doors creaked open and an attendant hurried out to greet her. At the same instant her communicator chimed, and she groaned as a text message rolled across one face, telling her which OP she had the dubious pleasure of reporting to.

"Warrior," said the flunky. "You are anticipated. I have sent word to the Chancellor to determine when he can see you. In the meantime, we have a tolerably hospitable lounge...?"

He held out his hand in an invitation to enter and looked hopefully at her. Claire nodded, then had to work very hard not to give the polite, attentive Grenlik a wide berth as she passed him.

She had no chance to discover how tolerable the waiting room was; a message was already waiting by the time she passed into the entrance hall. They were to take her to his workshop right away.

The instant attention did nothing to soften the edginess Claire had been riding since she had decided to jump in. Things between her and Tolks had ended fairly definitively. She couldn't think what he could say to undo things. Her mind wound itself into knots inventing fantasy arguments and responses, each more unlikely and confrontational than the last.

She almost cannoned into the back of the doorman, who knocked a door for her then bowed and walked quickly away. Nothing happened for long enough that Claire reached out to open the door herself, at the same instant the handle twisted and the door opened towards her. She took a hurried step back, and Nagrath smiled out at her like a benign uncle. "I tell them to warn new visitors about that every time, but do they remember? Please, come in. Make yourself comfortable." He looked around the cluttered room. "Somewhere."

Claire found a stool with a moveable stack of books on it and placed them carefully on the floor. Nagrath had already turned to a long workbench along one wall, so she dragged the stool over – close enough to talk but not enough to get in the way – and sat.

Nagrath's workshop was the antithesis of Tolks', and looked more like a dynamic example of chaos theory. Its only partially clear space was directly in front of Nagrath, and in it was the cube. Claire could still see the new shard sitting on the top of it, and a trickle of ice slid down the centre of her spine.

"Most unfortunate," said Nagrath, looking at her from the corner of his eye. "We have been able to perform some tests on the item so kindly donated by Humbard. It is, as you have already discovered, nothing to do with the cube."

"Then what is it?"

"A trap, my dear and specifically for you. I would hazard a guess that somebody is most determined that you not be allowed to fully reassemble this device."

"I'd say they almost succeeded. Won't it come off?"

"Not by any artifice we can devise and, of course, now that the trap has sprung we can no longer analyse it for specific magical signatures."

"I really messed things up, didn't I."

"You didn't help, but Tolks and I must accept some of the blame. We both have a tendency to treat you as a child, and to not invite you into our confidence as fully as we should. We must not be allowed to continue that practise, but perhaps I could ask you that rather than exploring or experimenting on your own, you could simply tell us when we are acting like stuffy old fools?"

Claire smiled despite herself. It was hard not to like Nagrath, and she had to force herself to remember there was nobody she

81

could trust — except Stuart, and him only because of the spell keeping him honest.

Nagrath slapped his hands on the bench and made her jump. "But! That is not why I asked you here. If this flinder is a fake, then we have to find the real shard. And I would like to perform a second experiment if I may ask. Over here, on the floor."

Claire followed him to a space she hadn't yet seen, hidden behind a catalogue of oddments stacked into an impromptu wall. On the floor were two maps; one of UnderLondon and another of a city Claire didn't recognise. Several metres separated them.

"Do you need to be meditating on the cube to locate the parts?"

Claire shook her head. "I'd rather not. Not yet, anyway."

"Absolutely. Please, take your time."

Claire caught her bottom lip between her teeth. She hadn't expected to do any magic today. She had been expecting to get chewed out and told to make her peace with Tolks. Still, the spell she needed wasn't terribly hard. A moment later she had woven it and sent it on its way. There was no echo, no answering pinpoint of deep blue light.

"It's gone," she said, hearing the despair in her voice. "They've moved it."

"There are two modifications I would like you to try. First, lighten the detector, but push it harder. Second, send out the spell as you did before, but focus on what is not, instead of what is."

She nodded. She had used the first trick herself some weeks ago, but the second idea was new and she couldn't see what it could achieve. She closed her eyes, changed her detector to be as light as she could make it and still have it work, then drew in a little more energy to power it. It flew fast and far, but still returned nothing. Claire was about to let it disperse when she realised it was miles and miles away, but still active, still coherent. She concentrated, tiny touches here and there when the weave started to unravel, turning it into a game to see how far she could get it to go.

And then there was a ping. A tiny sparkle of a return that so surprised her she lost control of the spell and it unravelled about her. Nagrath clapped, once, and Claire opened her eyes to see delight on the old Grenlik's face.

"Well done. Do you see it? There?"

Her gaze followed a slightly trembling finger and she was looking at the other unfamiliar map. A tiny char mark marred the surface, close to the centre. "Where is that?"

"You would call it "Edinbelow", I believe. It is in the focus of our presence in the Real of Scotland."

"So far!"

"Indeed. You are a most accomplished technician. Now, may we try the other trick? Are you fatigued?"

No headache pounded in her skull, no stabbing pains lanced between her ears. She was tired but that was as much being out of practice as anything else. She shook her head, then closed her eyes and wove the spell for a third time. This one was different again. Rather than gossamer thin, Claire made it heavy, detailed. She wanted to feel every cobble stone and lamp post as her detector passed it. This one needed most energy of all, and pain twinged behind her eyes as she threw it into the void.

It lumbered, soaking along streets like falling night. It slithered through buildings, oozed past Underkin and human alike. It moved so slowly she could recognise some of the landmarks, like the SFU offices in what should be the Tower of London, and the airship terminus on Broad Street. And if that was the canal, the she should be about to reach—

A pool of utter darkness, bottomless, terrifying, vast. Streets wide. Claire reached for the edges of the spell, desperate to shred it before the darkness could draw her in, and then it was gone. She tore the spell apart anyway. She knew what she had seen, and she was sure they had seen her. All the trust Nagrath had gained that morning burned away like mist.

"You knew."

The old Grenlik's face was a mask of incomprehension, but Claire was having none of it.

"You knew that there was a protection around Mt Primrose, and you let me blunder right into it, didn't you?"

Nagrath's eyes flickered up and down, a sure 'tell" in a cornered Grenlik. "I had my suspicions. Be assured, they will not have any reason to suspect you personally. The spell was no different from one any Grenlik would weave. They may even discount you, believing you damaged by their trap."

But Claire heard deceit and betrayal and stood up to step away from the map.

"Please," said Nagrath, "don't leave. There are things we must discuss. You are making use of powers you nor we understand. There is every chance that you are damaging yourself."

But Claire had already torn a hole in space and stepped through, and his words were echoes on the wind.

15

Claire brooded through the afternoon. Why couldn't anybody in Underland be on the level? Always plots and plans and nasty little secrets. If she could have turned her back on the lot of them, she would have done so in an instant. Except she couldn't. Morphs still possessed her parents. Though she was beginning to doubt whether any Underkin had the knowledge or skill to help her, Claire had no choice but to play their vicious little games until she could be sure either way.

Her chest ached as though there was a strap around it, and the air she dragged into her lungs tasted worn out and lifeless. She had already towelled herself dry, and lying around here wasn't helping. Her hands trembled as she planted them on the airbed to push herself up. She took a deep breath, then another. She couldn't let her grandmother see her like this.

Claire killed time sitting in the lounge with Nana May, watching a wildlife documentary. It wasn't particularly interesting, and her mind wandered. She hadn't been to the hospital for a few days, which made her think about her Mum, which led her on to Nana May, and how much they all looked like each other. Claire took her height from her father, but her appearance from her mother. Nana May and her mum could use each other for make-up mirrors. Her grandmother's skin was firm and smooth, and her eyes were so bright, so alive. They even had the same name; her father had so loved the strength of 'Stone' that it had become their family name, rather than his.

Claire's vision flickered. She hadn't moved, yet one instant she was looking at Nana May, the next at the TV. At the same time, she sensed a tiny tingle of white magic, and her throat tightened.

She hadn't asked for it, or gone looking for it. How had there been magic? And here, in the Real. She blinked, and her eyes focused on her grandmother.

She forced her eyes back to the TV, but the night habits of meerkats were not that interesting. Claire's vision flickered and white magic fizzed softly in her mind like space dust. Another flicker and she was looking at the TV again, but buried under the meerkats was another image; her grandmother's face. Goosebumps prickled along Claire's arms. She was inside Nana May's head, seeing through her eyes. Now what was she supposed to do?

The sensible answer was simple; get out and never try anything like this again. On the other hand, what if this was a fluke, a one-off? What if she could never repeat it? Could she really pass up the chance to look around inside someone else's head? It wasn't like she was going to go digging, or would tell anybody. For one thing, who would ever believe her?

Claire relaxed, and convinced herself to stop worrying and open herself to whatever was going to happen. She used a similar approach on the cube when she was learning to meditate; mindful, but passive.

There was something behind her, not in any physical way, but a sense of presence. Without trying to understand how, Claire turned to face it and gasped. Whatever it was, it wasn't real. Somehow her mind was translating the impossible into something she could understand.

In front of her was a shining sphere, colours swirling across its surface. A waterfall of silver streamers undulated from the bottom, fading into nothing. Above, a golden mist swirled up from the sphere to and around a complicated web, like a sponge or a coral

Claire moved closer to the sphere and heard a whisper of Nana May's voice. It was so clear she nearly looked over her shoulder, her mouth getting ready to say "I was only looking". Another voice, but still that of her grandmother, joined the first, then she heard a dozen more. She could make out snatches, fragments of sentences, sound-bites and concepts about the meerkats, the toilet, food things to do, aches. Claire pulled back. The voices all radiated out of the shining sphere. Could this be her gran's mind, her soul? It certainly seemed to be the bit that was doing all the thinking.

The surface of the sphere was smooth. Ghosts of images slid across the surface, as tenuous as a shadow in the oily skin of a bubble, fading in and out, slipping away before she could really see what they were. She flinched back, recognising herself, but as she had looked when she was no more than eight or nine. Was that how Nana May thought of her? Afraid to interfere, and let herself drift towards the mesh above.

As she got closer the mesh got too big too fast, out of proportion. Every moment a new level of detail revealed itself and, when she finally reached the edges, Claire felt like an ant crawling along the side of an office block. The mesh of tiny nodes strung together along the finest gossamer strands. Some nodes touched many threads, others only one or two, and some threads looked more substantial than others. The nodes differed too; those with strong threads shone with life, whilst others were grey, dull and shrunken. Still at the very edge, Claire gently 'touched" a node. She smelt coffee, and glittering sparks danced along the connecting threads; she tasted it, saw an image of an empty milk bottle, and a snapshot for a cafe and a woman she didn't know laughing. These nodes were memories.

Claire drifted carefully inwards, back through her grandmother's life, touching memories here and there, skipping sadly over the broken links where memories had died. One node she touched brought up an image of herself, and she stopped. Did she really look like that? The image was thin, with hollow cheeks and haunted eyes. She touched the image again, first realising that it was a composite, mixing how Nana's emotions and memories as well as what she saw, but there was something odd about it, like a guitar chord played a fraction out of tune. Claire tried another and found an altercation with a butcher in a supermarket. Although the tone was darker, it rang true. She went back to the memory of her, and the off-key jangle returned.

There were hundreds of connections from this memory. Far too many for her to check individually. Besides, each of them could branch at another memory, over and over until the possibilities made her head swim.

Was there a trick she could use from the magic Tolks had taught her? The cube complex; not nearly so much as a living mind, but still with convoluted, multiplex pathways. She focused her mind, then let herself flow passively out along the mesh, skimming across the memories without actually triggering any of them. She rode the matrix, seeing where it would take her.

Time became tricksey but eventually she sensed a shadow in the mesh of memories. She drew herself together then drifted cautiously closer. Though she knew the idea was insane, she couldn't shake the terrifying thought it might be another trap laid for her.

The shadow resolved into a cluster of black pearls connected by equally dark gossamer threads. Not the same lifelessness of forgotten memories, but a hard, brittle darkness. They had been interfered with, cut off. Claire looked farther in and saw other trapped memories, all connected to this one, scattered back across Nana May's past.

The dark pearls begged her to explore them, but she had other things to do that evening. A moment later she felt what should have been a wince as she realised she was completely disregarding her nana's privacy. Reluctantly, Claire let herself float back to the top to Nana May's mind. She could have "left" from where she was

—— after all, she hadn't actually gone anywhere —— but it seemed safer. A few moments later she was looking at the TV again, then there was a last twitch and Claire was back in her own head.

16

Her locker combination hadn't changed, and the door hadn't been busted open, which Claire counted as a result given the last time she had been there and the reputation she had collected. There were a few neutral nods from others using the room, and she returned them politely. She didn't need to be there and wasn't sure why she had come. She had all her equipment with her. She had only dropped by to make sure nobody had left any messages for her. The ventilation slots of the lockers made for great post boxes.

Or she could she putting off reporting for duty. Claire would have done anything to get a different Observation Post — except actually ask. She couldn't make up her mind if somebody was trying to be helpful or cruel assigning her there. She slammed her locker shut, gave her equipment a last check, then marched out of the building.

The Observation Post was on Eastcheap. Like all buildings with OPs, the main doors opened to a skeleton key issued to all SFU operatives. Claire looked at the rickety and unreliable elevator, sighed, and climbed the five flights of stairs.

Once she got to the office, her hand wouldn't turn the door knob. She was breathing too fast, her heart was hammering, and she balanced on a knife edge of going on — or turning away and claiming she had been ill. The way her luck had been going, it was inevitable he would be inside.

The door handle snatched from her fingers as someone within jerked it open, taking the decision from her.

"Stone! I mean, Warrior Stone. Sorry."

The girl was a year or two, younger than Claire and they had met before. Stuart had chewed her out for not being polite. The lesson must have worked, as the girl hopped aside to let her through first. Claire smiled, nodded, and walked into the silent room.

"Welcome back, Warrior Stone."

Claire's heart stopped. Exactly what she had been afraid of. She turned towards the Senior Observers desk, and Jack Cooper. Once partner-in-crime, confidant, and imaginary boyfriend. Now, awkwardness incarnate in a horrible twist that left him looking cool and calm and her feeling like a mouse in a barn full of owls. His face was polite, but his eyes were cold, and Claire knew whatever there had been between them, even friendship, had gone.

"Senior Observer," she responded, and the tension level in the room ratcheted up another notch. The OP was not as well staffed as it should be, but there was another Observer and two Runners sitting at a table, watching intently. "Anything I should be aware of?"

Jack flicked a glance at the rest of his staff and Claire felt their eyes turn elsewhere, though she could tell their ears were still straining for every word. "This station has seen a shout every night in the past week. Across the region, double that. We are taking the brunt of it."

"How many other Warriors on duty tonight?" she asked.

Jack found a sheet of paper on his desk. "Two, over to the west. One is already on a shout."

Claire nodded, then took a seat on the couch reserved for the duty Warrior. Crisp crumbs covered the cushions and she could see several discarded wrappers tucked down the sides. Taking her e-reader from her pocket, she pretended to ignore everything. A soft mutter of conversation slowly lifted the silence from the room.

An hour later one of the Observers came down from the roof to take a break and swap duty with someone else.

"Holborn took a hit about fifteen minutes ago."

"Is their flag up?" Jack asked.

The Observer nodded around a mouthful of confectionary. "And Covent Garden is still up too."

Two hits, both Warriors engaged. If anything else happened, it would be down to Claire. The tension in the room continued to rise until Claire could feel it prickling across her skin. It was all she could do not to run, up onto the roof and away from all the judgement.

And then she realised her skin really was prickling. The background magical field was distorting. Twice before Claire had sensed a Morph break through from Beneath, but it hadn't been like this, not a creeping dread. Just a—

Her head swam, like the vertigo of rising too quickly, but compressed into a single second. She staggered to her feet and pulled her PPG from its holster. She flicked it from side to side, taking the safety off and making sure the charge crystal showed full and the emitter was clean.

"Claire?" said Jack, voice cautious, but before he could say more there was a thump above their heads, followed by the sound of someone all-but falling down the stairs from the roof. The door crashed open and a young Observer, goggles still over her eyes, yelled "Cannon Street, by the station".

Lifting her hand to her neck, Claire checked her Kevlar was in place, then she was out the door and clattering down the stairs. As she burst out onto the pavement Claire took a moment and wondered if she had come back to duty too soon. Running down the stairs had left her breathing heavily, and she covered her hesitation by pulling her goggles over her eyes. Fractal lines of colour swirled over the dark lenses until they initialised, top half clear, bottom half obscured with a dark blue tint. She ran.

She found the silver splash of the Morph's entry point, shining bright through the lower half of the lenses, and followed the trail along Cannon Street. Fifty yards later she stumbled and crashed into the wall as the whump of another Morph incursion momentarily scrambled her thoughts. This one was close, too. She needed to find the first one and take care of it so she could deal with the second one before it got away.

The arrival of a third Morph made her miss a step as she turned into New Change Alley, running alongside the gardens of St Paul's Cathedral. Claire's foot caught on the kerb stone and she fell to the pavement. For a moment, she had to say down. The fall hadn't winded her, but her breath was burning in her throat and her heart thundered uncomfortably. She hauled herself to her feet, leaning against a railing, and the ground at her feet exploded in a shower of gravel. She ran.

She already knew what had hit the pavement. A Morph's primary weapon was its frog-like tongue, at the end of which was a hard ball the size of two fists. It could punch through thin walls, and break ribs. Somehow, a Morph had crept up behind her.

As soon as she was out of range, Claire slid to a stop, yanking her PPG from its holster as she turned — but the Morph wasn't there. It hadn't followed her.

Whump. Another Morph, so close it took precious seconds for Claire's ears to stop ringing. That was four! Claire caught a silver glimmer in the corner of her eye; a Morph, not running from her, but heading towards her. She aimed and flicked the trigger twice. The PPG coughed and two clouds of purple mist shot towards the Morph. The first missed, but the second brushed against it and the Morph dissolved into a puddle of goo, and the railing behind Claire's head rang like a bell. Her eyes flicked sideways long enough to see the bent metal, then she dove to the ground and rolled away.

Another Morph had crept up behind her. Claire fired the PPG again but the shot went wide. She only dared fire once. A PPG held six shots, and recharged from the magical field, but it took time; thirty seconds to get enough power for two more shots. And there were so many Morphs.

Whump. This was getting silly, and she was losing count. Was that four or five? Either way, she needed to make herself some space, and get out of this alley. She looked for the quickest way out. A Morph stood in the middle of the road and another moved into position behind it. Claire turned and ran, but stumbled to a halt in a half dozen steps when she saw two more Morphs blocking the other exit. In the cathedral's gardens, another shape ghosted towards a gate that led into the alley.

If she was very lucky she could take out one pair of Morphs, but then what? If she missed even one they would trap her. Her best chance was to get to the gate before the Morph in the garden did, and try and make her way out the other side. She broke left and sprinted as fast as she could, firing two discouraging clouds at the Morph inside the park as she darted through the gate.

The little park was dark and the paths meandered between tall shrubs. Claire zigged and swerved and dove behind a bush. Two deep breaths to stop herself gasping, then she eased open a gap in the leaves of the bush she was hiding behind and peered through. They had the gate blocked off. Three Morphs slimed into the park to join any already there and one stood guard to stop her escaping. She had a clear shot, and it might distract them enough for her to run across the garden and look for an exit on the other side. She eased the PPG through the foliage and fired two quick shots.

One connected. and the lead Morph exploded. The one behind, spattered with ichor of its companion, turned and rushed towards her, transforming into an angry Godzilla.

She burst out from behind the bush and ran as fast as she could. A Morph slid out from its hiding place, its mouth gaping obscenely wide. There were tall shrubs on either side of her, too thick to dive through. She raised the PPG, pulled the trigger, and nothing happened.

The Morph shot its tongue at her. Claire saw it start to move and jinked to the left, but guessed wrong. Off balance, Claire could do nothing except wait for the hard ball to hit. The Kevlar took most of the blow, the air sparking around her, but it still threw her to the floor. She rolled over to climb to her feet, but realised at that level there were gaps in the shrubs. She dropped to the soil and squirmed between the stems.

What was wrong with her PPG? As soon as she was back in the bushes, she checked it over. The charge crystal was dead and showed no sign of recharging. Claire groaned. Morphs disrupted the magical field, and made it difficult for things to work. PPG's were hardened against this, but there must be too many of them. She was in over her head. Her reputation was going to take a battering, but the safest thing she could do was jump out.

Even that was denied her. When she reached out to create the fold in space, she felt nothing. The Morphs must be disrupting even the tiny amount of magic she needed to do that. Bile and fear rose in her throat.

17

A sparkle of white glinted in the back of her mind. It would be so simple to use the white magic. She wouldn't need to jump out. A casual flick of her thoughts and the Morphs would be history. She could even send them back where they came from.

Except that Nagrath's warning echoed in her mind. It wasn't much of a coincidence that every time she made use of it, she ended up with an aching head, or things happening differently from the way she had meant. Evidence was starting to stack up that using it wasn't such a great idea. She had to get out of the mess herself.

The shrubbery was dense, which worked both for and against her. She moved cautiously and watched every step for twigs that might crack underfoot. As far as she knew, Morphs could hear and see, but had no magical ability to detect her. She paused. Nobody had ever told her that. She was making an assumption. Still, creeping along had to be a good idea.

The flip side was that though they could not see her, she could not see the Morphs. What she was hoping was that she would come up against the railing and could climb over it, but there was an equal chance she was heading straight into another trap.

Claire kicked something hard and heard a subdued "dong". She froze. Without moving her feet, she explored with her hands and touched the railing. The bush had grown over it, and there was even a thick limb she could use to help her climb over. She put her foot on the branch and shifted her weight.

The whole bush wobbled, and rustled loudly. Claire dropped to the floor as two Morph tongues hammered through the space she had recently occupied. Scrabbling on hands and knees she shuffled away, fist after fist blasting through the foliage above her.

The white magic glimmered at her again.

Claire swore as her hand banged into something sharp. When she tried to brush it out of the way, it wouldn't move. She tried again and her hand closed around a metal rod, about a centimetre in diameter, long and partly buried. She shuffled a half step sideways to go around it, then realised what it was. It was a metal spike, the sort of thing builders used to put up fences of bright plastic net. She wrapped her hand around it and pulled.

It was heavier than she would have liked, but then she wasn't intending to use it as a javelin. But it might make a good club. She turned and headed back towards the Morphs. If she could get close enough before they saw her...

The soft *phat phat* of a PPG drifted across the garden, and Claire heard the gelatinous pop of a Morph meeting its end. Another Warrior had come, but whoever it was didn't realise the danger they were in. The constant barrage above Claire's head had stopped, and she guessed those trying to find her had turned away to deal with the new threat.

"Stay back. It's a trap," she screamed, and leapt out from the bushes. Two Morphs were on the path, both facing away from her and moving towards the new threat. Claire jumped forward, stabbing the metal pole into the back of the beast closest to her. The point sank in an inch, then bounced back, throwing Claire to the floor. As she climbed back to her feet the Morph turned towards her, its mouth opening in the obscene gape she so hated. Claire raised the spike, but the fist already quivered at the end of the coiled tongue, ready to strike out. She had no time to force the pole through the tough skin. She gathered herself to leap away, but knew the Morph would still track her and score a clean hit. She wasn't even sure her Kevlar would protect her. She needed the unexpected.

Claire jumped forward, pole outstretched, driving the point into the Morphs gaping mouth. It let out a warbling scream, then burst. Morph goo drenched Claire, its peculiar stink of mothballs and dog food filling her nose and turning her stomach.

"Stone!" A voice cried out, familiar, warning. Claire had frozen. She had never heard a Morph scream before. She turned as the other Morph struck out at her. Her kevlar took part of the blow, but not all of it. She let out an *ooof* as she flew briefly through the air then, with the help of the foul gel, slide for metres along the path. She heard a distant *phat phat* and hoped another Morph had been taken care of. That left two. She risked a quick glance at her PPG. It was charging again, but still had no shots.

She ran back towards the Morph on the path, jinking from side to side. It fired at her and missed. As it reeled in its tongue she ran even faster, hoping to get there before it closed its mouth. She didn't, quite, but she used the stake as a club and hammered it against the Morph. She had no idea if she was hurting it but she had to get it to yawn, or keep it busy long enough that the other Warrior could come and deal with it.

Her arm started to tire. The plan wasn't going to work, at least not the way she thought it would. She made two more swings at the Morph, each weaker than the last, then rested the spike on the ground as if it was too heavy for her. The Morph yawned, seeing its opportunity to strike. Exactly what Claire had been waiting for. She swung the spike in a fluid arc and rammed the point deep into the Morph's mouth. Another scream, another goo shower. Another *phat phat* from outside the park.

Claire turned, expecting to see that the Morph was now a puddle on the floor, but whoever the other Warrior was, he or she had missed. Worse, Claire was sure she could see somebody on the ground and she was out of range for her PPG, even if it had held charge. The other Warrior was going to take a pounding if she didn't help. She ran.

Claire was mad angry now. Someone had set her up. There was no way this was a coincidence. Five Morphs, and all around her duty OP. Someone had blabbed, and someone was still out to get her. She had covered half the distance to the last Morph, and the white magic begged her to use it. She pushed it aside. She would use it when she wanted. Instead, she drew hard on the little ordinary magic there was around her and wove a spell; a spur of the moment invention, growing from her need and her heart and her anger. A millimetre long but razor-sharp blade of magical energy appeared on the tip of the spike and, with every ounce of energy left in her arm, Claire threw it.

She never believed it would go so far, or fly so true. It had only been a distraction, a threat to make the Morph turn away, to attack her. But it did fly far, and it did fly true, and it sliced through the Morph's membrane and reduced it to a puddle of slime on the cobbles.

Claire hurried over to the fallen Warrior, lying face down in the road. She heaved on a shoulder, desperate to see who it was and what injuries the battle had inflicted. Deaths were rare, but not unheard of, and Claire couldn't bear the thought of somebody else taking damage on her account again. The body rolled over and Claire gasped.

"Stone, you will be the death of me," groaned Jack.

Claire grabbed his arm and tried to help him up, but the goo dripping along her arms made her hands slippery. She scrubbed her palms on her trousers and tried again. "But, how did you get hold of a PPG?" She hauled him to his feet, awkward, unbalanced, doing everything to avoid jarring the cast on his left arm.

"Most people start with 'thank you'," Jack snapped, then raised his good hand in apology. "Uncalled for. Arm is giving me hell." Claire picked his weapon from the floor and handed it to him. He checked the emitter hadn't been damaged, then slipped it into its holster. "I requisitioned this out of stores when I saw how bad things were getting. I kept it in the OP, figuring there was going to be a night... well, not exactly like this."

They began to walk back in the direction of the OP, a subtle gap opening between them. "I guessed you were in trouble after the third Morph turned up, and there was no way either of the other Warriors were going to get here in time. Didn't realise it was as bad as this, though." He gave her a sly look. "You do know you are in for a whole world of new nicknames when it gets out you took out two Morphs with a blunt iron spike."

Claire groaned louder than she needed, to let him know he had scored a point.

"Thank you," she said, eventually. "I know things got weird between us, but—"

"Claire, I'd have done the same for any Warrior. Not that any other Warrior would have ended up being cornered by five Morphs."

And the gap between them was a mile wide as they walked back to the observation post.

Morph slime evaporated after thirty minutes. They took the long way back, arriving after most of it had disappeared from Claire's clothes. Claire ached so much she made no protest when Jack used the lift to take them back to the top floor. A buzz of conversation leaked through the OP room door, instantly silenced by the rattle of the handle. Jack walked in first and stood in the middle of the room, surrounded by a sea of anxious, expectant faces.

"Five shouts," he announced, his voice calm, but strong and clear. "Five kills."

18

The room erupted. Claire tried to explain that Jack had got two of them, but nobody was listening and he wasn't helping her make the point. She gave up, and let the exuberance wash around the room. These people had been waiting a long time for something to celebrate.

The mad huddle and cluster of high-fives gradually eased, but the demand for a retelling was insistent. Jack looked at her; she couldn't tell if he was giving the opportunity to take the glory, or if he was waiting to see if she had the guts to step forward. She smiled with as much warmth as she could find and made a small gesture with her hand. She would stand there with him, but the tale was his to tell. At least she could trust him not to make her look too stupid.

The javelin throw met with incredulity and demands for multiple repeats, but eventually Clare could get away to the couch, where she pretended to read her e-book for the rest of the shift, and trying not to let the happy buzz drive tears from her eyes.

The party atmosphere in the OP had been too much for her, and she spent the last two hours of her duty shift on the roof of the building, watching the night skyline. The next Warrior on duty offered her a "high five" as she walked into the room, word having already spread. Claire dutifully slapped palms, but felt a fraud for doing it. Jack had pulled her backside out of the fire. If he hadn't turned up, the Morphs would have killed her, or taken her somewhere guaranteed to be unpleasant. Her skin crawled when she thought about it.

Now she had snapped back, arriving the same instant she had

left the Real, but eight hours more tired. Showered, changed, and dosed with painkillers, Claire walked into the lounge carrying two mugs of milky coffee. The quiz show had finished, replaced by a sitcom featuring a couple of ancient has-beens and humour she didn't get. She sipped at her coffee and tried not to think; thinking took her to places she didn't want to go, exposed her to truths she didn't want to accept.

She caught herself staring at Nana May; not obviously, but sideways from the corner of her eye. It pleased Claire she had resisted the white magic during the fight. It meant it didn't control her, didn't own her. Flipping that over, did she own it? Would it come to her when she wanted it, or only when she needed it?

Again, Nagrath's warning whispered into her thoughts but this time she ignored it. This would be an experiment, carefully controlled. She reached into the place where the white magic usually appeared, but here was nothing there. How did one summon magic inside one's own head? She couldn't draw fancy diagrams on the floor, or burn candles. She could chant a spell, but had never needed to before. It had appeared, like when she had drifted into Nana May's head.

The experience quickly replayed in Claire's mind, fascinating her, scaring her. What a wonderful thing to be able to wander around someone's memories, so long as she didn't do anything stupid and break something? Still, it would be a cool thing to do again.

White magic fizzed in her mind in a moment of vertigo. Claire's vision flickered and she was looking through Nana May's eyes again. She twisted around and looked at the golden mist of Nana May's memories. Experimenting with white magic could wait. She was here, now, and might never get another opportunity. Besides, she wanted to take another look at those grey pearls of walled-off memory she had found.

It took her a while to find them, and there were more than she remembered. She tasted the memories around them and found the grey pearls scattered over some six years of Nana May's life, cropping up apparently randomly over the period. The closer Claire looked, the more she saw, until she was certain there were thousands of them.

Whatever was inside, it had not been forgotten. Even in the brief time Claire had been exploring she could see that lost memories were gaps, clusters of pearls with connections that had withered and removed them from the net.

The grey pearls were different. Claire focused down, looking at smaller and smaller detail. The connecting threads went around these memories, inlayed on the grey surface and looking for all the world like the magical circuits in Claire's goggles, or the delicate tracings inside the mechanism of the cube.

What if the pearls were protecting what was inside? After all, sometimes memories came back, perhaps by the awakening of a connecting thread. What if...?

Claire was consumed by an overwhelming urge to look inside one of the pearls. She promised herself she would be very careful, and not disturb the connecting threads, but she needed to see the memory inside. She reached out as delicately as she could to one of the earliest nodes, gently probing the pearlescent wall, trying to understand its structure. As soon as she made contact, the wall pulled her inside.

Claire floated in a universe of colour. One colour. How could a memory be a single thing? It took her a moment to understand. Every time she had touched a memory, it had been a composite of all the other memories associated with it. That's what the connections were for. Each individual, isolated memory was really like this. A single thing.

Disappointed, Claire began to pull back, to find the edge of the memory so she could leave its pearly shell. There was no fun to be had here if everything was chopped up into discrete memes like

103

this. At the boundary, she stopped and turned back.

I know this colour.

It was a dirty, untidy sort of yellow. Claire remembered, and the pearl shell popped. Sparks flew along every connection that the shell had been blocking. She smelt a smell she already knew, then sensed the feel of a Kevlar under her fingers. All around her pearls were dissolving and a cascade of signals stormed across Nana May's memory. This had happened to her once, and — horrified — Claire remembered the terrible shock, and the breath-taking wonder. She had to get out, and quickly. *What have I done!* Nana May would need her. After sixty years, Nana was going to remember.

Claire managed to catch the coffee cup a moment before it slid from Nana's nerveless fingers. Her grandmother's eyes were staring wildly at nothing, her breath gasping, short pants. Claire took her hands and rubbed them.

"It'll be all right, Nana. It doesn't last long. You'll be fine when it's over."

But it did last long. It went on and on and on, and Claire began to feel the first fingers of panic around her heart when she saw her nana's lips darken, and flecks of foam gather at the corners of her mouth. For Claire, it had taken seconds, but she had needed to reintegrate a few hours of stolen memory.

Nana May was remembering six years of Underland.

That was what Claire had recognised. The yellow memory she had found was the dirty, soiled colour of Underland's sky. Just as had happened with her, the first memory had released them all.

Nana's breathing eased. She covered her face with trembling hands, took a deep breath, and wailed like a child with a broken heart. Claire knelt on the floor and wrapped her arms around her Nana, flinching at how frail the woman felt. She wanted to chant *I'm sorry* over and over, but wasn't brave enough. There was no knowing how Nana May would react if she knew Claire had done this.

The wail faded into sobs, the sobs into gasps. Claire pulled back enough to see Nana May's face, and cold sweat broke out over her body. Her grandmother's eyes focused on nothing, flickering around as if she was reading, or watching a movie. Finally, Nana May closed her eyes and let out a long sigh.

"Are you OK?" Claire asked, feeling that the question was stupid and inadequate, but not knowing what else to say.

"I really am not sure," said Nana May. She opened her eyes and looked at Claire, then her gaze dropped to Claire's neck. "But you know, don't you? You've been there."

Claire nodded. "Yes, Nana. I'm a Warrior."

A sad smile tried to light up Nana May's face, but it made her look worse. "I was an Observer. I never felt right about killing them." She sat back on the sofa and puffed out another breath of air. "How could this happen? We were told that the memories would fade away, and yet…"

"When you saw my Kevlar, or the PPG?" Nana May looked confused, so Claire tapped her neck and her hip.

"Ah, we called them Mae West's and BR's, after Buck Rogers."

"Or it could be I just — handled a couple of Morphs. I might still smell—"

And together they said "mothballs and dog food" and Nana May chuckled.

"Oh, this is rather splendid. I wonder how long it will last?"

Claire had no answer, the memories could fade in an hour for all she knew. "Why did you cry, Nana? You sounded so sad."

Nana May reached out and touched her on the cheek. "Sometimes memories are bittersweet. I loved my time there, but there are always thorns. Tell me, what is it like now?"

Nana May quizzed Claire for hours, and Claire did her best to stay awake, even though she had been on duty. After all, she had been the trigger. She had woken all these memories. And yet, clamouring for attention and threatening to distract her every minute, there was a thought. It had worked for Nana May.

Who else?

The hospital was quiet today. Claire had left the house early, begging Nana May to stay behind. "I haven't been for so long, and I feel really bad about it."

"And you're sure you don't want any company?"

"Not today. I want to spend the day with them, or as much as I can."

"And a fossil like me would get in the way?" Nana May smiled to take any sting from her words, but Claire still gave her a huge hug anyway.

"Don't be silly."

Now she was on the ward, sitting beside her mother's bed. Two nurses bustled in and shooed Claire temporarily out of the way. She stood at the end of the bed and watched as they turned her mother onto her side.

"It's to prevent her getting bed sores from staying in the same place too long," said the younger nurse, and flashed her a genuine smile. Claire smiled back, though she didn't feel like it. A real smile in the hospital was a rarity. She found it a place of masks and polite condescension.

The nurses smoothed the bedclothes one last time and left her alone. Claire pulled the chair around to the other side of the bed, wincing every time it screeched against the floor, but determined she would be able to see her mother while she did this. She wanted to watch her eyes open, and to see her mother peering blearily out through them, bewildered as usual, then they would hug and mother would worry about father, and Claire would tell her everything was going to be OK.

She knew she was grinning like an idiot, but there was nothing she could do about it. She could fix this, and she could do it without any of the councils, or the academies, or anybody else trying to pull her secrets out of her. And once everything was back to normal...

The chair was like sitting on flat steel, but she did what she could to make herself comfortable and reached for the spark of white magic she would need. It was there, as though it had been waiting for her, or expecting her. She let it connect to her thoughts and winced at the static-spark pain. She forced herself to relax. Once this was done, and she had healed her father, she'd have no more need of it. She let her mind drift towards her mother.

And met a barrier. Her mind saw a mesh, or a geodesic sphere, all triangles and pentagons and vertices, glowing softly. She could see through it, but it would not let her pass.

Inside, a million miles away, dim and distant, she could see a lethargically sparkling core that she knew was her mother. Everywhere else was a boiling mist of black and purple. And it was laughing at her.

Claire pounded the arm of the chair, again and again until she missed and hit her wrist on the steel tube. This time, she had beaten herself. The spell that kept her mother safe and asleep was also stopping Claire from getting in. She touched the edges of her spell again, looking for a way past that wouldn't leave the Morph inside free to act.

"Yesss, human child. Touch it. Feel it. Can you see where it went wrong?"

"Wrong?" Claire gave herself a mental pinch. She knew better. She had read this scene in so many of her books. Never engage in conversation with the enemy. Trouble was, the books weren't so good with advice about not listening.

"Of course. The spell is too hard, too sharp. Look deeper. See how the mother-thing hides from it."

The spell was different to how she had expected, more than

107

what she had woven, but it was difficult to see exactly how. The white magic wasn't helping; it was showing her how to beat down her own spell, then launch a fiery attack against the morph-spirit.

"It crushes her. She has no room, no food."

Claire's heart turned to ice, even though she did her best not to listen. What if it was right?

"Without sounds, senses, her mind is starving. You are killing her. Break the spell. Release me. I will not harm you."

Claire was planning the sequence she would need to tear down the spell before her mind caught up with what the Morph had said, yet behind the words there were others, cold and angular, as if spoken in the crystalline light of the white magic.

"Release me, stupid child, and I shall scream and I shall rage and I shall bar you from the source of wherever you get your power and I shall watch while my master rips your mind inside out and I will feast on the carcass."

Claire drew her mind back from the spell. "Well at least while you're in there you can't hurt me, and you can't hurt my Mum."

"Hurt her?" The creature's laugh was cruel. "Stupid human. I feed on her"

Claire snatched her mind away, slamming the connection closed but not before the cruel laughter of the Morph began to run around and around her own thoughts. She slumped back in the chair, heart hammering in her ears, forehead and neck damp with sweat. What if it wasn't messing with her?

Oh God. What if it was telling the truth?

19

The doors in the roof of Broad Street station rumbled open. Warning blasts echoed around the cavernous space, deep and masterful from the dock, lighter from whichever vessel was about to leave. A basso thrum intensified, drumming at the air, then a twin-bagged passenger liner rose majestically above its brethren, tail rotors barely moving, but those on the four attitude control pods straining upwards.

Claire watched from the upper concourse of the station. This was, perversely, her "quiet place", or one of them. Somewhere to hang out when she wanted to relax, or at least stop stressing. Somewhere to think. Except today it wasn't working. Thoughts whirled in her head, moving too fast to stick together and make ideas.

A presence joined her at the railing. She ignored it. She didn't want to talk. The presence had other ideas.

"Miss Stone?"

Claire glanced towards the voice. "Lady Ostrenalia. I can't imagine you are a fan of airships."

The Sitharii looked out at the dock and when she turned back a faint smile hovered around her lips. "Actually, I find them intriguing, but I would imagine for different reasons." She turned her back to the rail and leant against it. "I was wondering why we had not seen you at Bedford Row."

"You had me followed here to ask me that?"

"Don't flatter yourself, my dear. If you don't want people to find you, don't have favourite places. Everybody knows of your fascination for airships." She looked around, mouth elegantly pursed into a moue of disapproval. "However, we——" She paused, then spread her hands and rolled her eyes. "Very well. I wanted to know why you hadn't come back."

Claire looked steadily into the Sitharii's eyes for a moment, then turned back to face the dock. "Things have been... complicated."

"They always will be, child." Ostrenalia's voice held an unexpected note of compassion, and Claire was sure she heard a soft sigh. "I can feel it on you, Miss Stone. I can feel it burning inside you. I can feel that you have already used the crystal I gave you. Already. You may think you are controlling it, but you aren't, and right now you have nowhere to run when things go wrong."

Claire hunched her shoulders.

"Sooner or later someone will get tired of waiting for you," Ostrenalia went on. "Tired of waiting for you to pick a side, tired of waiting for you to share what you know."

"Someone like you?" Claire didn't move.

Ostrenalia snorted an unladylike laugh. "No, Miss Stone. An unwilling student is a waste of time and effort, and in our field, a catastrophe waiting to happen. If you come to me and ask, I shall help. Others... well, not all that glitters is gold. Friends may not be, and there are some who believe they can recover the knowledge they desire through compulsion or experimentation." She pushed herself away from the railing and opened her purse, holding an envelope out to Claire. "This is for you."

"What is it?"

"I've no idea. It arrived at Bedford Row with a note asking me to give it to you should we meet. Do you know who it is from?"

Claire shook her head. The envelope was unmarked, and she certainly wasn't going to open it when she had an audience.

"Shame. I would have liked to explain to the sender how little I appreciate being used as a courier." She closed her bag with a snap. "Think about what I said, Miss Stone. I do not for one moment expect you to believe I am offering you my support out of some sense of altruism. I fully expect to personally profit from the venture in some way and at some time, directly or otherwise. But we are all monsters, in one way or another. I simply promise you that I have no interest in you personally. Which may be your safest option, under the circumstances. Do not wait too long."

The Sitharii swept away towards the street and Claire saw a Hrund climb down from an ornate carriage to hold its door open. The driver climbed back into his seat and, with a shrill *peeeep* and a blast of steam, the carriage moved away into the traffic.

Claire slipped her finger under the flap of the envelope and broke the seal.

"A golden ticket?" Stuart turned it over then back again. "An honest to god freaking golden ticket?"

Claire wasn't sure if it was his outrage that was tickling her, or if it was the ticket itself, but she had a fit of the giggles and couldn't stop. Stuart squinted and read the tightly printed script.

"I don't think so," said Claire, taking the ticket back. "The same phrase is repeated in Grenlik and Sitharii, and I'm guessing the other two are Hrund and Angel. Besides, I think I know who it's from, and why." She emptied the rest of the contents of the envelope onto her airbed.

"A scrap of a map with a hole burnt in it and a doodle in Grenlik," said Stuart. "Very enlightening."

"Want to come?"

"Come where?"

"Secret." Claire was enjoying herself. For the first time in a long while she felt as though there was something she could do, that she had a measure of control. Teasing Stuart was the sprinkles on top of the ice cream. "Road trip. Three or four days."

"Days? What about the snap-back?"

Some of the elation faded, but she clenched her jaw. "I can fix it. Can you?"

Stuart shrugged. "I guess."

"I need a yes or a no. I don't want to do this on my own."

"Do what?"

Claire chewed her bottom lip for a moment. It would have been fun to keep Stuart in the dark a little longer, but she needed to know she could rely on him.

"While I was with some Grenlix, well there's this spell and..." She took a breath. "There's this thing everybody is looking for. When we were trying to locate one in London, I accidentally found one further away."

"So who sent you the ticket?"

"I'm guessing somebody from the Grenlik academy. I'm being offered a chance to go and look for it."

"But why not officially, through channels?"

All the fun went out of the idea. Claire had been avoiding that thought, trying to focus on the fun of the adventure. Stuart had brought everything down to earth.

"Because they don't work."

"I thought everybody was playing ball — even the Angels."

"They pretended to, but..." Could she tell him how close they had come to killing her? Would he let her go? "They let everybody down."

Stuart pulled a face. "Nobody ever said it was safe to trust an Angel. So where do we have to go?"

"Edinburgh." Claire smiled, thinking he would like an excuse to go home, if only for a while. Instead his face dropped and he ran his hand roughly through his hair.

"Bugger."

Of the many possible responses, that was the one Claire had least expected. "Is that a problem?"

Stuart rubbed his hand across his head again. "Yes...no...might be. Look is there anybody else? I might not be the best help."

"Who?" snapped Claire. "Who do I have left? Jack will barely talk to me. I don't have Evie Jones, and Tolks has disowned me. Who else do I have? Who else can I trust?"

"Easy, girl," Stuart said, reaching out to take her hand. She stopped herself from jerking it away, but didn't return the pressure. He sighed. "It's — well, it may not be so easy."

"Why not?" Claire scrubbed the tears from her checks with fists.

"It's complicated."

Nana May frowned. "I'm not sure dear. I mean, going away with a young man for a week, and at your age..."

"Please, Nana. I promise we won't get up to anything. I need a break from... well... you know. Everything."

Her grandmother pursed her lips, tapping at them with a finger. "And tell me again where you are going?"

"Youth hostelling. In Whitby. Three or four nights. Then home again. It's girls and boys in different dormitories. Designed to prevent hanky-panky."

"But why so far away? Why not Southend? Can Stuart's little motorcycle go so far?"

Damn, she hadn't thought of that. Another lie. "It's stronger than it looks Nana. Kind of like you. Whitby is cool. It's got this big Goth vibe going on."

"You aren't going there to get anything pierced, are you?"

Claire smiled. "No, Nan. I just want to get away for a few days."

Nana said nothing and watched the TV for a few minutes. Claire held her breath, waiting for the next argument, or for approval, or to have to remind her nana what they had been talking about.

"This isn't anything to do with Underland, is it?"

That caught her by surprise. "How do you mean, Nana?"

"That place has a way of getting inside your life, of affecting you even when you aren't there." Bitterness glinted underneath her grandmother's even voice. "I know they say it isn't dangerous, but there are stories. People go missing, or they did in my time. Are they working you too hard? You looked very stiff this morning, as though you had been in a fight."

"Honestly, Nana, it was nothing."

"I know when you've been down there. I see you in the morning, nursing aches and pains."

Claire closed her eyes and bit the inside of her lip. "No, Nana. They know about Mum and Dad. They have me on light duties."

The lies layered on lies worked, and Nana May gave her reluctant blessing. Claire sent a text to Stuart to say they were on, then went to pack the smallest bag she could for the trip.

They stashed Stuart's bike and their crash helmets in a small lockup off the Seven Sisters Road. Claire didn't ask. The lockup made her think of Tolks' shop; slightly shady, but nothing overtly criminal. She didn't want to know what was going on, nor Stuart's involvement in it.

As soon as they were outside and Stuart had locked the door, he looked furtively up and down the alley. "Let's get out of here. Don't want anybody realising they don't recognise you."

A split second later they appeared in the locker room at SFU headquarters. Nothing new had been taped to her door, and there were no notes on the floor where they had been "posted" through the ventilation slots. Claire was relieved, but also disappointed that nobody needed her for the moment. But then, a little anonymity might help this side trip go more smoothly. It took her a few seconds to collect what she needed from her locker, then she was standing at the doorway, pointedly looking at her watch as Stuart ambled across the room to join her.

"What exactly is your hurry, woman?" Stuart grumbled. "I checked; the Edinburgh train doesn't leave for two hours. We have plenty of time."

Claire said nothing, but chivvied him along; first down to the private underground station hiding beneath Underland's version of the Tower of London, then up to the platform level of Broad Street Station. Stuart turned left, towards the train platforms. Claire stood still and wondered how long he would keep walking until he realised he was on his own.

Eventually he stopped, glanced left and right, then over his shoulder. "Whut?"

Clair grinned hugely and cocked her head in the opposite direction.

"But that leads to... oh you can not be serious"

Still smiling beatifically, Claire nodded. Stuart fell in beside her. "You know it'll take three or four times as long?"

"I do."

"And I thought we were in a hurry?"

"We are, but somebody else is paying and I may never get another chance or another reason." Claire stopped at the Dock Office and looked out through the tightly packed gondolas and lifting bags. "Today we fly."

There was a minor unpleasantness with the Sitharii manning the ticket office, who tried his best to insist their ticket only allowed them to travel steerage, but after Claire threatened to call whoever had issued the ticket and see what they thought, he duly assigned them two separate, non-adjoining rooms on the Caledonian, lifting in less than forty minutes and would they kindly make haste to slip number six before the captain called the gate closed.

Claire tried to run, but Stuart held her back to a brisk walk. Claire protested. "But I want to see."

"You're a bloody Warrior, and in uniform. Act like one."

Claire was ready to grimace, even poke out her tongue at Stuart for throwing this level of Adult at her, but his face was so serious she decided now was very much not the time. His face was fixed, emotionless, but she could see tension around his eyes and in the stiffness of his walk. He was, as usual, right. She straightened up and marched alongside him, struggling not to gawk up as the massive manoeuvring nacelle they were walking under.

A rating directed them to the upper deck, where a purser checked their boarding pass, then asked to see the golden ticket, then checked the pass again. "Welcome aboard, Warriors. Please, make yourselves comfortable in the lounge while we prepare your rooms."

They followed his directions forward and through a sliding door held open for them by a liveried Hrund. Claire bit back a squeal of glee. The lounge was also an observation deck, edged entirely with tall windows. At the front, the windows reached to the floor. Half way along each wall was a door, leading out onto a wooden platform that headed off towards the stern of the vessel. Large signs attached to the doors said "Not to be used unless safety net is deployed".

Claire dropped her bag into a chair and sauntered to the forward wall. There wasn't much to see, at least not while they were still docked, so she came back to where Stuart had already summoned a waiter.

"May I fetch you something to drink, Warrior?"

She shook her head. Stuart ordered coffee and the waiter drifted away. Claire sat. "Want to tell me why you're so edgy?"

"Want to tell me why we're drifting up to Scotland in this gas-bag when we could be there in seven hours on the train?"

"I already told you why."

"I don't buy it."

Claire blinked, surprised. "You don't believe me?"

Stuart gave her a long look, but at the end of it his eyes softened a little. "I'm saying I thought we were in a hurry. I thought you were in a rush because of your parents. I don't see the sense in

116

taking the entire day to get somewhere. You know this thing stops at Birmingham too?"

Claire didn't, but she didn't care. Stuart had slapped her in the face, using the parent card like that. He didn't have the right, not after the disgrace of helping Aslnaff try to destroy her in the past. Claire picked up her bag, suddenly wanting some distance between them.

"I think I'll go and see if my room is ready. Enjoy your coffee."

"Claire, wait. I didn't mean…"

She walked away to a background of Stuart swearing angrily under his breath.

20

Her cabin wasn't ready, but a steward dubiously directed her to the second-class lounge, on the lower deck. Though smaller, it was much the same as the lounge above, but with smaller windows and simple tables; no crisp white linen here, or delicate flowers in vases clipped to the tables. Nor was there a walkway around the outside of the hull.

There were more people, and Claire was attracting uncomfortable attention. She went back to the central corridor and walked aft. Thirty paces brought her to another door and, through that, into what was obviously steerage. Bare benches bolted to the wooden deck and porthole-sized windows barely big enough to let light in. Eyes turned on her with distrust and ill-will.

A junior purser rushed across the room towards her. "Please, Miss. I don't think you should be here. Are you lost?"

It took Claire a moment to snap free of the hostility. "Ah, no. Not really. I was looking to see if there was a better view anywhere."

"A view?"

Claire felt herself blush. "I sort of have a thing about engines."

The junior officer stared at her for a moment then shook his head. "Best you head back upstairs, Miss."

Claire nodded, face burning, and turned away. Before she reached the door, the purser spoke again. "I'll ask the Chief Engineer, Miss. No promises, though. He's not one for strangers, nor for ladies."

Claire flashed a grateful smile over her shoulder and headed back towards first class.

By the time she got to the lounge the only evidence Stuart had been there was a dirty coffee cup. Their rooms were obviously ready, so Claire found out where hers was and explored that instead. It was lovely, with a small en-suite washroom, all brass fixtures and china decorated in Wedgwood blue.

A writing desk doubled as a dressing table and an ornate chair completed the furniture, and she was disappointed to see that her window was a porthole barely larger than those in steerage. The bed was a little small, and a little firm, and there was a net along the side to stop her rolling out. They would either jump home, or take the train.

It took her a moment to realise that her little spat with Stuart was taking the edge off her airship ride, and her first reaction was to get angry. How dare he judge her, and how dare he spoil her first — perhaps only — airship flight? She dropped everything onto her bed, including her communicator and PPG, and stormed out of the room. She was going to watch the launch and if he was in the lounge as well, to hell with him.

The observation lounge was mercifully Stuart-free. She took a seat as close to the bow window as she could and watched as the airship hauled itself into the sky. It was anti-climactic, and left her feeling cheated. She was even denied a view of UnderLondon as they beat their way north-west; moments after breaking free of Broad Street station they were enveloped in yellow-grey cloud.

Claire sat in her cabin, wishing she had thought to bring a book. A knock on the door made her jump, then smile. Stuart had finally come to apologise. She was still angry with him, but her heart skipped a beat at the thought. "Come in."

There was a pause, then the polite tap repeated. Claire opened the door and peered over the head of a young Grenlik. "The Grenlik Engineer's compliments, miss, and he would be pleased to show you the engines at five pm, miss. Oh, and he said to say "briefly". Made me promise, too."

Claire smiled at the uncomfortable young rating. "Thank you,

Grenlik. Please thank the Grenlik Engineer for me and say I will be ready promptly at five minutes to five."

The rating scurried away before she could close the door. She glanced at her watch. Thirty minutes to kill. Not really time to do anything. Should she change? She looked at herself in the wall mirror. What she had on was as appropriate as anything in her bag and wouldn't get tangled in anything.

A gentle rap on the door at five minutes to five announced the return of the rating, who led her aft, through the first-class kitchens and to a spiral staircase at the very stern of the vessel. Two levels down a sturdy hatch opened out onto an engineering deck that ran the length of the hull.

She followed the rating to a bank of controls and gauges. Two older Grenlix sat at the board, like pilot and co-pilot. Behind them, on a raised platform, was a swivel chair upholstered in leather. The Grenlik sitting in this chair wore dirtier overalls than most others, yet he wore them like a King's robes.

"Grenlik Chief Engineer," said Claire, bowing slightly, and correctly following etiquette by neither offering nor requesting any names.

"Warrior." The engineer inclined his head. "I am told you have an interest in my domain."

Claire wasn't sure if the engineer had a sense of humour, or if he was really so stuck up he thought of the engineering deck as a "domain". Still, she wanted a look around, so she played the game.

"I do, Grenlik Engineer. I have a general interest in engines and mechanisms. This is my first trip on an airship."

The engineer studied her for a moment, but she couldn't read his expression. After a moment, he pushed himself up from his chair and stepped down from the dais. "Then let us try to make it memorable." He summoned another Grenlik and muttered to him. The replacement stepped up onto the dais and stood next to the chair. Claire got the feeling that only one backside polished that particular seat.

"This way," said the chief engineer, and led her off towards the stern. For half an hour they wandered around engines and control systems and drive shafts to the point where Claire was getting bored. She was even getting a headache. There was a noise, like a gnat whining in her ear, and it was driving her to distraction. She looked for a way to cut the visit short.

"And lastly, the power room." The engineer crouched beside an elongated trap door, grabbed an inset ring, and hauled it open.

Claire clapped her hands to her ears but it made no difference, the buzzing was in her skull, or inside her head, and it was a dozen times louder.

"How do you put up with that?"

"With what?" The engineer's face was blank.

"The noise."

The Grenlik cocked his head. "I hear nothing unusual."

"Shrill, like an insect."

"Ah, we do not hear high-pitched tones."

Claire winced. "Lucky you."

"Do you wish to continue?"

Claire was about to say "No", when she realised there was a harsh, jagged edge to the sound. "What's down there?"

As an answer, the engineer waved his hand at the open door in a gesture that said "go down if you want to see". Claire looked below. A flight of narrow stairs led down into a space filled with confusing flickers of blue and purple light. She was about to decline the offer, but the expression on the Grenlik's face hinted at a contemptuous 'thought not'. Also, the noise was wrong. It was the sort of noise that shouldn't come from a well-functioning machine. If the Grenlik couldn't hear it, perhaps she should take a look.

Three rows of long crystals stretched half the length of the hull, mounted in heavy wooden frames and clamped in place. Elegant end-caps engraved with magical circuitry cupped either end of each crystal, and thick cables disappeared up into the deck above.

Down either side a pair of crystals each five metres long gave off a deep violet light that made her eyes ache if she looked at them too long. Along the centre were conventional energy crystals, but Claire thought they looked too big for the job they needed to do. "What are those?" She pointed to the crystals along the edges.

"Lifters." The engineer gave her a look that that implied she should know such a simple fact. "Do you think these things can get off the ground with these tiny gasbags? They would need to be ten times the size."

"So these help? So why do you need the gasbags?"

"Because they can reduce the weight, not eliminate it. Hyperbolic function. They give nine tenths of the lift. Any more costs too much energy. The gasbag takes the last fraction."

"Which is why you need the over-size energy crystals - to power these lifters."

They had been ambling along the deck, and Claire realised the horrible whine had abruptly become much louder. She winced and turned her head from side to side. The sound was coming from a specific point, directly ahead. She took another step forward and cocked her head again.

"That noise is coming from here," and she pointed at the forward port lifting crystal.

"I hear nothing. If there was a problem, I would have been told."

Claire didn't argue. All crystals vibrated. She could feel the contented hum of the power crystals on the air, comforting and warm, and a slightly more enthusiastic hum from the other lifters. This crystal was screaming in agony. She raised her hand to it, not touching but hovering a couple of millimetres away, then focused her thoughts and let them slip into the crystal's matrix. It was nothing she had learned. This was more of the instinctive magic,

122

the stuff she knew as if somebody had downloaded it into her head when she wasn't looking.

The matrix was tense, its rigid structure trying to twist. She followed the stress lines deeper, diving ever closer to the crystal's heart, torque wrenching at the structure until its pain became her own. And then she saw it. A brilliance in the otherwise uniform energy field.

She let herself get cautiously closer. It was a crack. No, it wasn't even a crack yet. It was a misalignment, a flaw in the crystal lattice. Disrupted energy arced and spat across it, adding to the stress, generating a disruption to the flow.

"There is a flaw here." Her voice sounded odd as she heard it through the crystal, sharp edged and brittle.

"There is no flaw. These are the finest lifters money can buy, painstakingly tested and align—" The Grenlik Engineer sounded deeply offended, but Claire didn't give a damn. She didn't have time. As she watched, a pressure wave rippled across the matrix; not outward from the flaw, but upwards from beneath. She ripped her mind free of the crystal, grabbed the engineer by the back of his jacket, and threw them both beneath a frame.

21

There was a crack like a mountain breaking in two and a pressure wave pushed them under the power crystal and out the other side. Sirens screamed and the deck tilted under them, dipping forward and right. Claire saw a hand in front of her; the Grenlik was already on his feet and offering to help her up. She grabbed and pulled, but snatched her hand away when the engineer tried to pull her towards the ladder.

"We have to go. We have to abandon ship."

"How?"

"There are parachutes," but the engineer sounded uncertain, and Claire wondered if he lacked confidence in their quantity or quality.

"Can't we fix this?" Claire was edging closer to the damaged lifter. The crystal had broken in two, one half still pulsing violet, the other dark. Bright sparks and arcs of heavy-duty magic twisted through the gap between them.

"Are you mad? Touch anything and it will burn you to a crisp. Get away from there, girl."

But Claire was already tugging at the clasps that held the end-cap onto the darkened section. "Help me. If we can get this off, and maybe kick the dead crystal out of the way, we can stop the other one leaking."

"It will kill you."

Claire shrugged his hand from her shoulder and turned her head until she could look him in the eye. Grenlix were difficult to read, but her time with Tolks had given her and idea of their expressions. The Chief Engineer was afraid, genuinely, but there was a hint of deception in his eyes. Claire brushed it aside. She was probably seeing what she wanted to, or expected to. She glared at

"… It would split like a glacier calving," Stuart agreed. "And what exactly did you do this time?"

Claire squirmed like she was in front of the head teacher for a misdemeanour and resented Stuart for it, even though she knew the fault was not his. "I got them to move the broken stuff out of the way then put the plug back on the end of the crystal."

"And?"

"And what?"

"Don't try to lie to me, Claire Stone. I've been lied to by real artists, and you aren't one. Did you use more of that damned stuff? The white magic?"

"Why do you…?"

"Because you have black smudges around your eyes that don't look like grease-dirt to me."

Claire hesitated, then nodded. "I had to pump up the broken crystal. It had leaked too much…"

But Stuart wasn't listening. He had thrown his hands in the air and made a noise that was half grunt, half snarl, but obviously disgusted. Now he was pacing back and forth across the cabin, hand stuck in his pockets, forehead so tense he had a unibrow. Twice, he opened his mouth as if to speak and Claire waited for the tirade. It never came. He sat down on the bed, not as close, and sighed.

"Get some rest while I try to find out where this wreck is going now." He left. No kiss, not even a held hand. Just an odd look back from the door as he unlocked it.

Claire lay on the bed, staring up at the ceiling, fists clenched by her side. She had saved everybody; saved the airship, even. And he looked at her like she had done something wrong.

Two bright spots of pain stabbed at the back of her eyes. She winced, closed them, and forced herself to relax as a generalised headache washed backwards through her skull. Maybe she should try to rest. For a few minutes, at least.

She had no sooner nodded off than Stuart was shaking her shoulder to wake her. If he had wanted her to rest, then he should have given her... but why was it dark enough to need a table light?

"What time is it?" Claire blinked sleep from her eyes.

"About ten," Stuart chuckled softly. "When you nap, you really nap."

"Where are we?"

"About a half-hour out from Waverley. The Captain said, and I quote, 'this service is to Edinbelow, so that is where this vessel is going while I have air beneath me and steam to drive me". Then he and two Hrund insisted I leave the bridge."

Claire snorted, then shook her head gently. No aches, no pains, and no nosebleed. Result. Maybe she was getting the better of this perverse power that fate had seen fit to gift her. She climbed off the bed, put her hands on the hem of her tee-shirt, and looked expectantly at Stuart. He simply settled back in his chair and smiled, raising his eyebrows. Claire pulled a face and poked her tongue at him. "Out."

Stuart laughed and kissed her on the cheek as he left. Claire pulled off the tee-shirt and threw it on the bed, then sniffed at her pits. Deodorant would do, for now, as there was no time for a shower or bath. Trust a boy not to wake her up until the last minute. She walked to the hand basin and splashed some water on her face to help her wake up. Then she saw herself in the mirror, and froze. She looked like an old woman; twenty, at least. The dark smudges under her eyes were black now, and puffy. Her lips looked pinched and dehydrated, and her eyes dull and lifeless until tears sparkled in the corners.

What was she doing to herself? Was this the price she had to pay to get her parents back? Years taken from her? She pulled back her shoulders and glared defiantly at herself. If that was what it took, then she would pay it. She bent forward, cupped her hands in the cool water and threw it at her face. As soon as her skin was dry she reached for her makeup bag, and took out the small tube of concealer she kept there for break-outs. Giving in was not an option.

"Can we get a map anywhere? A street map."

Stuart frowned. "Not that I know of. Edinbelow is much smaller than in the Real. Don't really need them."

"Library?"

"Don't think they have one. What about your Grenlik friends?"

Claire hesitated. Stuart wasn't aware how much she didn't trust the Grenlix, and she wasn't sure now was the time to tell him. Besides, she still felt bad about how much she now loathed them. To taint a whole people with a sin committed by a few was a despicable thing, and there was a nasty word for it in the Real.

"Best not to involve them. Politics. They may not know what's going on down south and..." She let her words trail off, knowing she was digging herself into a hole. She looked up and down the street. To her left loomed a mountain, bigger even than Mount Primrose, and to her right a castle crouched on the top of a hill. "Where are we?"

"That's Mount Holyrood," he said, jerking his thumb. "And the castle is the SFU and police headquarters. This is Meadow Street."

"There are that many Angels here?"

Stuart looked sour. "They're like frickin' termites. They run everything; police, crime, brothels, even the SFU."

Claire's eyebrows tried to crawl up and over her head. She hadn't expected that.

"The Grenlix are restricted to a couple of Hives along the back side of Princes Street. Virtually no Sitharii except for women. There's rumours the bastards even have human girls working for them."

Which should have been impossible. Underkin couldn't touch

humans; it hurt them like stinging nettles. Claire shook her head and pushed the thought away. It wasn't why they were here.

Without a map, she would have to do it the hard way. She could use her magic like sonar, sending out a ping and watching for the echo. From that, they could get a direction at least. She needed to calm her mind to be able to focus on the spell.

It was all but impossible. The street wasn't that busy. There was foot traffic, and the occasional steam lorry or omnibus, but it wasn't as though they were at the edge of a football crowd. She tried again, this time managing to build the spell. It was sloppy and unbalanced but she let it go anyway.

There was no return ping. Nothing.

"I need somewhere quiet," Claire said. "Somewhere I can concentrate."

"There's a squash bar on Cockburn Street. Come on."

It wasn't a steep hill, but to Claire it was as though she was climbing the side of a mountain. As soon as they began to ascend, her legs ached loudly and she couldn't get enough air. She pushed on, trying to hide it from Stuart. He would only worry, or worse, fuss.

The shop was rougher than the squash bars she was used to in London. This place looked more like a biker's cafe from a noire 60s movie, all bench seats and tables with cracked Formica tops. Instead of a Hrund serving, it was an Angel, and they were both served deeply suspicious looks long before their drinks turned up. Claire noticed that Stuart earned an especially long glance. At least it was quiet enough for her to do what she needed to.

It was still hard. Much harder than it ought to be, anyway. She wondered if the density of the magical field was weaker in Edinbelow, but pushed the idea aside. She was making excuses. Deep breaths helped, a little, and she slowly cleared her thoughts.

With exaggerated care, Claire put together the elements of the spell, ignoring the outraged observation that it was taking her longer than the first time she had ever tried it. Focus. Concentration. She checked it over again, making sure she hadn't forgotten anything, then gently fed power into it from the local field. When the spell tugged at her to be about its business, she let it go.

It drifted outwards, not so fast but looking hard for anything that was a shard, or that matched the flavour of the cube into which the shards would fit. Claire held it in her thoughts, minute after minute, feeding it a trickle more magic to make up for the distance travelled, then a little more as it got farther away and more tenuous. Eventually, after more than ten minutes, she could no longer hold onto it and the spell evaporated into the background field.

"It's not here."

23

"Whut?"

"I can't find it."

"Hell, girl, you found it from London. How did you lose it?"

"I didn't lose anything," she glared at him. "If the shard was anywhere near this place I would have detected it."

"Hidden?"

She shook her head. "Concealments show up as holes. You can feel when there are places you can't look."

"So do it again. Look farther. "

Claire couldn't meet his eyes. "Can't."

"Again, whut?"

"Because I'm fried. Because my head feels like cotton wool and I can't concentrate." She slammed her hand on the table, her eyes glaring at him gimlet-sharp. "Because the damned white shit is trying to get me to use it other than the regular stuff. The bloody thing is not here."

"Did you check before we left?"

Claire curled her lip at him, folded her arms tightly across her chest, and stared out the window.

Stuart grabbed her arm and hauled her from the chair. Claire let out and angry "Heyyy!" and tried to pull her arm from his hand. He tightened his grip, hurting her, and hauled her towards the door. "Out. Now."

Her feet tangled in her chair, sending it clattering across the floor. Her arms windmilled as she lost her balance, but Stuart pulled her onto her feet. Behind her, the Angel who had served them shouted. The accent was so thick she couldn't make out what it was, but it was angry.

As soon as they were outside the shop Stuart hauled her into a narrow passageway. It was exactly the sort of place she would never go down on her own if she didn't have to, close and dark and threatening. The houses on either side leaned inwards, blocking off what little light the dirty yellow sky offered. She caught a glimpse of a name board — Anchor something — gone in a flash of grimy bricks.

She stopped fighting, and ran with Stuart rather than dragging back from him. He eased his grip but didn't let go. At the end of the alley they turned left, dodged across the busy road, then dove into what she first thought was the gate to someone's yard, but which turned into another narrow passage. This one was totally enclosed, and dark apart from the faint yellow glow at either end. They broke out into daylight, sloping downhill at first, then pattering down a flight of steps onto a cobbled street barely worthy of the name.

"Where are we going?" Claire had to fight for the air to speak. Half the run had been steeply uphill, and her throat was burning. She finally pulled her arm free of Stuart's and stumbled to a halt. She bent over, hand on her knees to stop herself falling, gasping for air.

"As soon as you did your wee rant back there, yon Angel in the back was hard at work on his communicator, and staring at the both of us while he did it."

"And?"

"If we're lucky he was calling the po-liss."

Claire opened her mouth to speak, but Stuart's expression silenced her. He looked scared. Properly scared.

"Are we done here?" His voice was hard, urgent.

"Why? And why all the running?"

"I tried to tell you. This isn't a nice place. What's our next move?"

Claire tried to focus, but her head was spinning from the run, and from a weariness below that was deeper and more pervasive.

"I don't... I'm not sure."

Stuart rubbed his forehead. "Can you jump? Can you jump all the way home? They say it's possible."

"They said you commuted from here."

"Oh." His face fell. "That's where the rumour came from. Well, could you?"

"Could you?"

"I can make my own way back."

Claire was worried now. The urgency wasn't leaving Stuart's voice. Whatever was chewing on him, it was getting worse - or at least wasn't getting better. She built the image of her room in her mind - not at home, but her impromptu sanctuary at Nana May's. She layered in the smell of her airbed, and the slight mustiness from the accumulated crafting junk that Nana stored there. It would be a huge jump, and she needed all the detail she could think of to make the location lock tight.

Tentatively, she tried to wrap the magic around her that would pull her from this place to that. Not making the jump, but opening the connection. Her mind screamed pain at her and pushed the thoughts aside like they burned.

"No. Not back home anyway. What is our problem?"

Stuart looked up and down the street, balanced on his toes as if he was expecting to run. "I'm not sure. Not exactly, anyway. Things aren't like London up here. They're... looser." He drew a breath. "There are folk here who want words with me. Unkind words. And I can't be sure but I have a feeling that damned Angel was as interested in you as me." He shook his head. "We need to get away from here."

"Train?"

"The station will be crawling with his people by now."

"Who?"

"Willie. Willie Marr. The flint-hearted bastard who runs things down here."

136

"A human runs the SFU?"

"The SFU is a joke, and is run by an Angel. Willie Marr runs the gangs. Look, this is too complicated to go into. Wee Willie has eyes everywhere, and word is out on us already. I'd hoped we could crash in, do what we needed and run, but we've sabotaged that. We have to leave." He held out his hand. "I'll take you up top. We might be able to shake his people more easily up there."

Claire reached out, opening her thoughts so he could steer when they jumped. As their fingers touched, something punched her hard in the chest. An instant later there was the sound of a pencil dropping to the floor. Claire looked down to see the quarrel from a hand-bow roll across the pavement and into the gutter.

"Shit." Stuart staggered as he too took a bolt. Only their Kevlar's, the amulets of personal protection, had saved them from injury, and they could take two or three hits before they failed. He grabbed her hand and ran, but slid to a stop before he had taken a half-dozen steps. Two figures stepped out of the alley Stuart had been heading for.

Claire turned, looking back down the street. Two more bodies walked out of the lane they had run from moments before, and farther up the street, more appeared. As she watched, what few Underkin there were disappeared into shops and houses, or scurried quickly along the pavement and away from whatever was about to happen.

Something else was wrong, and she ground her teeth as she tried to figure out what. She looked again at the figures standing in front of them. She had dismissed them as Angels, but now she looked again, looked closer, and her heart stopped. They weren't Angels. They weren't teenage boys.

"Those are men!"

24

Another handbow bolt slammed into Claire's kevlar, driving her into Stuart's arms. A faint tingle against her skin warned her that the amulet was exhausted, and would grant no further protection until it had time to recharge. Stuart lurched against her as another bolt also struck him.

"My kevlar is down," she hissed in his ear.

"Mine will be when they shoot again."

"Again? They're just softening us up, right?"

She felt him shake his head, and his body twisted as he tried to shove her behind him. It was a gallant act, but pointless. They had enemies on all sides.

Stuart cried out and dropped to one knee. Claire squatted beside him and looked down. Bile filled her throat as she saw the quarrel buried in his thigh. It was all happening again; friends were being hurt for her, risking their life for her.

"Run." He grated the word out through clenched teeth. "They may just want me."

"I can't..."

"Go." His voice softened. "Please. I can't bear to think what these bastards would do to you if..."

He screamed, his head ripped away from her by the bolt that appeared in his shoulder. The cry cut off as his head cracked against the pavement.

Claire swung her head from side to side, trying to keep all the men in view. Those armed held their weapons casually, but she knew that if she tried to run she would simply collect a bolt in the leg, or worse her back. Her hands shook when she saw that those who didn't have hand-bows were carrying long knives that glinted evilly in the sick glow of Underland's sky. Almost as evil as the grins crawling across their faces.

"You stay there, girlie."

"Wouldn't want to hurt you if you tried to run."

"Not our job."

"Yet." Sick chuckles all around.

"Unless we get lucky later."

Stuart struggled to rise, but sank back to the ground with a groan. The closest of the men was near enough for her to smell now, stale sweat and beer, with a hint of smoke that wasn't tobacco.

"You pissed off the wrong man, warrior-boy. Mr Marr is not pleased with you." He turned to his companion. "Did the bounty say alive or dead?"

"Don't think they care."

A smile grew wider, and hand-bow rose to point at Stuart's heart. "It'd be worth it to get to kill him."

The hand-bow thrummed and the bolt skipped off the cobbles next to Stuart, bright sparks striking from the steel tip. The men laughed and mocked the shooter, but he was staring at Claire. "Do that again, missy, and we'll do you; right here right now. Right in front of your boyfriend. And we'll make him watch. Clear?"

Claire met his eyes and held them. The tiny push she had been able to conjure up was barely enough to deflect the bolt, but it had saved Stuart. She was terrified. She could feel her arms trembling even though she was leaning on them and her heart pounded so loud she could hear nothing else. Still, she was damned if she would give the bastard the satisfaction of making her look away first.

His cold eyes wrinkled at the edges a fraction of a second before he laughed, but Claire was still too slow. He had been distracting her. Arms grabbed at her, hauling her to her feet, and a cold line pressed against her throat. She froze.

The man who had tried to shoot Stuart was in charge. He stepped closer to her, touching her face with the back of a filthy finger. He stroked it down from the corner of her eye to her neck then, snake-strike fast, he back-handed her across the mouth. She slumped, terrified that the knife would slice her neck. They held her up and he hit her again, this time from the other side, and she felt the knife return. Her mouth filled with the taste of copper and she gingerly poked her tongue at the hole she had bitten in her cheek.

The man turned back to Stuart. He raised his foot and nudged the bolt in Stuart's shoulder sideways. Stuart howled and his back arched. Claire heard herself scream "No," but knew they would only enjoy it more. The man kicked at the bolt again, then raised his boot until the sole was hovering over the fletching at the top. Nausea bubbled in Claire's throat as the thug lowered his boot and pressed the quarrel deeper into Stuart's flesh. Stuart howled.

Time twitched. For an instant, the knife against her neck grew so hot it stung. She wasn't surprised. She knew the grip was glowing white hot. The thug to her left screamed and the knife went away. So did he, swearing in a voice filled with panic.

She twisted until she was facing the man to her right, the one holding her arm. She braced herself, then struck him in the chest with the palm of her hand. There was a flash, a tug on her other arm, and he flew backwards. She turned away before he landed.

Two hand-bows thrummed, the sounds merging into one. Claire didn't have time to move her hands, but the bolts both buried themselves in a pillow of solid air six inches from her breastbone. She looked at them, then reached out and took one in either hand. All I need is the fricking Neo shades she thought.

The two who had shot her had already turned to run. She guessed they would be bringing friends, but by the time anybody else got here, it would be over. Still, there was a point to make. She flicked the quarrels up, setting a spin on them. Raising her own hands, she caught them at the top of their arc, now by the shafts and not the points, and threw them like knives. Each buried itself in the thigh of a gunman. More swearing ensued as they scrabbled away on their knees.

Now she could focus on the man in charge, who was only now realising his plan had gone desperately wrong. He was off balance, trying to look over his shoulder but his body couldn't twist. She decided to help him. Again with open palm, she struck him in the small of the back, angling the blow upwards so that his weight would lift away from Stuart.

His arms flailed as he flew. Claire thought it looked like he was flapping, trying to fly away from her. He landed face first and slid along the cobbles. By the time he had rolled over, eyes shining hate for her, she had conjured a ball of energy in her hand.

"Pretty, isn't it," she said, her voice flat. And it was. It sparkled with half the colours of the rainbow. He struggled to his knees, facing her, obviously planning to return and deal with this uppity girl from the soft south. She tossed the little bomb to the cobbles a foot in front of him. A soundless detonation gouged a hole a foot across in the road and he fell onto his back.

"Go away." Claire said. "You are annoying me."

He scrambled to his feet and ran, leaving his fallen to fend for themselves. Claire knew he would be off to find replacements, but by the time reinforcements arrived, there would be nobody here.

Stuart was out, but she could see his chest rise and fall, and his eyes winced every few seconds. It was time for them to leave. She pictured her bedroom with such clarity she might already be there. She had no hesitation now, no doubts. She was not using the white magic, she was the white magic. She had unconsciously opened herself to it fully. The choice had been Stuart's life, and possibly her own. Now they were one. She took his hands, ripped a hole in space, and slid through.

Claire's aim was so precise that they emerged not only in her room, but with Stuart lying exactly along the centre of her bed. It huffed in alarm as it took his sudden weight but did not burst. His eyes flickered open.

"We're safe. Lie still."

His head rose form the pillow but she held him down with a firm hand. Instead, his eyes darted nervously from side to side, then widened as he realised where he was. Claire took her hand from his brow and laid two fingers across his lips.

"This may hurt. Sorry, but I need you with me, not stuck in some hospital."

His eyes stopped their flickering and fastened onto her. The calm, dispassionate tone had surprised her, too, and she wasn't entirely sure where it had come from. Or the decision to fix Stuart herself.

She went to his shoulder first. The bolt had punched through his jacket and shirt, and there was no way she could get either off without wiggling the quarrel around and doing him more damage inside. If she drew the bolt without getting rid of the clothes, it would take longer to get to the wound.

She drew two quick arcs with her finger, either side of the bolt. The magic knew what she wanted, or had it told her what it wanted? Either way, the fabric beneath her finger misted into nothing, leaving two small donuts of cloth she could easily lift away.

There was a little blood, but not as much as she expected. The bolt just poked into his skin. She thought she ought to feel sick, or at least squeamish, but there was nothing more than analytical curiosity.

"This may hurt."

"Whut? No…"

But before he could move, or raise a hand to stop her, Claire placed one hand lightly on his chest, the bolt poking up between two fingers, then grabbed the end of the shaft and pulled. Stuart should have screamed, even fainted, but he hissed like an angry cat and looked surprised. Claire laid the bolt to one side and looked at the now-puckered hole. Blood welled up and trickled down Stuart's chest. Claire touched a finger to the hole, pushing it inside, and let the magic do what it needed to.

There was no element of control. In no sense was she guiding the magic. She wouldn't know what to tell it if she could. But it was part of her now, or her it. Stuart closed his eyes, groaned, and his face lost all its colour. Claire lifted her finger, and left a scab.

"I must do the same to your leg."

Stuart didn't open his eyes, but he nodded. Claire repeated the procedure, with the same sound effects, then knelt back on her heels and watched. The colour came back to his face and his eyes opened. He didn't say anything, but looked at her with a thousand unspoken questions.

"How do you feel?"

He flexed his leg and his shoulder, then again with more vigour. "Aches. Cold, too, but it all seems good." None of the questions in his eyes went away. If anything, there were even more.

"Good," said Claire. "We need to find food."

Claire got to her feet. Stuart rose less gracefully, and got to the bedroom door in time to watch her collapse and fall to the bottom of the stairs.

25

"So, what now?" Stuart seated himself on the sewing chair. Claire dropped onto the airbed, then grimaced when she hit the floor through the under-inflated mattress. The fall down the stairs had knocked her unconscious for a few moments, and when she awoke she had no memory beyond arriving at Edinbelow and finding no shard. Though Stuart had filled her on the details, they were unreal and incomplete. Her Nana had banished her to bed with a prescription for sleep and paracetamol, and hadn't allowed Stuart to visit for two days.

"You're still missing at least one piece, maybe two. Are you going to back to your Grenlik friends?"

"Not sure I have any of those left," Claire grumbled. She searched under the table for the air pump and connected it to the bed. "Here, make yourself useful."

Stuart dutifully began to step on the inflator. "You fallen out with your buddy at the Grenlik university?"

"Academy, and I don't know. Haven't heard from him for days though. Weeks, in fact."

"Did you leave on good terms?"

Claire opened her mouth to answer, but had to think back. She wasn't sure. She seemed to be in a bad mood with everybody. "Probably not," she admitted.

"Then he might be waiting for you to cool down?"

Claire grunted. It was possible, but it wasn't how she wanted things to play out. They should be helping her, coming to her with ideas. It still seemed as though all they were interested in were their own projects, and their own skins.

"The last shard I know about now is the one the Angels had in Mount Pleasant. If I could get inside I might be able to find it."

"And exactly how will you get inside Mount Pleasant?"

"Are you planning on running out of questions any time soon, Stu?"

"He might, but I doubt I will." Nana May stood in the doorframe, leaning on the edge. She pointed at the foot pump. "And for future reference, that thing sounded far less innocent from the lounge."

Claire went bright red, but Stuart grinned and wagged his eyebrows at Nana May. She glared at him, then chuckled.

"How much did you hear?" Claire asked

"Enough to know you are being less than honest with me, Claire Stone, and I won't have that. Not in my own house and not while I am responsible for you. Downstairs, both of you. I'll make us some tea and we can get to the bottom of this.

Stuart followed Claire down the stairs, and was thus no help at all. Claire idled as much as she could, frantically trying to figure out how little she could get away with revealing. They sat in the neat, tiny lounge, side by side on the sofa.

"You're on your own here, girl," said Stuart. Claire flashed him an angry look but he met and held her eyes. "The lady is your kin; it's up to you what you tell her. I'll say nothing so I don't mess up your story, but I won't lie to her for you. I'm with you, but I'm staying schtum."

Claire let the glare fade, trying to be angry about but not being able to fault his logic.

"Besides," he added. "You might try telling her the truth."

This surprised her, and earned Stuart another glare. She was so used to keeping secrets and telling lies that being open felt alien.

Nana May came in a few minutes later, three mugs on a tray, sugar and biscuits. She arranged herself in her armchair, swept some imaginary crumbs off her skirt, and pinioned Claire with gimlet sharp eyes.

"Right, young lady, what have you been up to?"

Claire told her everything — more or less. She left out the white magic, and she left out the battle with the Morph Lord, but a highly compressed outline of everything else went in.

It was catharsis, even when she had to admit that she had put her parents into hospital. That was the point where her voice failed her, where her throat squeezed so tight there were no more words, and when the tears ran down her face. Nana May levered herself to her feet, waving away Stuart's offer of help. She stopped a foot in front of Claire.

The retelling weighed down on Claire's heart, as did a deep dread of what her Nana was going to say. Was she going to throw Claire out? Would she call the police?

"Could you have done anything differently?"

"I...I could have backed down. When I was warned."

"And how many others would have been hurt if you did? Could you have done what you did differently?"

Claire shook her head.

"Did you, and do you, honestly believe you were acting in the general good at the time?"

A nod.

"Then why are you punishing yourself, child?"

And then she was kneeling in front of her Nana, arms around frail bones, face buried deep in the comforting cardigan as she wailed like a child.

At some point Stuart left the room. Claire didn't realise until she felt her grandmother's arms drawing her back towards the couch. Stuart appeared moments later, delivering fresh tea at the perfect moment.

"Now, what is it you and this young man were discussing upstairs."

"A thing we need is being hidden in Mount Primrose."

"That place hides many things," said Nana May, shocking Claire with the bitterness in her voice. "And some are best left there."

146

"We were trying to figure out how to get in, Mrs M," said Stuart. "Apart from anything else, though, our Claire is a little thin on allies at the moment. Or there's many as say they are, but few she feels are trustworthy."

"Are you trustworthy, young man?"

Stuart gave wry chuckle. "Aye, missus. Absolutely guaranteed."

"Are there any other real people you trust. Friends from the SFU?"

Claire shook her head. "Going in directly as a Warrior did me no favours."

"What about the other Warrior. Evelyn?"

Claire's eyes filled with tears again. "They took her away, Nana. They used magic to burn out her memories and change her before they dumped her back in the Real."

Nana May pinched her bottom lip between finger and thumb for a moment, then put her arm on Claire's leg. "But we are having this conversation, young lady."

Claire looked up, into her Nana's smile, and felt her eyes open as wide as saucers. Nana May winked.

"And when you've attended to that, I'll show you the jump-point I know inside Mount Primrose."

26

Claire got to the cafe early. Very early. She had sent instructions in a letter – 'If you want to know more about your mother, come to the Hanlow Centre Juicy Bar at eleven. I will find you.' The letter had been unsigned, but if the recipient was still as Claire remembered, she would arrive a good ten minutes early. Claire had been there since half past ten. She didn't think she would be recognised; her hair was so different now and she made herself up with way too much slap again. Still, she sat at the back, concealed, but with a clear view across the rest of the shop. Her smoothie shook precariously in her hand as she picked it up.

At a quarter to eleven Claire sat up straight in her chair. There was a prickle in her mind, like a half-remembered smell. A knot of people walked into the cafe. She recognised none of them, then realised one wasn't part of the group. She was thinner than Claire had expected, unkempt, and with sunken eyes. Claire raised her drink to hide her face from the suspicious scan the girl sent around the room. She bought a drink, and found a seat against the far-left side of the shop that allowed her clear sight of the door too.

Claire relaxed, as best she could, and dug around at the bottom of her mind for the bright thread of white magic that hid there. Gently, she teased it into life, not taking anything from it, but making it aware she was going to use it. Imagining herself as a swirl in a breeze, she let her thoughts waft gently across the room.

With a disorienting flicker, another viewpoint replaced her own. It took Claire a moment to realise she was looking through the wrong eyes. She extracted herself and tried again, but with the same results, albeit on a different person. She pulled her thoughts back to her own head. Her target was watching the clock. It was already five to eleven. She was running out of time. At best, she had five minutes grace after the appointed time.

Delicacy wasn't working. She could drift her mind around the room for another half hour and still not end up inside the right head. She drew a little harder on the white magic, focused her thoughts very clearly, and let her mind wander again.

Her eyes snapped to a new view, which swung suspiciously from side to side, then back to the door. Damn. Had she been too clumsy. Was her host somehow aware of her, warned about her. Would it make a difference? Claire turned her *self* around and looked back into the mind she had broken into. How different it was to Nana May's. No golden sparkling cloud here, but a snarled knot of dark reds and blues, and firecracker snaps rather than Christmas light twinkles.

With another part of her mind, Claire could feel herself rubbing her thumbs against the tips of her fingers. What the hell was she doing? She had blundered around in Nana May's memory by accident and luck, and it was a wonder she hadn't damaged anything. Here she was doing it again, standing at the fringe of some dark and forbidden forest. She should stop. Get out and stay hidden at the back of the shop until it was clear to leave. Or jump down into Underland and hide there. This was a textbook bad idea.

But she didn't. The eyes she was looking through flicked up to the clock again. Eleven exactly. Now back to staring at the door. Out of time. She turned back to face the angry mesh, and dove in.

Where surfing Nana May's mind had been like drifting through clouds of sunshine, this mind fought back. She was pushing through a bramble patch, threads connecting memories burning her like hot wires and knotted in front of her to keep her away.

She forced herself farther in, farther back in time. At least she didn't have so far to go; Nana May had sixty years of memories to wade through, but here were a few months, no more than a veneer. It took seconds to reach the first nodule, the root of the

149

contagion that surrounded her and infected this mind. It wasn't smooth and dove grey and pearlescent. It was spiky, lethally sharp and black cancer dark, sucking energy and life into its surface and daring Claire to touch it. Dark fibres, thick and rough, radiated out from the black surface, alien, not native to this mind, yet touching everywhere and crawling with dark pulses of energy.

It was daunting. Claire pulled back, frightened, and looked farther down the memory stream. Perhaps there was another way, a different place she could go to find a chink in the armour. Wherever she looked, the black nodes dominated; many, many times more than she found in Nana May's brain. This was not as simple as poking at the single memory. She had, as usual, underestimated the problem She should get out, before she did any harm.

And yet, this chance would never come again, and the rewards — oh, the rewards would be so wonderful. Claire made herself a thin probe of thought and reached out to the surface of the nearest node.

A shock like static struck out at her as soon as she made contact, and lightning-fast a foul sheath of black began to crawl back along her probe. She cast it from her, watching the black skin sag and wither as the magic within it dissipated. A faint echo of trembling hands reached her from her body.

Claire drew a little harder on the white magic, this time building a lance, not a probe. She had to find out what was inside, whether it was a memory that could help her. She stabbed at the ugly blackness.

The lance struck, and stuck. Blackness tried to creep back towards her along the shaft, but Claire trickled more energy into her probe until the contamination from the darkness burned away. She sensed a flinch but not, this time, from her own body. She drove the probe harder against the dark shell, shifting the angle of attack from side to side like she was trying to force a spoon into frozen ice cream.

Stalemate. The darkness could not reach her, but she could not breach it, at least not like this, and time was trickling away like sand through her fingers. The web around her was becoming agitated. She could hear arguing, ten or twenty voices all the same, all talking at once, gradually coalescing into one concept, one decision. The net exploded into activity. Claire's own body frantically demanded her attention, and she let enough of herself drift back to look through her own eyes. She was being looked at, angrily, with hatred. She had been recognised.

There was one thing left to try, but it was dangerous. She was playing with matches in a firework shop. All she wanted to do was light a sparkler.

Rough hands grabbed her arms, shook her. Angry words. Burly man coming towards them from the counter, and a girl behind the counter was talking urgently into a walkie-talkie.

"Bitch. I know you. Hey, bitch. You stabbed me, didn't you."

Slap! Across her face. She had to decide.

Claire drew on the dark magic and stabbed the disgusting darkness hard.

Slap!

It fought back. She could feel it squirming, thickening under the point of her lance. How could it fight back? It wasn't alive — was it? She touched the source of the white magic again and pushed harder, made the top of her lance hotter and sharper. In another reality, she was picked up by her jacket, an angry face spraying spittle at her from enraged lips.

"Told you if I ever saw you again I would mess you up. You fricking stupid?"

She had to back out. This was becoming a self-preservation issue. And she had been so close. Her anger pulsed down the white magic lance, and the darkness caught fire.

27

Claire's head bounced off the wall. The burly manager was trying to pull the other person off her, and a security guard was helping. Another guard, a woman, had a grip on Claire's arm, but it seemed to be one of restraint rather than support.

"Enough!" The guard holding the other person bellowed. "Now exactly what is all this about?"

"This bitch cut me."

"Where? I can't see any blood."

"Six months ago, you dick."

"I saw everything," said an elderly lady from two tables away. She pointed at Claire. "This one did nothing. She was sitting and drinking, minding her business."

"Shut up Gran," chipped in a youth from two tables in the other direction. "I saw her givin' evils."

Claire hadn't a clue what he was talking about, but from the glint in his eye and the twitching lips, knew he was stirring it for the craic.

"I think you both need to come to the office. Don't make a scene."

But the other person had slumped into a chair, face blank, eyes twitching restlessly from side to side but looking at nothing. The last thing Claire had perceived as she had fled back to her own body had been a glowing white line, consuming the darkness, moving ever quicker, spreading along the infected connections. Had it had worked after all? She dared not risk peeking inside again. She need her wits in the now, right here.

"Do you know this young lady? Hello?"

The guard shook a shoulder, but there was no response. The face was changing now, cycling between horror, anger and wonder.

"I asked if you knew this girl?"

A brief, unsuccessful attempt to gather wits. "Told you, she stabbed me. In the shoulder."

"But do you know her?"

"Of course," Confusion. Realisation. "She's... Claire?"

Claire bottled it all up. Put a lid over it like the containment for a nuclear reactor, and nailed it down. She caught Evie's eyes, and gave the tiniest shake of her head. Evie sat back, relaxed, and said nothing.

"It's OK," said Claire. "I'm sure it's mistaken identity or something. I'm not hurt."

"Can't have this sort of thing going on in the mall," said the male guard.

"Look, there no harm done. Forget it."

"Somebody spilt my drink," said the shit-stirring youth and Claire glared at him. He grinned at her.

"Has to be reported," said the male guard, taking Evie by the arm again. "And my manager will have to decide if the police get called. We 'ave a zero-tolerance policy 'ere."

"Zero tolerance towards what?" Claire asked.

"Anything. Come on."

Claire let the other guard march her out of the cafe. Evie followed, dazed and unsteady on her feet.

Security let them out fifteen minutes later. Claire had tried her best to convince them that Evie had forgotten to take her medication that morning, and when the security footage showed that Evie had indeed launched herself at Claire for no good reason, the officious little men capitulated and let them go, adding a two month ban of the mall for petty revenge. Evie was still pale, with bright spots of colour on her cheeks. When Claire took her hand it trembled, and her skin was like ice.

Evie let her lead her to the train station and onto a London-bound service. That was worrying in itself. Had she hurt Evie? The girl had never been one to be led. Fifteen minutes into the journey Evie raised her head. "This isn't the way to your place."

A glimmer of hope. "I'm staying with my Gran for a bit. I thought we should talk. Someone will give you a ride home, if you don't mind motorbikes."

"Oh." Evie's eyes went back to flickering across whatever scenes were playing in her mind. Claire tried not to stare at her; the last thing she wanted was to fall back into Evie's mind. She had already interfered enough. She turned her eyes to the window, one moment a field of poppies, the next a cluster of middle-class houses and a vintage white Rolls on a drive. She hands hurt, and she realised she had clenched her fists so tight her nails were digging into her palms. Had she done the right thing? Had she even had the right to mess with Evie's head this way? She needed Evie, or felt she did, but did that justify the hurt she had cause, and was still causing.

Evie gasped and Claire turned away from the window. A moment later she was on her knees, in front of her friend, hands on her forearms. Evie wasn't breathing. There was a choking noise from her throat, and her eyes stared fixedly into nowhere as tears ran down her cheeks.

"What is it, Evie? Talk to me."

Evie drew a deep, broken breath. "The goggles. They burned."

Several weeks back, Claire found out that "new" goggles provided by ex-Administrator Aslnaff were specifically designed to accelerate the memory erosion all humans eventually suffered, and there had been hints that there were other, special devices to make it happen even quicker.

"They forced them on me. They strapped me to a chair, and they forced them on me. They burned. I could feel them shredding my memories, feel them being taken away. When I screamed, they taped my mouth up. The more I fought, the more they used them, until one day they left them on and it burned and burned and burned—"

Claire was crying too, now, and Evie's hands crushed hers. She shouldn't have interfered. Evie had suffered enough. Now she couldn't speak again. Her mouth formed shapes, and Claire could see her throat working to make sound, but there was nothing more than a croak until—

"BASTARDS!"

Evie's hands clenched even tighter and Claire cried out in pain, then in joy. Fire burned through the eyes of Evie Jones.

"I will find each and every piece of shit who did this to me, starting with Aslnaff, and I will stamp on their balls—"

"Do Grenlix even have balls?"

Evie cut off in mid-flow and looked as Claire as though she was insane. Claire quirked a grin, then both girls were laughing. Warrior Jones was back, and their gods — if they had any — help Underland.

28

When Claire and Evie arrived at Nana May's house, Claire was on the edge of chewing her nails. So much could go wrong so quickly here. She opened the door, heard voices in the kitchen, and found her Nan taking tea with Stuart. Claire held her breath.

Stuart did a double take, straightened on his stool, and nodded respectfully to Evie. "Welcome back, Warrior Jones."

Claire's throat closed up and the threat of tears pricked at the corners of her eyes. Now, if Evie could complete the mutual arse-sniffing without growling...

"So you're the replacement?"

Stuart grinned. "Yeah. She traded up."

Evie snorted, and everything was well. Claire let out the breath she wasn't aware she had been holding and put the kettle on.

What started as simply bringing Evie up to speed on what had happened since her eviction from Underland took a left turn and ended up being a plan to infiltrate Mount Primrose. Even more of a shock to Claire, Nana May took over.

"No," she said, simply, when Evie speculated whether they could jump a squad of Grenlik raiders up to the Real and then back down to the Angel lair. "This will not be a paramilitary mission."

"But Nana, you don't know—"

"What a bunch of underhand scoundrels Angels are? Of course I do. Leopard's spots rarely change, Claire. No, if you want my help, it will be on my terms."

"Which are?" Evie leaned forward and put her elbows on the breakfast bar.

"Girls only."

"Now hold on."

"Girls only, Mister Grey." Nana May's voice was firm. "And

no weapons. Mae West's, certainly, and a small defensive magic or two, but nothing offensive."

"Why?" Evie asked.

"Because there's less chance of finding a fight if you don't go in looking for one. Besides, none of your weapons will be effective against Underkin, and do you really think a — "Morph"? Is that what you call them now? — Anyway, one could not emerge inside the Mount, and even if one did, we would be within our rights to exit and leave it to the Angels. It would be, after all, on their territory."

A flash of rebellion seared through Claire at the thought of letting a Morph get away anywhere, but she was beginning to see the logic of her grandmother's argument and, as it seemed she was not going to take any dissent on the matter, Claire gave in.

Nana May's jump was sharp and clean and surprised the heck out of Claire. Glancing over at her friend, she guessed the look of profound respect meant Evie felt the same.

They had arrived in the corner of a library. Claire and Evie shared another look — a joint memory of the place they had used to practise jumping when Claire had first worked in Underland. This, though, was older.

Scrolls piled high like honeycomb in diamond-shaped hollows gouged into the rock. Looming away into the distance were wooden bookshelves, twice as high as Claire, each twenty feet long. Before and behind them were two more, connected at the top by a metal rail. In the distance, Claire saw a ladder hanging from the rail, and immediately wanted to ride on it.

The air was dry but didn't taste dead. Light came from glowing sconces on the wall and at the end of each bookcase, powered by magic. Motes of dust glittered softly, drifting in delicate air currents. The loudest sound she could hear was Evie's breathing.

"Now what?" her friend asked.

"I guess I ping for it. Be ready to jump out again if I trip any alarms."

It was the weak point in the plan; they had to use magic to find the shard, and yet Claire couldn't know if there were any traps that would detect its use. The catch was, of course, that if she used magic to search for magic detectors she would trip the detectors because she had used magic. She had given herself a headache trying to resolve that one, and had simply concluded that they would have to hope for the best. For all they knew an alarm had already sounded.

"Remember, at the first sign anything is interfering with the magical field, get out." They had agreed on 'every woman for herself' if anything went wrong, but Claire resolved she would make sure Nana May was safe before she jumped herself out. She had already lost two members of her family. She had no intention of losing a third.

She built her detector of gossamer-thin magic, as light as a fairy's wing, and sent it on its way with a breath. No sonar pulse this, but a tiny question hovering barely above the background magic field. It crept away, questing amongst the books, seeping through the stone floors and seeking secretly as it passed.

Claire left it alone, no guidance, no reinforcement, silently waiting for news. A soft echo came back, more quickly than she had expected, and she immediately let the spell dissolve. She pointed a finger. "Over there. And close. Really close."

The three of them crept up to the end of the bookcase and Evie peered around the corner. Claire felt naked without her duster jacket and her PPG, and she decided the question of where Nana May had found a dark grey cloak at short notice could wait, at least for now. She got another surprise when Nana May insisted on leading.

"I'm sure I know the place better than you. Now, don't crowd me, girls. Stay a few paces back."

Nana May led them onwards, her bearing showing that with each aisle and corner she grew more confident, more sure of where she was. She turned a corner and there was a startled grunt, not from her, but from someone farther up the aisle. Claire saw the open hand behind her grandmother's back in time to stop herself, and Evie, from blundering around the corner too.

"*Nash met too stifnak Golan Pet?*"

Claire's jaw dropped. It was rare to hear an Angel speak in their own tongue, but here was her grandmother using it, and — as far as Claire could tell — competently. Her voice drifted farther away and Claire began to fret. What was she doing? If they lost contact it could be disastrous. Claire sneak a quick peak around the corner. Nana May was leading an Angel away from them, up to the next corner, ambling unhurriedly. Claire saw the Angel gesture to the left, and took a gamble. Gathering up Evie with a wave of her hand, Claire walked silently across the aisle to the next row. A moment later Nana May appeared at the far end, but walked straight past. Claire hurried to the next aisle, and saw Nana May turn and bow, hesitate for a moment, then start to walk again. This time, her left hand made a discrete beckoning gesture. Claire moved them quietly across two more aisles, then they ran up to re-join Nana May.

"And that was?" Claire began, her tone frosty.

"Cool," Evie added, holding her hand up for a high five. Nana May looked confused and left her hanging.

"Don't get distracted, Claire," said Nana May. "I believe I found us someone to help."

There was an odd tone in her voice, but the hood of the cloak covered her face and Claire couldn't shake the feeling there was something more. Her grandmother didn't seem inclined to share, at least not at the moment, so she filed it for later.

"The man you are looking for is Golan Pet." Nana May moved off, her step confident. "He is the Senior Librarian here." Again, an odd note in the voice, almost pride. "If anybody can help you here, he can."

"Help us?" Claire's head snapped towards her. "When did we decide we needed help? I thought we were going to sneak in, snatch whatever it is and run."

"And how are you going to do that if the only magic you dare use is lighter than a faerie cobweb?" She shook her head. "Human's doing magic. Whatever next?"

A few minutes later, Nana May led them into a deep shadow. Ahead, Claire could see the corner of a desk, and it was there that her grandmother pointed. "Up there, Claire. Be polite, and don't try to bully anybody. Librarians are so nosey, he'll probably talk you to death before he raises an alarm, but not if he senses a threat. Go on."

Claire took two steps away and looked back, confused. Evie hadn't moved either, and was staring at Nana May.

"Go on. Me being there might make things... complicated."

Claire squared her shoulders, spared her grandmother one more quizzical look, then jerked her head at Evie and strode towards the desk.

The Angel peered up at them, took a pair of pince-nez from the end of his nose, polished them assiduously, and replaced them. He fell back in his chair and flailed for a large brass bell at the side of his desk whilst making odd, meaningless noises.

"Please," said Claire, hands open and held wide. "I'm not here to cause trouble. I need your help."

Evie, in the meantime, stepped to the side of the desk and moved the bell; not too far away, but enough that the old librarian would need to get out of his chair to reach it.

"What do you want?" the Angel finally managed to get out.

"Are you Golan Pet?"

The Angel nodded, and Claire decided a little subterfuge might be in order.

"I was told you were the only person who could help us. Morphs have possessed my parents. I don't know how to get them free."

"Oh my."

"I need the last piece of the *Krezik Chet Knar*."

"What?"

"Your master, Humbard, gave us what he thought was the shard, but it turned out not to be." She decided to gloss over that his boss had tried to kill her with a fake. "We were told you might be able to tell us where it is."

"Why. It won't do you any good, young girl. It can't be used unless—"

"Unless you are the *Krezik Zha*. I know. I am."

"That's not what I was going to say. Had you not interrupted me..." His face went pale and he shrank back still further. "Oh, my. You're her, I mean she. Oh goodness."

He looked from side to side like a frightened rabbit, then lunged for the bell. Evie got her hand to it at the same time, and struggled to hold the clapper still.

"Please," Claire begged. "I'm not here to hurt anybody. I need to—"

"*Kith'en cha fremm targen*, Golan Pet?"

"I most certainly am when they are bloodthirsty monst..." Golan stared behind Claire, absently letting Evie take the bell from him. She placed it on the table and looked in the same direction. Claire didn't move. She heard the rustle of fabric behind her and knew Nana May was standing beside her.

"Do I... your voice is..."

Claire saw movement from the corner of her eye as Nana May raised her arms to push back the hood. "It has been a very long time, Golan Pet."

29

The Angel squinted, stood, leant forward over his desk, and squinted again. "May? But how can that be? You were, I mean you are..."

"Old? Time could have been kinder to you too, Bookworm."

Golan Pet drew his hand across his mouth. "This is all most irregular."

"This child is my grand-daughter," said Nana May. "She has abilities far beyond what any Underkin could consider normal. She opened my mind, and gave Underland back to me."

The Pet dithered for a moment, moving items around on his desk between stealing glances at Nana May. Eventually he stilled, head cocked to one side, and a shy smile curling his lips. "Have you been well?"

"Not in front of the children, Golan, and this is neither the time nor the place. My grand-daughter is telling the truth in every way. Can you help us? Before the Council decides to step in?"

He scraped open a drawer, pocketed something from within, and eased it shut again. "Follow me."

The Angel led them deeper into the library, stopping at a metal grille set into the stone wall and retrieving a key from his pocket. The grille opened silently and he ushered them within before closing and locking it again. He confused Claire. She had expected furtive scurrying and sneaking, but this Angel was marching — or to be more truthful, doddering purposefully — around the place as if she was asking him for a book on stamp collecting.

Beyond the grille was a corridor, cut deeper into the stone of the mountain. Around a corner were a row of metal gratings set into one side of the corridor. Claire's skin tingled, but she made no attempt to analyse any of the magic woven around them. If any of them were detectors, it would give them away and could trigger alarms or traps. She pushed all thoughts of magic away from her mind, and hoped the static spells in their kevlar amulets wouldn't set anything off.

Golan Pet stopped at a grille, produced a key that could have been the same as the one he had already used, and unlocked it. This time there was a soft squeal as the door opened, and he made no attempt to close it once they were inside.

"I'm afraid the seating is limited. I will be a moment."

Along the back wall of the room were book shelves, floor to ceiling, stuffed with scrolls and tomes that looked ancient. Against the left wall was a plain table with two chairs, and set against the right wall a tall wooden unit with dozens of drawers. For a moment, Claire thought it might be an old-fashioned index, like the one hidden away in the basement of her local library, but then she saw the tiny keyholes. Golan Pet paused for a moment, running his fingers over the drawers as if trying to remember the one he wanted. He came to a decision and pulled another key from a different pocket.

The box he placed on the table looked exactly like the one Humbard gave them, but when she opened it the shard was a different shape; not a hexagon, but an irregular wafer about the size of a grain of puffed rice.

"As I said, the artefact is of no use to you, even if you are able to integrate it with the rest of the *Krezik Chet Knar* key."

Claire tore her eyes from the box. "Why? I am the *Krezik Zha*."

"*A Krezik Zha*," Golan replied. "There have been others."

"Others?" Claire realised her mouth was hanging open and that she looked like a quizzical idiot. She rearranged her face, and hid the sudden anger that built inside her. Another lie, or at least concealed truth, by those she thought she could trust. Like so many other emotions she had been forced to confront, she pushed this one aside into the boiling pot of frustration, and closed the lid.

There was information she needed her.

"Yes, Warrior, at least according to certain texts. They are, however, somewhat evasive as to the exact number."

"Then why didn't they find all the pieces and put the *Krezik Chet Knar* back together."

"But they have been."

"I don't understand."

"The *Krezik Chet Knar* was shattered into a thousand grains and scattered around the cities of Underland. You just happen to be looking for the last piece."

"So what else is there?"

Golan raised a finger, opened his mouth as if to speak, then smiled. Claire smiled back. She couldn't help it. It was exactly the same gesture Mr Lee, the archivist at her local library, had made when she had asked him a question he liked. That was all so far away now; the random research trips into the bowels of Hanlow library. She thought again. No, only a year. She felt so different, so much older, and sad for her loss.

A book crashed onto the table and puffed out a cloud of dust. Claire jumped, and Golan Pet muttered "Sorry. Heavier than I remembered."

"I can't read the title," said Nana May, peering at the book first through her glasses, then without them.

"It is in old Grenlik. Very Old Grenlik, in fact. Apart from one section near the back."

He placed thin cushions on either side of the book to protect the spine as he opened it, then searched carefully through. After a number of pages the paper changed colour, as did the script. "Here," he said, and stepped back.

Nana May peered again. "Golan, this is equally impenetrable."

"Really. I am surprised. After all, it is in your tongue."

Claire edged her grandmother aside. It did look familiar, even though it was still illegible. It reminded her of an ancient bible laid out in a museum or cathedral.

"What is it?"

"These are the final words of Medrin, the last human mage and creator of the *Krezik Chet Knar*."

Claire's mind wound back to the day she had met the Grenlik council, and to the history they told her. "What else is in the book?"

"Both the Old Grenlik and the English are difficult to understand." Golan stroked his fingers gently along the edge of the pages. "Many of us have tried, but with little success. Certainly, we believe that Medrin's pages may be a description of the *Krezik Chet Knar*, and even how to use it. As for the rest…" He spread his hands in a helpless gesture.

Claire stepped back a little and waited until she could catch Evie's eye. She mouthed the word "box". Evie looked confused and Claire realised "box" and "books" would look the same. She outlined a little square with her finger. Evie looked shocked but nodded. Claire edged to the other side of Nana May as Evie did the same with Golan Pet. They locked eyes again, a huge question lingering in Evie's, but Claire gave the slightest of nods.

She saw Evie move from the corner from her eye, but was too busy focusing on her own job to pay attention. She flipped the side of the book closest to her up, over and closed, then she reached forward and gripped the it with both hands.

Nana May's face had an instant to register shocked horror. "Claire, no."

But she had already jumped out.

"Are you mad?" Evie threw the shard box onto the airbed and Claire's heart stuck in her throat as it bounced wildly off the edge and the underneath of the large dresser next to it.

"Look, I need this stuff."

"Why?"

"To get my mum and dad back." Claire realised she was shouting and took a breath. She glanced at Evie but had to look away. There was a challenge in her friend's eyes she couldn't meet.

"Jeez, you've changed."

"I haven't. It's just…"

Evie let the moment hang for a few seconds. "Exactly. You're harder, mate. You used me and your aunt."

"Gran"

"Whatever. Anyway, I'm not sure the new you is an improvement."

Claire's mouth hung open for a moment, then closed and her teeth ached from how hard she was clenching her jaw. Bitch. She had no right to say anything, not after the way she had used Claire in the early days. She tucked the book firmly under her left arm, grabbed the shard box with her right and glared at Evie. She felt her top lip curl slightly and a part of her warned her she was going too far.

"I'll do what I need to. Nobody else is going to fix this for me."

And she jumped again.

The rushed jump slipped sideways and she stumbled as she appeared in Nagrath's study. A young Grenlik on the floor in front of her struggled to disentangle himself from a chair, and two other youngsters leapt out of the way. On the opposite side of the desk Nagrath's brow-ridges flicked outward in surprise and Claire saw his eyes take in the book and the box.

"Out."

There were protests but Nagrath flapped his hands

"Out, out and if a word of this is breathed to another soul there will be expulsions."

He didn't acknowledge Claire's presence until he had herded the three students out and locked the door behind them.

"An unexpected surprise, Miss Stone, but always a pleasure. I take it you have news of some significance?"

Claire dropped the desk and the box on the desk. "Where's the *Krezik Chet Knar*? I want to fit the shard in now."

Nagrath placed his hands on his desk and peered up at her. "I don't think that's wise."

"What? I got you the damned shard, and your precious book, at least I think it is. Let me try." To be so close to curing her parents twisted her guts in a knot and a confusing swirl of anger and tears left her helpless.

"Think what happened last time, Miss Stone. Consider what might happen if Humbard has had constructed an even more fiendish trap for you? What could you accomplish if he this time managed to erase your mind, or worse, to seal it forever behind impenetrable walls."

He slid the book and the box towards him. "We must test this shard most cautiously, and put potent safeguards in place before you attempt the final assembly. The book, which I confess appears to be genuine, must also be assessed and verified. If it is what it appears to be, the whole Grenlik nation will be in your debt, but let us save our celebration until we are sure."

"And what should I do?" Claire felt small, foolish, like a baby who had bought a magic stone for a grownup and was handed back a pebble. Nagrath smiled at her. She saw pity there, and understanding. Or thought she did.

"Wait, child. As patiently as you can."

Nana May wouldn't speak to her. Since Claire had stolen the book from the Angels, there had been a brief altercation where Nana may pointed out that the only reason Claire was still in the house was that she had nowhere else to go. Since then her grandmother had stayed firmly behind the closed door of her bedroom, or had spoken to her in clipped, closed sentences when she had no other choice.

Claire phoned Stuart and arranged for him to take Evie home. They sat in deeply uncomfortable silence, toying with unwanted coffee in the kitchen. She wanted to shout, to argue. What else was she supposed to have done? Nobody else had been helping her, except the Grenlix. She had given them what they said they had needed. What was wrong with that.

Stuart arrived after the ten longest minutes in Claire's life. Evie all but snatched the spare helmet from Stuart's hand. "Let's be away then, biker boy."

"Ah, what?" Stuart looked at Claire for explanations, but she had none. She couldn't meet his eyes. Evie would tell him. Her version, anyway. She held her hand up in a half-hearted wave, then pushed the door closed and went upstairs. A moment later she realised she hadn't heard the buzz of Stuart's departing bike. They were outside, talking about her. Her two best friends. Maybe. She didn't blame them. Wouldn't blame them if they avoided her. She sat on her air-bed, feeling her backside hit the floor and not caring it had leaked again. She stared at her hands, waiting to cry but finding no tears. She didn't move, even after the sun set and darkness filled the room.

30

Claire was in the air, flying backwards at an alarming rate. From the scream to her right, she assumed Evie was in a similar state. Whatever she hit, it was going to hurt, and she covered the back of her head with her hands. As she tucked her chin into her chest, Claire saw the Grenlik Academy in front of her.

She landed on her buttocks, then tipped onto her back. Her duster took the brunt of the fall, but she was moving so fast friction began to burn her backside and her shoulders. She pulled her head in tighter, to keep the gravel from skinning her fingers, and hoped there was no wall she would crash into.

She scuffed to a stop, waited for a moment to be sure the world had no more surprises in store for her, then rolled to her knees.

"What the hell just happened?" Evie was sitting on the floor, arms around her knees. She looked none too happy.

"How do I know," said Claire, rising. She walked across to Evie, held up a hand, and hauled her to her feet. "Why don't we go and find out?"

Claire's boots crunched on the thin gravel as she strode up to the front door. It was closed, which was new in itself. She reached out towards the handle, but a memory of being thrown across the floor popped up in her mind. Tolks had done it as part of a training exercise, boobytrapping a door handle. Her hand froze in the act of curling to grip the brass lever. A moment later a spell tingled its way down to her fingers.

There was a trap on the door. Exactly what it was, she couldn't tell, but somebody had hoped to catch her, or someone else, off their guard. She glanced over at Evie and shook her head.

Evie raised her eyebrows. "Should I try?"

Claire raised her hand to the bell-pull mounted on the wall.

That, it seemed, was safe. She brushed it with her fingers first, then wrapped her hand around it and jerked. A bell jangled, so she yanked on the bell-pull three more times.

The wait was long enough that she was getting ready to heave on the handle again when a panel slid open in the door and a pair of suspicious, piggy eyes peered through. "What?"

Even though the owner of the eyes had spoken Grenlik, Claire understood. She was, however, damned if she would either bend down until she was on the same level as the panel, or use her rusty Grenlik to try to buy entrance.

"Open the door."

"No."

"Open the door. I am Warrior Stone. I'm here to see——" She bit off the word, almost committing the cardinal sin of openly naming a Grenlik. She struggled to think of a unique quality she could use to identify Nagrath. "I am here to see the Chancellor who sometimes wears boots of red leather."

"Wait here," and the spy-hole slammed shut.

"I thought you were in with these people," grumbled Evie, still trying to brush pale dust from her coat.

"So did I." Claire's heart was beginning to thud inside her chest, and her stomach roiled. Bad news was hovering beside her, outside of the corner of her eye, waiting to pounce. After a rattle of bolts, the door opened. Yashik stood conspicuously inside the threshold. On either side of him a Grenlik with hard eyes held an illegal repeating handbow; one pointed at Evie, the other at Claire.

"Ah, Stone." Yashik beamed widely until Evie corrected him.

"*Warrior* Stone, Grenlik."

Claire opened her mouth to scream "no" as the Grenlik facing Evie raised his handbow to point at her head, but Yashik raised his hand and, after an uncomfortable moment, the weapon lowered to a less threatening but still alert position.

"Warrior Stone, then. And presumably the assumed – retired?

— Warrior Jones?" He drawled the honorific into a deadly insult. Claire didn't move to see if Evie nodded. From the slight moue of distaste on Yashik's lips, she assumed Evie was not being gracious.

"As you wish." Yashik's expression became more business-like. "You may leave."

"What?"

"A simple enough instruction, Miss Stone. You, and all your kind, are free to leave Underland at your earliest convenience. You are no longer required."

"I want to see Nagrath." Claire knew she was breaking protocol but she didn't care.

"That Grenlik no longer has any position or authority in this academy."

Claire's bluster deflated like her mattress. "I don't understand. He was supposed to be helping me."

"Stupid girl. We don't need you anymore. Any of you."

"Moron." Evie snapped and took a step forward. The handbow rose again, but she ignored it. "Who will keep Underland free of Morphs? You think you can do it with those fake goggles? We know you couldn't find both cheeks of your arse with those."

Yashik raised a hand. "We really don't care. Why should we? The Morphs are no threat to Underland, except for a slight instability of the local magical field. As they are passing through; why should we interfere?"

"But, in the Real…"

"Is none of our concern. But if it truly troubles you, take comfort that we fully expect to have resolved the unfinished business of Beneath in two years, or perhaps three."

Claire's balance failed her for a moment and she took an involuntary step backwards. Three years of uncontrolled Morph incursions into the real world. Three years of infections, hundreds a day, or more.

"How?"

172

"You really have to ask? Because of you, girl. Because of your three priceless gifts." He paused, but continued when Claire didn't respond. "Oh, come now. You brought us the only surviving copy of one of the greatest works of our mages of old. You bring us the final piece of the *Krezik Chet Knar*—"

"But you can't use that," Claire interrupted, her voice too loud and too high. "Only a human can use it."

Yashik spread his hands. "Perhaps. But with our lost knowledge regained we may find a way — especially with the help of your third gift."

"Third?" She could see the connection to the book and the shard, but what else could he be talking about?

"The greatest gift of all. The crystal full of interstitial energy. It was remarkably easy to guide you into journeying to Edinbelow. The false signal was simple to create, as was the so-called "emergency" on board. We knew you wouldn't be able to resist leaping to the rescue. Now that crystal is in our most secret laboratory, and our brightest and best are digging out all its little secrets. I have every confidence in them."

"But my parents. You said you would help…"

"I, personally, said no such thing. Those with whom you made such an agreement are no longer in any position to fulfil it."

"But you could help."

Yashik paused to consider the thought, or seemed to. "I suppose I could. But then…" He smiled, wide and feral. "You have nothing I need."

31

Evie caught Claire as she launched herself towards the open door. She growled and tried to pull free, but Evie pushed her back. Yashik laughed and turned away. A moment later the door closed with a hollow boom and a gunfire rattle of bolts. Claire twisted and ripped her arm free, then continued the turn and swung an open slap at Evie's face.

Evie leaned sideways and did something with a leg and a gentle push, and Claire was sitting on the floor again. Evie picked up a half-dozen fragments of gravel, hefted them, and lobbed them in a gentle underhand towards the door.

The rebounded like bullets. Claire collected one in the arm and one in the chest. They stung like paintball rounds. Another kissed her cheek and left a wasp-sting. She touched her fingers to the pain, and they came away bloody. Evie squatted beside her.

"Let me see." She poked gently and dabbed with a dubious hanky. "Superficial. Won't scar if you don't pick it."

Claire didn't care. Her world had ended. Someone else she had trusted had betrayed her. That, together with her own stupidity, had taken away her last chance at rescuing her mum and dad. A sob ripped her heart out, then another, then she was wailing into Evie's shoulder, her friend's fierce arms the only thing stopping her from breaking into a million pieces.

"We have to go," Evie said, too soon. Claire shook her head. "Get a grip. Stand up and walk out like a Warrior."

"Screw being a Warrior, and screw this place," Claire wailed.

Evie unwound her arms and gave her a gentle shake. "Do you want them to win? Do you want them to know how much they hurt you?"

Claire's shoulders stiffened, and she gulped hard at two more sobs. Evie pulled away, then there was a hand, waiting to haul her to her feet.

When she tried to walk, the world tilted after the second step. Evie grabbed her arm and pushed her upright again. They took half a dozen more steps, and Claire began to wonder where they were going. The gates head of them were just as locked as the door.

"Are you ready?" asked Evie. Claire was about to ask for what when she sensed her friend getting ready to jump out. Without thinking, she did the same. "Three... two... one..."

Nana May still wouldn't speak to her. Claire kept to her room while in the house. Neither Stuart nor Evie were keen to spend any time with her, so she had taken to bussing to the local megamall and wasting time in there. She was sure the local rentacops were watching her as a potential shop-lifter, or something equally distressing.

She spent a lot of time in UnderLondon, too, pulling extra duty shifts, or hanging around. Remembering Ostrenalia's words about being predictable, she tried to find places that weren't on her previous list of favourites. Right now she was in a park on the south side of the Thames, not far from where the Tate Modern would be in the Real. She was watching the bustle of a ferry jetty, standing beside the noticeboard that told potential customers of sailing times and prices.

The hand-bow quarrel thunked into the wooden post less than six inches from her head. She flinched sideways, ducked, then spun about to see who had fired it. An anonymous crowd passed behind her, some glancing at her to see why she was behaving so oddly, others looking down their noses at the crazy human.

Right after her heart started beating again, which felt like the better part of a minute, she cast a glare over her shoulder at the bolt, then turned to study it more closely. The hairs on the back of her neck were already prickling; even though her Kevlar should have been able to absorb the energy of the bolt, it was still discomfiting that someone got that close behind her and nobody else reacted. She pulled at the bolt. It was deep in the post — more evidence of how close her assailant had been before he or she had fired — but she wiggled it free.

Something was wrapped around the shaft, held in place by — of all things — an elastic band. Her heart sank. Before she even found out what this was all about, she knew that another human was involved in it at some level. Even after Aslnaff planned to hurt or remove every human in Underland, her own species were still getting involved with the wrong sides.

She rolled the band off and unwound a note. The quarrel she put in her pocket. Perhaps Tolks could find out... She stopped, grimaced, and threw the quarrel into a waste bin. The paper she smoothed out against the side of the notice board, and laughed. Until she read it.

Foolish.
You warn once, we take your parent
Now you warn again.
Walk away
Or we take your Heart.

The text was made from newspaper cut-outs, as if out of a black-and-white gangster movie. Claire crumpled the paper in her fist and swung her wrist to throw it in the same bin as she had dumped the bolt. At the last minute, she held back, untwisted the paper and read it again. The words hadn't changed. When she looked closer, she noticed the letters weren't actually glued to the page; it was either a photocopy, or a printout using a clever font. She folded it more carefully and put it in her pocket, not entirely sure why, then walked away from the river.

As Claire stepped out of her room that evening she caught the scent of Underland on the air. It wasn't the first time. Unless Evie or Stuart were unexpectedly in the house, it meant that Nana May had jumped in again. The scent was so strong that Claire peeked over the bannister to see if her grandmother was still on the stairs.

She didn't know the protocol for this. What would the authorities do if they caught Nana in Underland? Was there anything they could do - and would it stop them if there wasn't. There weren't even stories about grownups somehow falling through, let alone being able to get there deliberately, and yet there were people obviously too old wandering the streets of Edinbelow in gangs.

If anything did happen, she would of course jump right in and start creating mayhem, but most of the time she didn't even known when her gran was off visiting.

Her breath caught in her throat. Was that what the message meant? Who the message meant? She had thought the note was threatening to do her harm, to rip out her heart. What if it meant they were going to go after someone else close to her? Her legs wobbled and she sat down on the top stair. How could she go through that again?

"Claire? Is that you?"

But she couldn't speak. Her breath was a solid mass in her lungs, impossible to move. Her heart had stopped between two beats and trembled in her chest. Or what if it meant Evie? Or Stu. Her throat tightened further and she wanted to throw up.

"Claire? I need to speak to you. Now."

Nana May still sounded mad. Claire forced a cracked "Coming" past her lips and took a moment to draw a deep breath. A hand still crushed her throat and her heart pattered like running footsteps. With a firm grip on the handrail she made it down the stairs, and a hand on the wall helped her towards the kitchen. At the last moment she pulled herself upright and rubbed at her cheeks to force some colour into them.

"Hi."

Her grandmother gestured to a stool on the other side of the breakfast bar. "Sit. We need to talk."

Heart sinking in an entirely different way, Claire took the indicated stool and schooled her face into what she hoped was an expression of polite interest. What she really didn't need right now was another lecture on how disrespectful she had been and how shameful her actions had been. She knew. She really knew, and in ways Nana May couldn't possibly understand.

"I have been spending a lot of time with my friend, Golan Pet. He was very put out with you, and with me, and I had to do a great deal of fast talking to even get him to speak to me again."

Claire braced herself for the lecture.

"He wants to see you."

Now that made her sit up and take notice. And not just the idea, but the way Nana May delivered it.

"Why? Cos I already feel really bad about what I did but I don't think—"

"Be quiet." There was steel in her nana's voice, unexpected and unavoidable. Claire closed her mouth so fast her teeth clicked. "This isn't about salving your conscience, my girl. He had information he believes you need to know, and I can't even get a hint out of him as to what it might be. When can you jump in?"

Claire had no snap-back deficit to wait out right then, but she skirted around the answer. "Nana, how well do feel you still know this friend?"

"Golan and I go back a long time."

"I know, but you haven't met in what, sixty years?"

May scowled at her "Forty-odd, thank you. Get to the point, Claire."

Heat rose in her cheeks, partly embarrassment, but partly anger that Nana May would speak to her so. "Could it be a trap?"

178

Now it was her grandmother's turn to show colour, two spots of angry red high on her cheek bones. Bloodless lips pressed into a razor-sharp line, and her eyes flashed. Then they softened and looked thoughtful. Claire reached into her pocket and took out the message.

"The last time I ignored a warning like this, it cost me Mum and Dad. How much do you really trust him, Nana?"

Her grandmother reached across the breakfast bar and, with the very tips of her fingers, turned the note around and drew it closer. She peered at it as though Claire was a cat and had brought in a half-consumed sparrow.

"This is disgusting."

Claire nodded. "I'm certain it was produced up here. Underland doesn't have laser printers or photocopiers yet. So that means someone up here is involved. What I can't be sure of is if any Underkin are involved, or if this goes directly to Beneath." She looked up from the note and firmly into her Grandmother's eyes. "So I'm sorry, but I have to ask again. How much do you trust him?"

"I trust him. At least I trust him to not be planning anything himself. He never was that devious. Now he's too wrapped up in his books." Claire had drawn a breath but Nana May held up her hand. "I don't dismiss that somebody might be pulling his strings. But I don't think so. I do believe he thinks he really needs to speak to you. Which, under the circumstances, I don't think you should ignore."

Claire took back the note, folded it, and returned it to her pocket.

"No time like the present."

Nana May jumped first, wearing her hooded cloak. The agreement was that if she didn't jump back out within five minutes, then Claire was to join her.

When Claire jumped, she used the pattern of Golan Pet's office door. It was closed, and she was outside. Her grandmother and the Pet were off to one side, standing shoulder to shoulder and holding hands. Claire raised an eyebrow, but her grandmother's answering look was cool, and silently said their business was nothing to do with her.

On a table between them, sat a book, propped up by reading cushions. A pair of cotton gloves lay on the table directly in front of the book.

"Please put on the gloves before you touch the book. It is over a millennium old."

Claire stepped over to the table and sat down on the obviously placed chair. "What is this?"

"Another history, like the one you stole."

Claire winced, but said nothing. The Pet continued.

"This is not an original, but no more than a second, if not first-generation copy. We still believe it is faithful and accurate."

"Of what?"

"It is a Hrund account of the same period. I confess I experienced a certain curiosity mixed with my anger, as to why you, and those you work for, would be so interested in acquiring such a volume. I found two more."

"Two? What about the other?"

"Later, perhaps. Your time here may be limited. I suggest you start."

"But I don't..."

As Claire looked at the meaningless symbols on the page they swirled, not moving - not exactly - but rearranging themselves in her mind, becoming legible.

"Here are the words of Hendred, official recorder to the Eternal Council, now broken and dissolved.

"I must make record of the events that led to the downfall of the Grenlik domination of our land. For so long, they spread their iron fist across the realm; punitive taxes, the interdiction on the learning of majic by other races, the restriction of teaching to all but a few.

"My task, Recorder, was to bear witness. To write down deeds they thought momentous, or worthy — at least in their own minds. To make permanent record of their victories over those in the realms below us, the deceptions practised on those above. For years I made note of their scheme to enslave human warlocks, and to use their alien magic to practice dominion over the land and to subdue all other Underkin beneath the Grenlik yoke, and to make war on Beneath. Only when the world Above had been depleted did the Grenlix direct the slave-mages to break the forbidden walls, and to touch the eldritch and dark power of Interstitial Magic.

"All bar three of the human mages perished in the construction of the *Krezik Chet Knar*, a device of such deviltry that it would permit the wielder to focus and control the Interstitial magic, even to the ability to influence and defeat the very boundaries between the worlds.

"They assembled a mighty army. With Grenlik battle-mages to the rear, and conscripted foot soldiers from all other Underkin to the fore, they commanded the walls between the worlds be rent open such that they could unleash terrible war on the denizens below.

"And with that command the last of the human mages summoned forth the last of their energies, but not to entice the *Krezik Chet Knar* to break down the walls between worlds, but to erect a shield around one of their number.

"The Grenlik battle mages fought to destroy the shield, first singly, then in massed ranks, but the human mages gave up their last life force and with it, held the shield. One, named Medrin, worked feverishly upon the *Krezik Chet Knar* and, as the last of his brothers burned away, did he turn back to his Grenlix masters and, screaming his defiance, cause the *Krezik Chet Knar* to explode in a catastrophic detonation.

"The battle-mages of the Grenlix were eliminated, killed or rendered ineffective by the violence of the magical detonation. The conscripted ranks below, now aware that their masters were incapacitated, turned on them and wrought bloody insurrection. The libraries and colleges of Grenlik were razed and their lore destroyed in root and branch.

"We are alone. Medrin perished, though his body was never found. Neither was any part of the *Krezik Chet Knar*. There are no powers or skills with which we may contact other worlds for help, were there any realistic prospect the smallest iota of aid would be forthcoming.

"We must find a new way. A better way."

A tear dropped onto the back of Claire's glove, and she heard Golan Pet gasp. A moment later she realised his concern was not for her, but for the book. She lifted her head.

"How do we know? Or how did we not know?"

The librarian looked at her, confused.

"How does this have any more validity than the words in the Grenlik book?"

Golan nodded. "I make no such claim. I simply bring the material to your attention. However, if this is more definitive than the Grenlik volume…"

"But I don't get why you bring it out now. Why doesn't everybody know about it? Why aren't the Grenlix hated, cast out?"

Golan Pet shrugged. "The volume was filed under comparative mythology. Without cross-reference and verification, there was no way to know that this had any validity outside of academic curiosity."

Claire clenched hands began to ache. She was angry, at the book and at Golan Pet. It didn't make any sense.

"Think of your history, Claire," said Nana May. "And of what you know about this place. There are any number of examples of despicable events that should have ended in genocide, but where the villains survived. The Grenlix were broken, they faded back, became a minority, yet managed to make themselves useful. They carved out a niche, pulled themselves back. Even now, nobody trusts them, and they are still looked down on, even after a thousand years or more."

Claire's hands gripped the edge of the table, her knuckles and nails white, and her muscles and bones aching.

"And I just gave them back the means to take over all three worlds."

32

They jumped back to the kitchen. Claire ran up the stairs and slammed the door to her room before falling back against it and sliding to squat on the floor. A few moments later the door shoved her in the back.

"Claire. Come out of there, we need to talk."

"No. Go away. I've ruined everything. Everybody hates me. I *ought* to be hated."

"You have to talk this through. Golan said there's more, another book you need to see."

"Leave me alone. Go, or... or I'll jump in and never come back."

There was a silence from the other side of the door long enough for Claire to hope her grandmother had actually gone away, but then there was a thump against the wall and a groan. "If you wish, child. I'll sit right here until I feel you jump, or until you come to your senses."

Claire said nothing. Tears streamed down her face, but she didn't sob. Anger and self-loathing consumed her. She pounded her fist on her thigh, harder and harder. Her fingers dug into her arm, scraping her nails across her skin, drawing blood. She did it again, digging deeper, the sense of rightness striking deep into her soul. She deserved to hurt, needed to. She was worthless, and everything she had done had made things worse and caused other people pain. The only way she could atone was through hurting herself more.

"I shall say only one more thing," said May. "I know you are angry, and particularly with the Grenlix. I am too. But remember that these events happened over a thousand years ago. They are different people now."

Claire's hand stopped at the top of its beat, ready to drag along her arm again, then slowly descended. The tears dried up, her anger replaced by a cold fire, as when she had fought off their attackers in Edinbelow. Except this time she wasn't afraid of it.

"Leave me alone, Nana. I have some thinking to do."

Even she could hear the difference in her voice, and the surprised grunt from the other side of the door suggested her grandmother had heard it too. There were sounds of movements, of involuntary complaints about a body that wouldn't follow instructions any more, or at least not willingly, and then the creak of the top stair bearing a load. Nana May had gone downstairs.

Claire began to plan.

There were three steps up to the door on Bedford Row, but Claire stared at them as though they were the foothills of Mt Fuji. She chewed gently on her bottom lip and for the n-teenth time tried to convince herself this was the right thing to do.

The cold fire had burned lower overnight, fading as she slept. It was still there; she could feel it just within reach, waiting for her to realise she needed it again, but for now staying out of her way.

She had come to the conclusion she had no real friends left amidst the Underkin. The exception to that might be Ostrenalia. Perhaps. Friends was certainly too strong a word, but it was better than 'the only person left who would talk to her'. And that was how she found herself staring up at the front door of 23 Bedford Row. She scaled the steps and pulled on the door-chime.

The Hrund housekeeper looked down her nose at Claire again. It was so unusual for a Hrund to have such a stinky attitude, but Claire pushed it aside. The procrastinator within wanted to let it distract her, to steal her focus, but she blinked hard and spoke firmly.

"I have no appointment, but if Mistress Ostrenalia is available, please tell her that Warrior Claire Stone would appreciate a few moments of her valuable time."

As formal and as posh as she could make it. Maybe that would impress the snooty Hrund. The barely audible snort suggested not, but Claire refused to let her expression fade to timid hope or disappointment.

"Wait here," and the door closed firmly in her face.

She put her hands behind her back, fidgeted from one foot to another for a moment, then leant against the handrail at the side of the steps. A pair of Sitharii males, looking like funeral directors in in their long grey coats and long grey faces, stared at her as they walked past. She looked away, feeling embarrassed. A young Grenlik driving a steam donkey along the road called out.

"Try round the back, human. They might answer the door then." And his scornful laugh faded into the chuffing and puffing of his engine.

Claire caught her bottom lip between her teeth, one moment deciding to end her humiliation and leave, the next remembering why she was here. The latch rattled and Ostrenalia was framed by the doorway. To her side, and behind her, the Hrund shot Claire a look of supercilious malevolence.

"Miss Stone. Please, come in." Ostrenalia flicked a glance at the housekeeper, who averted her eyes. "My profound apologies for the inconvenience. We will go directly to my workshop. Enis, you will bring tea there immediately."

Ostrenalia made polite chit-chat until the door of her workshop had closed behind them and they had settled in chairs.

"Am I to assume that this is not a social call, Miss Stone?"

Claire didn't answer for a moment, but rubbed the tips of her fingers against her thumb and caught her top lip between her teeth. "No, it's not. I…" She shook her head and put clenched fists on the arms of the chair. Ostrenalia's eyes flicked down, but she said nothing. "I need to know more about… this."

"Very well. By 'this" you mean the manipulation of intense

magical energies?"

"Yes."

"Can I ask why you have decided to acquire this knowledge now, rather than when I first offered it to you?"

Again, Claire was slow to answer. "Would you be offended if I asked you not to push that? At least, not yet. I have a job to do, or I think do. It's not really something I can talk about."

"Intriguing."

Claire turned her head and looked at the Sitharii from the corner of her eye. "I'm prepared to return the favour." Her skin tingled uncomfortably as she realised the parallel between her current situation, and how she had become entwined with Tolks.

"Even more fascinating." Ostrenalia was smiling, but Claire couldn't read her face. A smart rap on the door stilled the conversation while the housekeeper shuffled in with a tray of dainty cups and even daintier cakes. Ostrenalia said nothing until the Hrund left, taking time to pour tea for each of them, then to sit back with her cup, saucer, and an expression not dissimilar to that of a cat asked a favour by a mouse.

"Very well. I shall teach you flow management and storage for the rest of the day. What you learn will depend on how fast you think, and how much skill you show."

"Thank you."

Ostrenalia held up her hand. "In return, I shall ask you three questions, which you must answer to the best of your knowledge and ability."

"Closed questions?"

Ostrenalia lips quirked up at the corner. "Agreed. No demanding you tell me everything you know about Grenlik magic, or similarly phrased queries."

"I agree. Three questions. After I have finished the business to which I must attend."

Claire fought to keep a straight face. For all she knew, she would die, or never return to Underland. If she did, it really wouldn't matter. Her business wouldn't be over until she had saved her mum and dad, or had died trying. Ostrenalia didn't know that, and there was no need for her to.

Ostrenalia finished her tea. "Very well. Let us begin." She snatched a cake from the tray between delicate fingers, popped it into her mouth, then stood up and stepped over to her workbench. A cage of bronze metal that looked as if might have once housed a gyroscope was suspended between two crystals that extended out from the wall. Each was as thick as Claire's biceps and ended in an intricate filigree of the same metal as the spherical cage.

"This," explained Ostrenalia, "is a miniature reaction chamber. The crystals feeding it on either side can channel enough magic to keep one fifth of UnderLondon running for a week. Let us begin."

Claire's education was blindingly fast, concepts barely explained before Ostrenalia was on to the next thing. Two hours of intense theoretical instruction that left her feeling that there had to be blood, if not brain, oozing from her ears. She couldn't hope to remember a fraction of it, and by lunchtime she was dreading a snap exam and instant expulsion.

That was when Ostrenalia switched from theory to practice. Small scale at first, but inside an hour Claire was dealing in magical currents that would have fried her to a crisp the day before. As she juggled the power with her mind and her hands Ostrenalia's instructions made more and more sense, and on a couple of occasions her stomach flipped when she realised how close she had come to blowing herself up at least twice, meddling with what she barely understood. When the Sitharii called a halt, Claire didn't want to turn away from the table. Only when a long, slender hand tugged gently, then more firmly at her shoulder did she finally turn away, exultant at the progress she had made.

Ostrenalia looked unconvinced, even worried, and a large bucket of ice water drenched Claire's exuberance. "Frankly, Miss

Stone, I am unconvinced."

Claire's shoulder's drooped and tried to keep anything that might have looked like disappointment from her face. Ostrenalia waved a dismissive hand. "Forgive me. I did not mean that as any slight upon what you have achieved here today. You show significant aptitude for high energy magic. I was referring to the wisdom of trying to teach you so much in so short a time."

"You said we had all day." Claire protested. "You can't stop now. I can do it."

Ostrenalia shook her head. "Neither your dedication or ability are in question. Miss Stone. Your objectivity… perhaps."

"I don't understand."

"You have a phrase, I believe; "absolute power corrupts absolutely"?"

"Yes, but that means politics, or business and stuff."

"It could have been written for high energy magic. There is an enticement to it. It beguiles you. It entices you to try that little bit longer, to manipulate that smidgeon more power than you did last time. To pack the next crystal a whisker tighter than the last one, and to force that tiny bit more in. Until you cannot. Until you overextend yourself that fraction too far and your work unravels and you have long enough to realise your mistake before the magic unravels you to your components and wreaks havoc through the local field."

"I'm always like that, about most things."

"Step away from the bench, Miss Stone. Let us take a short recess and evaluate our position."

Claire turned back to the workbench, and heard a soft intake of breath behind her. She closed her notebook, straightened her pen beside it, and spared one more glance at the test chamber before stepping down from her stool and joining Ostrenalia in the middle of the room. The Sitharii's expression was neutral, but Claire was sure she could see a measure of approval in the woman's eyes.

Was that the test? That she could tear herself away from the experiment? It hadn't been easy, but Claire was damned if she knew whether that was down to some addictive property of high volume magic work, or if the subject was simply compelling — which it most certainly was. This was better than physics, or the watered-down stuff they trickled into her at school. But, if it reassured Ostrenalia, she would play along. She peered around the room until she found a clock. It was coming up on three and as if on cue her stomach suddenly announced it was tired of being empty.

"A little late for lunch, a little early for tea," Claire muttered, feeling her cheeks start to burn.

"I'm sure we can compromise," said Ostrenalia, with a small smile.

33

Claire did her best not to fidget through the light meal Ostrenalia had brought to the workroom. There was little to distinguish it from the earlier tray of tea and cakes, except that the range was wider and the portions larger. Claire nibbled and sipped and tried not to let her eyes wander back to the bench. Well, not too often, anyway. Logically, the next thing Ostrenalia should show her was how to fold energy into high capacity stores; a bit like putting the jenga blocks back in the box, or playing Tetris with dynamite.

As soon as Ostrenalia had begun her lesson, Claire realised this was what she needed to know. The Sitharii had obviously been astonished Claire's solution saving the crashing airship, so she followed Ostrenalia's program exactly, not showing off what she had already figured out and trying to be sure Ostrenalia's ego was suitably flattered at all times.

The interminable snack ground lethargically to an end. Claire forced herself to wait until Ostrenalia rose and invited her back to the work bench. If she looked too eager, she knew the Sitharii would call an end to the session, possibly to all her training, and being forced to stop now would be intolerable.

Claire took a step back, mentally checking herself. Ostrenalia might be closer to the mark than she wanted to believe. Was the lure of the magic taking her over? The white magic was already influencing her more than she ought to allow; was the heady power she was manipulating adding to that feeling of addiction? She set her jaw. It didn't matter. She needed this, and nothing was getting in her way.

She sat down in front of the containment sphere. Ostrenalia reached inside and placed a crystal into a clamp at the centre of the concentric spheres. The target was the size of a three-deck liquorice sweet. "Now, Miss Stone, I shall open the aperture half way. You will manipulate the flow through the local field and use it to fold the energy onto the underlying crystal matrix until I close the aperture. I shall give you sixty seconds to prepare."

"But that tiny thing is nothing like big enough to hold that kind of energy."

"Are you suggesting I cannot properly assess the capacity of a crystal?" A delicately drawn eyebrow arched dangerously, and Claire felt Ostrenalia looking for an excuse to bring things to a halt.

"No. Of course not." She didn't hide the blush. It helped her look contrite.

"Then your sixty seconds start now."

Claire scanned the crystal. It was simple, but regular and uncompromised inside. There were no fractures or flaws she needed to avoid. When Ostrenalia released the magical energy, Claire was ready, quickly and neatly folding the energy into the lattice of the crystal. When Ostrenalia shut off the flow, Claire was astonished to see she had used a fraction of the crystal's potential storage.

Ostrenalia leaned forward and Claire sensed her reaching out with her skills, probing the crystal. There was a flicker of emotion across the Sitharii's face. Claire kept her eyes fixed to the top of the workbench, but she was sure it was chagrin. She pushed down hard on a flicker of smugness as Ostrenalia swapped the part used crystal out for one the same size.

"Let us see how you cope with full aperture."

Claire tried to look nervous. If that was what Ostrenalia wanted to make her feel better that was what Claire would give her. She knew she could do it. She had done it.

She flicked her thoughts at the crystal expecting it to be as robust as the first one, and her mind froze. At least a quarter of it was unusable; either the crystal matrix was twisted or it was

192

obscured by flaws — and the flaws crept throughout the whole of the crystal, which would force her to keep changing where... and then there was the magic, gushing through the conduit before she was ready. She wrapped a controlling spell around it and squirted it into the crystal, but she was rushing and made a mess, wasting space.

It was impossible. She tried to gather her thoughts and get ahead of the game, but the flow was relentless, never giving her a moment. Within half a minute she knew she was in trouble. The crystal was already more than half full. If she couldn't find somewhere to dump the excess, it would feed back into the containment sphere.

Why hadn't Ostrenalia put an end to this? Was she trying to make a point? Claire forced her awareness to widen beyond the confines of the crystal, and found Ostrenalia had problems of her own to deal with. The control mechanism at one side of the containment sphere was failing. Magical energy was hissing and spitting from the metal filigree at the end of the feed crystal, and Ostrenalia was unable to contain it. If it failed completely, the workshop would flood with energy. If they were lucky the safety net strung across the ceilings would absorb it and spread it harmlessly about. If not, Bedford Row was in for a cataclysm worthy of the early evening news.

In the instant her attention wandered, the tiny storage crystal slipped from her control and began to unravel. The best she could do was moderate its discharge and stop it from releasing its energy explosively, but even that was burning her mind.

"Get out," Ostrenalia cried. "I can contain this for only a few minutes."

Claire's flawed crystal cracked open. Raw magic sprayed out into the containment sphere. Battered from within and without, the sphere began to crumple and one of the circumferential rings shattered, flying out to the left and right.

Calmness settled over Claire, and everything looked as though illuminated by blue-white light. Time stretched out in front of her. Ostrenalia's movements became a panicked slow-mo. She looked at the fracturing end of the control mechanism, and at the crystalline pipe feeding it, searching deep inside the structure. Now, if only she had somewhere to put it.

Her hand reached up to the crystal at her neck, the one Ostrenalia had originally given her. She dove into the structure as if it was a swimming pool filled with light. The lattice was perfect. So perfect she could even... In a split instant she took the energy she had already dumped into it and compressed it a thousand thousand times. Her right hand snapped the chain holding the gem around her neck and clenched around it, and her left hand clamped down on the power feed, several inches behind the failing control filigree. A channel of deeply concentrated magic sprang into life between her hands.

"Fix it," she grunted, as time resumed its normal flow.

"But that's not possible." Ostrenalia gaped at her, eyes and mouth wide.

"Fix it anyway," Claire ground out between clenched teeth. "Quickly."

Ostrenalia hesitated a second more, then fell to work on the containment sphere and the control. Claire, tense at first, began to relax. It was so easy. Too easy. She folded the energy tighter and tighter into the pendant; enough to run the city for a day, two days, a week, all folded so tightly and so neatly that it took up only a part of the capacity of the crystal. The white magic was protecting her hands, giving her the control to do what she must. It was as if she was doing what it wanted, and for a second the absurd notion that it could have somehow caused the component failure crossed her mind. She chuckled, and drew deeper draughts from the raw magic feed.

By the time Ostrenalia finished sealing off the controller,

Claire's pendant was still only fractionally full. She gradually let the energy back up against the controller, testing that the repair would hold, then lifted her hand away. The actinic beam to her fist sputtered and went out and Claire fell forward onto the workbench, catching herself on her elbows.

"Let me see your hands," Ostrenalia insisted. Claire opened her left, which was pink and blistered from its contact with the magical feed, but kept her right fist closed firmly.

"Let me see the other, and let me take that pendant from you. I can see its safely disposed of."

Claire put her clenched fist firmly into her pocket. "No, thank you."

"But it's dangerous. What you did was not possible, and that crystal is dangerous. Why would you want to keep it? And how did you do it? Your hands should be blackened stumps, if you were alive at all."

"I think those may be two of the questions you can chose to ask me later," Claire said, smiling. "Assuming there is a later. Thank you, Madam. Your instruction has been most beneficial."

She was done here. She gathered her thoughts, bowed to Ostrenalia, and jumped out.

34

Nobody had spoken to her for days, which was in danger of putting her into an even deeper snit until she realised that they could be waiting her out and hoping that her mood would improve; or to put it another way "giving her space". Claire spent a lot of the intervening time practising packing her crystal with energy. It wasn't that rewarding; if she worked in Underland there wasn't that much loose magic to play with, and if she worked at Nana May's, she was juggling with white magic. At least that got easier each time she tried. Still, the crystal was getting close to full, and it was time she forced her friends to stop doing whatever they were doing and face her.

She picked up her phone and scroodled around the screen, dropping messages into the inboxes of both Evie and Stu. Who was doing what where, and was there any chance she was invited?

The wait turned into a nail-biting torment. The hoped-for instant responses did not materialise. Claire scolded herself for being impatient and, more, for letting it get to her. Just because she was feeling twitchy and in need of reassurance, she shouldn't be reading anything into a three-minute wait for a message.

After ten minutes she put the phone on charge. After twenty she checked the ringer volume and carrier signal, and that the phone's memory wasn't full. Then she sat on her part-deflated mattress and stared at it from across the room, willing it to make the portentous clang of the Cloister Bell.

After another ten minutes the anger set in. They were deliberately ignoring her. She didn't need them anyway. She gathered up her night clothes, her shower bag and a towel and headed off to the tiny toilet. Two minutes later, towel wrapped around her still-dry body, she scampered into the bedroom to check the phone again, then stomped angrily out.

After the shower, hair still damp, Claire scowled at the phone as she tugged the charger from the wall, throwing both onto the airbed so she could plug in her straightener. Only as the phone left her hand did she see the tiny indicator LED was showing purple; there was a message.

She stabbed at the screen, dried her hands, and tried again. Eyebrows rose. It was Evie.

"U ok? 2 l8. Call 2mrw"

Not the effusive open arms she had hoped for, but about what she expected from Evie, who shunned tech wherever possible. Pretty much all she could expect under the circumstances.

The phone bonged again, and a pop-up window announced a text from Stu. She let out a long breath, swiped and wiggled, and prepared to eat humble pie.

"You were warned"

Claire scrabbled at the screen as she sent another text.

"Stop messing about - that's not funny."

No reply - at least, nothing immediate. She scratched at the screen again.

"Mrs Grey? Claire Stone. Is Stu there? I've been trying... Oh. How long? Since yesterday. Did he say... Of course, if I hear from him I'll get him to call you."

The person on the other end of the line hung up as the words left her lips and for a second she wondered if she really had been speaking to one of his family. The accent sounded suitably impenetrable, but she hadn't really been introduced.

She fumbled through her duster pockets until she found her Underland communicator and jumped in — not into the SFU changing area, but into Tolks' shop. She looked around, blinking owlishly in the darkness then cursing herself for not thinking. He could have been doing anything in here.

Fortunately, the place felt deserted. No light shone under the door to the workshop, hidden in the blackness at the back of the shop. Even the air smelt more stagnant than usual, as though nobody has opened a door or walked through the room for days, or even weeks. She squeezed the communicator and spoke Stuart's name. The communicator hummed the odd little tune it used to say it was trying, but gave up after two or three minutes. As she was about to jump, the little box twitched in her hand and a text message rolled across the face.

"Stay away. Do nothing. Behave, and we may negotiate. Only warning."

She jumped home.

Evie, unkempt and strained, arrived moments after Claire's panicked call. Using Underland as a hop through — to jump in then immediately jump out to a different location — left one feeling jangled, but Claire barely noticed her friend's appearance. It took just a few minutes to bring Evie up to speed by showing her the paper note and the two messages. She cursed inventively for two solid minutes on the unreliability of Underland and all those who live in or beneath it. She might have gone on longer if it hadn't been for a perfunctory knock and the door to Claire's room opening.

"Little late for guests."

Nana May's face wore its now habitual politely neutral impassivity. Claire made the effort not to sigh. She hated that things had broken down so badly between them, and knew family duty was the only thing keeping a roof over her head at the moment. She didn't blame her grandmother; Claire wasn't sure if she could have offered shelter to someone as horrible as she felt.

A whisper of cold reason suggested there was a way to deal with it, if she would set aside these mawkish emotions. Claire hesitated, not pushing the thought away, at least not yet, but not letting herself listen either.

"They've taken Stuart." Evie ground the words out between her teeth. Claire was simultaneously and irrationally annoyed that Evie has stolen her dramatic announcement, and surprised at her friend's passion. Once, she would have expected Evie to look on Stu as competition.

Nana May looked thoughtful. "How sure are we of this?"

"I can't get hold of him by phone," said Claire, then explained the rest.

"And he's not likely to be playing a prank."

"Not if he wants to reach his next birthday," rumbled Evie.

Nana May flipped dismissive fingers at Evie and looked directly at Claire. She shook her head.

"I don't think so."

"So who are 'they'?"

"The Grenlix?" Evie offered.

"What, all of them?" Nana May used the "grown up making a point" voice, and Claire watched Evie start to bristle.

"No," she said. "They may have helped, but they didn't start it. None of the Underkin started it."

"Then who?" Her grandmother looked confused.

"The demons beneath. Morphs."

"But they're mindless. Blobs of stinking jelly with hunt and kill reflexes."

Evie grimaced and jumped in before Claire could. "Not all. Most of them, yes, but I've heard stuff."

"Nana, what about the ones they sent for Mum and Dad?"

Her grandmother pursed her lips and frowned but still didn't look convinced. Cold anger began to leak out from somewhere near her heart, implacable and emotionless.

"I fought a demon, a Morph Lord. In Aslnaff's office, before I moved here. He was smart. And devious. And they've taken Stuart."

"Then you must tell the authorities. If they already know about this… person, then they should act."

Claire shook her head. "They didn't want to know about Evie, they won't want to know about this."

"Then wait," said Evie. "They'll tell us what they want and we can make a deal."

Claire stared at Evie for a moment, eyebrows raised, and wondered if she might have broken something when she was burrowing around inside her head. Caution had never been one of Evie's strong points.

The emotional chill was creeping up her spine now, invading her thoughts. "No," she said. "I have to go down there and get him back."

Nana May and Evie spoke at the same time.

"Don't be absurd."

"You are joking."

"What if they do to him what they did to Mum and Dad?" Claire demanded.

"What if you stick your nose in and they kill him?" Evie planted herself in front of Claire, fists on her hips. "And how are you going to get there. And what army will you take to fight them with?"

"I have power they don't understand."

"This shite magic? Right. Stu told me all about that. Told me the after-effects, anyway. Sounds to me like you don't understand it either"

Claire ignored her, so Evie turned to Nana May. "You have to stop her. She's not listening to me."

The chill reached to her neck and Claire let the white magic fill her, welcoming it in. She was the white magic again. She could do anything.

"I don't think she will listen to me any more than you," said Nana.

Claire checked her equipment. She had already put on her heavy boots, grey camo pants and a tight black top. Over that she clipped her standard issue equipment harness. Most Warriors never wore them, but she clipped on a selection of the magical distractors Tolks had helped her make oh-so-long ago when it was such a different world. Crystals and bulbs and complicated coils of wire to confound traps and senses alike. She could have done it all herself, but why waste effort when a tool was available.

"What are you going to do, Claire?" Evie sounded scared.

"The Grenlix have something I need. I want it back."

"We should talk this through. Come up with a plan."

"I don't need a plan."

Evie grabbed her arm and Claire managed to stop an instinctive surge of magic that was going to throw her aside. She looked at the hand on her arm, then into Evie's eyes. She didn't let go.

"They can't stop me. I have to go."

"But Stuart said every time you use this stuff you end up hurt somehow."

"I accept it now. It's always helped me, but I didn't remember. We're working together now."

"And what are you prepared to do, Claire?" asked Nana May. "How far are you prepared to go?"

"As far as they make me."

"'Don't make me hurt you'? Is that it Claire?"

Claire smiled. Her grandmother didn't understand, but she could do something stupid, as might Evie. With a thought, Claire took away their ability to jump between the worlds. For a half-hour. She would be back by then. She took hold of Evie's hand, still gripping her arm, and squeezed her wrist just hard enough to make her hand open. Claire smiled at Evie, patted her on the shoulder, and stepped through into Underland.

35

In the middle of the yard, fifteen feet or so from the door, the facade of the academy looked odd. The colours were wrong. It was garish. The soiled yellow light of Underland was exaggerated, distorting things.

She had, briefly, considered appearing somewhere deep inside the academy, but it was easier to arrive in the open than to fight through a barrier "in flight". She stooped as she walked towards the door, picking up a stone and flicking it ahead of her. Instead of whizzing back at her, the stone stuck in mid-air, dark sparks of purple fizzing from its point of contact with whatever the Grenlix had erected as a screen.

A step away from the stone, she stopped, raised a finger, and poked at it. It felt as though she was pushing through jelly, and the screen crackled furiously around her finger. An inch later the stone dropped to the floor and rolled unenthusiastically forward until it touched the door.

Now she knew everything she needed to bring the barrier down. She withdrew her finger and placed her palm lightly against it. The air winced at the angry hiss of conflicting energies as the white magic teased apart the weave of the spell. The hiss turned to crackling, like an ice cube dropped into a drink, and a tracery of dark lines grew outwards from her hand.

When the web of cracks covered an area large enough for her to pass through, Claire tapped at them with a fingertip. The space in front of her shattered, each sliver vanishing with a tiny glint of white light before it hit the floor. She stepped through and up to the door, listening to the prickle-crackle fading away on either side as the rest of the barrier crumbled.

The doors presented no obstacle; Claire simply aged the metal of the bolts to rust. A hard shove and they swung inwards on stiff hinges. A Grenlik, presumably guarding the door, held a handbow pointed at her. Doormen were always too young or too old, and this one was the latter. The point of the bolt wobbled back and forth as he glared at her.

"That's far enough, human. You aren't allowed in here, not any more. Be off, now, or..." he waved the weapon meaningfully.

Claire reached out with the white magic and divided the taut string. There was a noise part way between twang and *pfunt* and the bolt slid from the track and fell to the floor. The Grenlik stared at the ruined weapon for a moment then dropped it and reached for a hand-bell on the table beside him. She joined the bell to the table before he could lift it. "I think they already know I'm here," she said, and flashed him a thin smile. The Grenlik flinched and backed away.

Claire wanted the *Krezik Chet Knar* cube, the last shard, and the book of Grenlik Lore. The latter was of no real interest to her, but it was wrong to leave it in their hands. She knew where the *Krezik Chet Knar* and the shard were. They burned in her mind now, like beacons. The book she could not sense, but she guessed it wouldn't be far from the other two.

The shard was still separate from the *Krezik Chet Knar*. Perhaps they had been afraid to perform the final assembly. Whatever the reason, they were below her - exposing another lie by Nagrath that the academy had no basement - and towards the back of the building. The stairs in the lobby only went up, so she turned back to the doorman. "How do I get down?"

He had backed away, already behind the table and making for a corridor off the right of the lobby. He shook his head. Claire frowned at him.

"I can dig straight down from here, if you want? Or you can tell me where the stairs are. Your masters have already set up traps for me, and I expect they would be displeased if you wasted their effort."

The doorman pointed to a hallway to the left of the staircase, his finger trembling. Claire gave him another smile and he ran.

The doors to either side were all locked. She could feel life behind each of them, vibrating with fear and anger. She walked quickly along the wide corridor. Nothing they had was any threat to her. If anything strong enough had been put in place, she would sense it before it became an inconvenience.

The hallway narrowed to a corridor, still with doors facing each other every ten or twelve paces. These were not locked, and were empty of people. A surplus of magic hung in the air and made it taste bitter and metallic. They had flooded the local field, trying to hide things beneath the glare. Claire felt the white magic within her become more alert.

Iron bars blocked the end of the passage. Behind them, a metal cage lift shaft sat next to a spiral staircase. In the middle of the iron bars was a gate with two ponderous locks.

There was, thought Claire, an unusual quality about the last pair of wooden doors before the grating. They looked the same as every other door that had stared at each other from either side of the corridor, and yet these two troubled her. She reached out, using her own magical skills rather than the white magic, and felt for the deception.

The doors were not there. They were illusions. She let whoever had set the trap a moment of satisfaction before stepping forwards to trigger it. On either side of her, hidden behind the deceptions, two cannons roared.

Claire reached into the white magic and stopped time. Almost.

That Underland even had cannon came as a surprise to her. Industrialised magic powered everything down here, harvested from the outside the cities. Chemistry was new. Out of mild curiosity, she examined the trap a little closer. They used magic to ignite the gunpowder, and the cannon were expelling a cloud of marble-sized munitions. Grape shot. It would reduce her to a bloody mess of ragged flesh. Assuming it reached her.

She stepped past the cannon fire, building a half-circle wall of solid air behind her to catch any strays or ricochets, then allowed time to resume. Plaster flew as the shot pounded into the opposite walls and the cloud of smoke and dust handily concealed her as she made a thousand years pass for the locks in the iron gate.

Indistinctly through the smoke she could see short figures hurrying down the corridor towards her. She stepped through the grating and took a moment to merge the gate with the frame around it, then she wove the wall of air through the bars that spanned the width of the corridor.

Eight or ten Grenlix appeared out of the dust, each with a repeating handbow. Each fired as soon as they saw her, but the bolts slowed, then hung in the air. She let them fire three or four times, then with a lazy thought severed all their bowstrings. She hesitated. She could do the same to their necks, and with as little effort. A little snip with scissors of pure energy. They wouldn't even bleed much. Her hand began to rise, two fingers extending.

She clenched her fists and let her hands drop to her sides. That wasn't why she was here, tempting though it was, and she refused to descend to their level. She couldn't take that step, no matter how furious she was and no matter how they had hurt her. She turned away and walked towards the stairs.

A welcoming committee waiting for her; a wall of Grenlik mages, with Yashik standing safely behind them, arranged in a defensive arc in front of a double iron door.

"Far enough, human."

She stopped a dozen steps from the line of mages. Each had a hand raised, holding a ball of bright fire. Inside, Claire flinched. Even though these creeps weren't a shadow of the battle mages of the past, they would pack a hard punch. The white magic swirled inside her as if it understood and was offering reassurance. She took a step forward.

The mages threw their weapons as one. Claire raised her hands in front of her, cupped like a baseball catcher, and gathered them in, drawing each missile into the bowl of her hands and moulding them into one. The mages looked at each other in confusion, then attacked again. Still Claire collected the energy, blending it together until she had a magical bomb the size of a football; enough energy to punch a twenty-foot-wide hole up to the sky.

They stopped. There was nothing left for them to draw upon. Everything in the local magical field had been exhausted, concentrated into a ball of boiling energy sitting an inch above Claire's hand. She glared at the mages, who shuffled nervously from foot to foot, then she raised her other hand above the fireball and squeezed. The ball got brighter, until it was painful to look at directly, then it shrank.

In truth, Claire was shunting the energy to the crystal around her neck. The Grenlix magic was tiny by comparison to what was already there, but it was somewhere to store the energy and she thought the effect made her look even more powerful, as though the Grenlix were children, or amateurs. When the last of it was safely stored, she dusted her hands together, then she glared at the mages.

"Run." The word came out flat and angry; not loud, but deeply intense. There was a second of glancing at each other, and over shoulders at Yashik, then they scattered like cockroaches in daylight. Yashik shouted at them to stay and fight, then the arrogance and anger in his face turned to fear. He glanced to either side, then at her, and tried to escape.

Claire made a minute gesture with a finger. Yashik ran into a wall of solid air. He bounced off it, stumbling, then span about and ran the other way. Another gesture, another wall. She twirled her finger, like she was drawing on a tablet, and the walls turned into a circular fence. She pinched her fingers together, and Yashik's prison contracted until his arms pressed against his sides and his shoulders began to hunch.

"Not you," said Claire, making sure he was paying attention before she uttered the next words. "You have something I want."

36

Yashik struggled, refusing to look her in the eye, and she could feel fractions of spells forming in his mind. She snuffed each out like a candle. Eventually, he had no option but to look at her.

"You are an abomination," he snarled. "Humans are abominations, traitors to their cores. You have no right to the power you wield."

"And you do?" Claire was genuinely surprised that he could hold such an opinion, knowing what she did. "You made me what I am. If you had kept your bargain, if you hadn't tried to steal this from me, none of this would be happening. Or if you hadn't used me to steal the book for you. All you had to do was help me."

"The book is ours by right. The only help I would offer a human is to leave our world and never return. To wipe every memory of us from each of you and lock you out."

"And so you developed the modified goggles?"

He raised his head. "I did."

Claire pinched her fingers together again and Yashik cried out. "Do you have any idea of the hurt those things caused. The damage they did to people, to my friend?"

"Worth... the... price..." Yashik forced the words out as Claire forced the air from his body. The pain overwhelmed his self-control, and she plucked the location of the book and the shard from his thoughts. She reached out with the power and felt them, hidden in a steel- and magic-lined safe, buried in a wall of solid rock. The protective spells were prodigious, but nothing she couldn't handle, not with the white magic backing her up. She squeezed harder, driven by her pain, and that of her friends.

"Child, no!"

Claire looked up, surprised. The voice had sounded like Tolks.

"You must not kill him. Is he truly worth the stain you will carry on your soul for the rest of your life?"

She looked around again, and eventually spotted a door to her right; small, nondescript, with a six-inch grille set in it at head height for a Grenlik. A face pressed up against it, but she couldn't be sure if it was Tolks or not. She turned back to Yashik and squeezed a little harder. He let out a short scream, which Claire found surprisingly pleasing - so much so she wondered if she could make him do it again.

"Claire, listen to me." The voice was definitely Tolks, thought it sounded weak and strained. "I know you no longer think of me as you did, but trust me in this. You must not kill him."

"Must not?" Claire turned her full attention to the window in the door. "You have the nerve to tell me what I can and cannot do? I've seen the books. I've seen what you people were, what you did. Whether you were once my friend or not, you don't get to tell me what I can do."

Fury was building inside her. Up to now, her rage had been cold, meticulous, planned, but Tolks had set a match to it.

"You are changing, child. I saw the beginnings some time back, but I dismissed them as growing in confidence as your abilities developed. I was wrong. I did not know what danger you were in." His voice dropped. "I failed you. Failed to protect you when you were most vulnerable."

Claire snorted. "Oh, spare me the pity, Grenlik." She saw Tolks flinch when she pointedly didn't use his name. "You betrayed me. You all betrayed me."

"Not all. We didn't know. We thought we had preserved lore and knowledge from the past, until you recovered that book. We were wrong. So very wrong."

Talking through the grille was suddenly frustrating. Tolks and Nagrath had promised to help, and had failed her. Like all their people they were corrupt and self-serving, and she wanted to confront him face to face. Whilst making sure she didn't lose her grip on Yashik, Claire reached out with her magic and aged the lock of the cell to rust. "Get out here and face me." The words ground out between clenched teeth.

There was a pause, then the door scratched against the floor as it opened outwards into the main chamber. Two Grenlix shuffled out, naked apart from loincloths — and bloody bandages wrapped around their hands. Claire blinked, hard, shocked by the apparent brutality inflicted on them. For a moment, her heart softened, but an effervescent wash of energy up her spine hardened her eyes and face.

"This magic is not what it appears, child. It is not helping you. It is using you."

"So you say," Claire's voice was flat, but the words sounded childish and she resented them. "It has been more of a help to me than many I could mention."

"The Claire Stone I know would never have considered harming someone, let alone murder. How many people have you hurt, child? How many have you done deliberate injury to?"

She didn't answer. She hadn't hurt anybody here, at least not yet, but an uncomfortable memory refused to let her ignore it - throwing hand-bow bolts into the legs of those who had attacked them in Edinbelow, and when they had been running away. She rolled her shoulders, pushing the memory aside.

"I tried all the good ways, all the nice ways. I listened to people tell me they would help, to trust them. All lies. All indifference and betrayal. Everything gets left to me, but now I have the will and the strength to do it."

Tolks raised a hand to his mouth and bit at the bandage. The other hand he held out to Nagrath, shaking it slightly. His master fumbled with the binding while Tolks worried the other free with his teeth. Claire's teeth snapped together, and it took all she had not to let her feelings show on her face. His hands were angry red, charred black, oozing blood and clear fluid in equal measure. Had the injuries been hers, she knew she would have been kneeling on the floor screaming.

"This is what your white magic does to those it hasn't chosen."

"And I should believe you why?"

"Say anything and I shall have you burned alive," Yashik hissed.

Claire squeezed him harder, stopping only when he screamed again. "Your last warning," she said, then turned back to Tolks. "Still waiting."

"Yashik and his people took control as soon as they knew you had delivered the book. He already had the crystal you had infused with interstitial magic. Nobody had managed to touch it, or work with it. I suspect many died. Excuse me." Tolks limped over to the table and hooked out a chair with his foot. "The room we were held in is bare. It is a pleasure to sit on something other than the floor, and... I am in some discomfort."

"Still waiting."

"The book contained lore on interstitial magic. Above all it said it was dark, fickle, and controlling. It also said that one either had to be expertly skilled to use the magic..." he paused, looking down at the floor before raising his eyes to meet Claire's. "Or chosen by it."

Tolks lifted his hands. "They made me—" he waved an arm in the direction of Nagrath. "Us, experiment with the crystal you charged. This is the result. The magic fights back. It will not be used unless it wishes to be. The magic punished even the simplest attempt at manipulation, as did he if we refused to try." He jerked his head at Yashik.

"Are you trying to make me pity you?" Claire's crossed her arms over her chest.

Tolks shook his head, but it was Nagrath who spoke. "He seeks to warn you, Warrior, and he speaks the truth." He sighed. "There were hints about events far in our past, but I chose to ignore them.

211

If you have seen corroboration of these, then I do not blame you."

"And so you expect me to give up? To abandon my parents?"

"No, Warrior, that would be futile, and you have the right to try to undo what has been done. Tolks, and I, need to warn you not to trust the magic. It is eating away at who you are, at the values you hold dear. The more it can take away your conscience, the easier it is for you to commit the next atrocity. Search deep. How many times have you been tempted to hurt or kill someone since you arrived? Does it feel good when you squeeze Yashik?" He grimaced, and added "Not that the *castrak* doesn't deserve it."

"I still don't believe you." Inside, a tiny ember of doubt glowed as she again let her mind roam back. No. Don't weaken. Stay strong. They want you to doubt, want you to fail. The ember flickered and died, but not before it begged the question if the defiance was hers.

The door to the cell was still open. She flung Yashik inside, then stared through the door in confusion. She had expected him to fly into the room hard enough to bounce off the wall, and damn her if anything broke. The effect was similar, but the violence was not there. His landing was hard, but not bone-crushing. There was disappointment, but it was distant, as though not quite hers

The door slammed shut. As an afterthought, Claire made it impermeable and did the same to part of the wall around it. The grill shrank to the size of a postcard, and Claire willed that nothing should pass but air.

"If we're done here, I have things to do." The comment was rhetorical, and she strode towards the great iron door without waiting for comment. They opened without tricks, and beyond was a workshop, or a laboratory. Not as simple as the one in Tolks' shop; more like the workroom of Ostrenalia, but less elegant. The tome she had stolen from the Angel library lay open on a bench on her left. Magic still lingered in here, even though she had drained the field outside. Traps still clung to the energy stored in them, though the low field density was doing its best to leech it away. A crooked smile twisted Claire's lips. All the easier for her. She walked farther inside.

Scattered around the floor were thick mats. When working on delicate magics, stray charge could sometimes ruin hours of effort. She had seen the mats at Tolks' workshop. They collected any wayward energy and carried it safely away to the background field. There was a large one set in front of the wall safe she knew held the *Krezik Chet Knar* and the last component. It was a logical precaution.

"Be wary, child."

She looked over her shoulder. Tolks had entered behind her, and Nagrath stood in the doorway. She turned away.

"Yashik and his mages spent long hours working in here. Once we had proven the interstitial magic would not be tamed, they layered trap after trap in this room."

Claire said nothing, but raised her hand, palm forward, and sent forward a pulse of energy. Explosions sputtered, shafts of virtual spears half-heartedly stabbed across the path she would have taken, and a cage of pure force rose from the floor, but shattered into purple sparks before it could become solid. "Yashik cannot stop me. You cannot stop me."

"I am not trying to stop you," said Tolks, but she was walking away, deeper into the room, and his words fell on empty air. She stopped a couple of steps from the wall safe and let her mind wander through the lock, the door, the walls of the safe, and the rock around it. She sensed a dozen or more traps of varying ingenuity and effect, all depleted by the weak magical field. None took more than the merest thought to defeat or destroy. Very carefully, lest her magic affect anything inside, Claire let ages pass for the bolts and levers holding the safe door. Once they had rotted to dust, she stepped forward, hand outstretched to open the door and claim her prize.

213

As she stepped fully onto the mat, it shifted slightly beneath her and there was a loud click. A simple mechanical trap, well hidden with childishly simple illusions. She had been too confident. She had missed the obvious, as Tolks had scolded her for in the past. She threw her mind forwards into the door, to see what she had triggered.

Another click, milliseconds later, but from above. She was looking in the wrong place. She had relaxed, convinced she had won, and let her grip on the white magic loosen. Over her head, a huge shape fell through a simple paper sheet, painted to look like the roof. Copper sheathed, with complex coils and windings, and a sharp downward-facing point. Claire tried to stop time, but the magic was too far away from her. She managed to slow it enough to allow her a step to the side, so whatever it was would land beside her, but that was all.

As the pin-sharp point drew level with her eyes she realised that this was the lifting crystal from the airship, the one she had charged with white magic to keep them airborne. Except now whatever was inside the crystal boiled angrily.

As a last defence, Claire tried to put a solid pad of air underneath the crystal, to block it from whatever it was supposed to do. She had taken a half turn away from the safe, her hand outstretched, but it was too little and too late. The needle point tore through the meagre cushion she had made and drove deep into the mat.

37

Darkness rippled from the crystal, a negation of energy. Again, Claire tried to react, but the darkness was as fast as her magic — and it had a head start. Streamers of darkness, edged in violet, rose around her body. Her own magic held it away from her, but barely. She began to understand what she had done to Yashik, except her torment was dark sparks of pain prickling at her like a million nettles. She could see thorns growing out of the mesh, stretching towards her.

She couldn't move; she hadn't the strength, and the dark net held her in place. She fought against it, but the white magic wasn't helping. It was still there, but apart from her, at a distance. The bond between them had stretched, and in a flash of insight, Claire realised what Yashik had done. She glanced away from the net surrounding her. The coils and windings around the crystal were glowing, some with an ugly purple, others golden or white hot. Her own magic was attacking her, but inverted and twisted.

Fire and pain exploded in her thigh. She gasped but dared not move. Another thorn had formed, this one in front of her face, and it was growing towards her eye. There was little she could do, but Claire shifted her defensive focus to the new threat. More pain, this time in her left arm and against her breastbone. She cried out.

There was movement. Time was out of joint and Tolks moved like an astronaut on the moon, but his face was angry and determined, and as he walked he re-wrapped the bandage around his burnt hand.

"No!" Claire screamed as realised what he was going to do, but there was no way she could intervene. Tolks stepped up to the crystal and wrapped his arms around it. She could see smoke curling up from his flesh as it charred. His lips curled back and he made a growl deep in his throat. Then he lifted.

Claire had no idea where Tolks found the strength, but he raised the brass-clad point clear of the mat. His bandages were aflame now, but the anti-magic still enveloped Claire, travelling to the mat through him. She could do nothing to help, nothing to stop him.

Tolks took a step back, then another, and was on the bare floor of the room. Claire pushed at the residual magic holding her in place, but she was too late. The anti-magic was free of all control. It had a path to the earth, to the background field, and with no constraints. An angry violet glare enveloped the crystal, and Tolks, growing brighter and whiter in seconds.

Still Tolks held the crystal. Claire didn't know whether he wouldn't or couldn't let go, but as the anti-magic finally released her, the fire around Tolks and the crystal flared outward. Tolks howled, once, and the crystal imploded.

Energy boiled outwards, dark and ugly, ripping at the local magical field. Even though it was no longer wrapped around her, the twisted force still reached for her. How, though, she could fight back? In an instant, she built a barrier between herself and Yashik's evil; irresistible force and immovable object. They struck, and tore a hole in the world.

Interstitial energy poured, uncontrolled and immeasurable, through the rip in reality. Claire didn't think, she reacted, the lesson Ostrenalia had taught her driving her into action. She gathered and packed, folding and compressing the raging energies, forcing them into the crystal at her neck. The breach began to seal itself, but the white magic seemed to flow all the faster, as if it wanted to force itself through into Underland. Claire held her boundary around the two forces, folding and packing, folding and packing. Even the dark, twisted energy was crushed into the perfect matrix of the crystal.

The rift imploded, its sudden absence as loud as a balloon

bursting. Claire was suddenly empty, the crystal in her hand burning hot, yet still she clenched it. For a second, perhaps two, there was a wave of uncontainable grief filling the sudden void, but it faded away before she could begin to understand it. There were no emotions. She simply had a job to do, and now she could get on with it. The door of the safe was hanging open. She pushed it aside, reached in, and claimed her prizes. Three more steps and she closed then picked up the book of lore. As she turned away, she saw Nagrath at the door, his face numb, as if he was unable to believe what he had seen.

Evie punched Claire's arm as soon as she appeared in her temporary bedroom.

"Ow?"

"Don't ever do that again."

"What?"

Evie stared at her, and after a moment, Claire's cheeks start to burn.

"You use that shit on me again and you are on your own. Do you understand me?"

Claire nodded. Back in the real, the determination and focus brought out by the magic affected her less. The image of Tolks burning in the crystal fire clamoured for attention, but there at least the white magic still helped, pushing the image aside, walling it off. There would be time to deal with it later. For now...? For now she was so close. There wasn't time to stop. There wasn't time to deal with Evie's whining. Claire stepped around her, then made a clear space on Nana May's sewing table by sweeping most of the stuff onto the floor with a long arm.

Evie muttered a protest, but Claire ignored her. She still had the cube in one hand and the boxed shard in the other. She placed them both on the table then opened the box. The shard was irregular and very unlike all the others she had found. She lifted it from the box and held it over the cube. Nothing happened. Before, the cube had provided a slot, or some opening to insert the new component, but today it was inert; smooth, featureless, and lifeless.

Claire reached out with her mind. Inside, the cube was a labyrinth of tiny mechanisms and magical channels. Tolks had used it to teach her how to meditate, or so he had said, allowing her mind to wander through the intricacies and follow its complexity as far as she could. Now, for a moment, she wondered if he had known exactly what was likely to happen and had set her up. Brought her to the cube, which in turn had led the magic from between the worlds to her.

Like the sadness, she pushed the anger aside. She would deal with how she felt about Tolks when there was time to do so.

"What's supposed to happen?" Evie was leaning over her shoulder, peering at the table. Claire fought down an urge to push her away, to punish Evie for invading her space, interfering in her problems. She didn't answer, and a moment later heard a grunt and sensed Evie step back. Claire leaned forward, resting her elbows on the table, and touched the cube with her mind.

She bounced off. The cube was closed to her. She tried again, willing the white magic to infuse her thoughts, but it refused to respond. The false shard seemed glued in place too, so seamlessly welded to the cube that there wasn't even a gap to slip her fingernail into.

"Can you even do that here?"

Claire's eyes opened wide. Evie might have a point. They added all the other shards to the cube whist it, and she, had been in Underland. She had assumed that since she could still use the white magic in the Real that the cube would behave as it always had. Perhaps she had been wrong. She put the shard back in the box and closed it.

"Claire, where are you going?"

But she was already gone.

The room was dark, but Claire knew the layout so well she stepped to the nearest workbench without feeling for it with her hands and deposited the cube and the shard box. A moment later a ball of cold light appeared in the palm of her hand, throwing sharp-edged shadows around Tolks' workshop and guiding her as she walked towards the door.

From the shop outside came a thump and bitter swearing. Claire reached the switch that fed magic to the lights and turned them up as Evie burst through the door.

"Thought so." She stomped across the room and perched on Tolks' stool. "Time to talk."

"About what?"

"Shall we start with your questionable sanity?"

Claire raised an eyebrow — a small part of her really annoyed that now she could do it — and turned to her workspace. She didn't have the time or the interest for this right now.

A wooden clatter made her jump, then a hard hand on her arm spun her around. Evie pressed in close, her face furious. "Don't you dare turn your back on me."

The stool, lying on its side on the floor, had a broken leg, and for an instant Claire mused on how mad Tolks was going to be when he found out.

"What did you do to get that?" Evie jutted her chin at the treasures on the workbench. "Why did you need to push us away? Why couldn't we help?"

"I have no time for this." Claire twisted away, trying to turn back to the bench, but Evie's fingers dug into her arm. Again Claire managed to stop the surge of energy that would have thrown Evie across the room, and possibly through the wall. Her thoughts froze, just for a moment. That was the second time, and it had been harder? It had taken more effort, more will, not to hurt

219

her friend.

"Make time," Evie snapped. "Did you kill people to get this? Are you so hopped up on your own self-importance and that damned magic that you would murder to get this stuff? Do you think that's what your pare—?"

Claire's hand was on Evie's throat without her being aware she had actually moved. Her fingers dug in to either side of Evie's windpipe, an inch below her chin. Evie made a choking noise and stood very still. Her eyes gaped wide, but there was more anger there than fear. Claire forced her fingers to relax a little, but did not let go. "Do not presume to lecture me on behalf of my parents."

"I wish to hell you hadn't fixed me," Evie ground out. Claire let go. Eve rubbed at her neck and swallowed. "Better never to have known you than have to remember you like this."

Claire turned away, but Evie hadn't finished. "Can you hear yourself? 'Do not presume to lecture me'? That's not you, Claire. You don't talk like that." Evie leaned on the workbench, leaning forward as if trying to make Claire look at her. "So why? Why did you find me and fix me?"

Claire stopped. She had "rescued" Evie for help, but now realised she didn't really need her. Out of guilt? That she had been responsible for causing Evie's expulsion and torment? But that debt was repaid. Now she was becoming an inconvenience. Claire raised her head from her work and stared deep into Evie's eyes. She could go back in, change things. Make her go away. She realised there was an easier way. A quicker way.

"Practice."

She saw Evie take the step back. She saw the hurt overwhelm the anger. They didn't register. Claire turned her eyes back to the cube and the shard. It was ready now. The spurious chip had flaked away and a cradle extruded from the top face, delicate, perfectly shaped to accept the new fragment. With tweezers from the tool

Evie had first woken her memories of Underland, sitting outside the girl's toilet at school so very long ago, everything came back to her.

The memories had never gone. She had always known everything she had done. Now, as though a summer shower had cleared the dust and fug from her mind, she felt it. She couldn't draw air to breathe, and her chest ached as though her heart had stopped. She had been so cruel. She had used people so mercilessly, especially those trying to help her. She had become everything she despised. And now, all she had left was the shame.

"It's all gone," Claire gasped, scrubbing at her tears.

"What is?"

"The magic. All of it. I've got nothing. I can't feel the cube, there's no local field, no white magic. Nothing."

"Oh crap," said Evie, after a moment, and then, "Ah, do you think you can jump us out of here. I just tried, but..."

Claire built the essence of her room at Nana May's in her mind, but from the outset it felt wrong, empty. She'd never really been aware of the subtle power that enabled the jump, but she could tell it was missing today.

She shook her head, and hauled herself back onto her feet. It was no harder than climbing Everest.

"So much for our social life," said Evie. "So, what's the plan?"

Claire looked around her again. She wanted to curl into a ball and ignore the universe. She had made such a mess of everything, hurt so many people, and still couldn't save her parents. She was helpless and hopeless. "I have no idea."

"Well we can't stay out here. Let's head for those hills, or whatever they are."

"We have to look for the *Krezik Chet Knar*. And what if this is the only place we can get back from. We'll never find it again."

"Stay out here for the whole day and it's a safe bet we won't need to, seeing as how we'll be dead."

Claire scowled at her. "Melodrama, much?"

"I don't know if those are hills or mountains. I don't know if they are fifteen klicks away or fifty. Either way, if we don't reach somewhere with shelter, and hopefully water, getting to the end of tomorrow won't be a problem."

"You a closet girl-scout or something?" Claire was annoyed. Evie was right. Again. Out in this dry heat they would be lucky to make it to nightfall without shelter. She took off her long coat and draped it over her arm. "Come on, then."

Evie shrugged and set off in the general direction of whatever was looming on the horizon. Claire glared at her back for a moment, then trudged after her.

Though she tried to convince herself to deal with it all later, sharp claws of fear were soon squeezing Claire's heart, and at the same time waves of self-loathing swept through her thoughts as her brain insisted on rubbing her nose in what a bitch she had been. Despair shrouded her, as stifling as the air around them and just as difficult to live with. The hills, or mountains, or whatever they were, looked not an inch closer and Claire was sweating hard. She glanced down at her watch, then realised she had no idea what time they had set out. She looked at her watch again and groaned. The second-hand wasn't moving. She shook her wrist, then rapped at the glass with a fingernail, then a knuckle. The hands remained obdurate, motionless.

"Hey, my watch is bust."

"So sad."

"Well, what's the time?"

"No idea. Mine's bust too."

Evie's infuriatingly casual response meant she had found out some while ago, and Claire couldn't fathom why she hadn't mentioned it. This horrible place, or the act of getting here, was messing with that as well as denying her magic. Claire gritted her teeth. "We must have been walking for hours."

"About thirty minutes."

"What?"

"You aren't counting?" Evie made it sound like Claire had forgotten something obvious.

"What?" she snapped back. "Mile markers? Lamp posts?"

"Steps. Three steps is about two seconds. Well, that's my guess anyway. 2700...2701...2702"

"Will you stop that."

Evie kept walking. "Nope."

Claire took a few fast steps to catch up. "How do you know all this rubbish?"

Evie stopped, frowning. "Survival programs. Look, I can't chat and count. We've come about two kilometres. If those are hills, I'm guessing they could be about 10 klicks off. If they're mountains, it could be forty, or even sixty. The air here is so dry it's going to pull moisture out of every bit of you that's even vaguely damp, so shut your mouth, put on your coat, and walk."

Claire put on her long duster, wincing as it scraped over arms already tender from the relentless sun. Evie had to be wrong. This would make her hotter. She set her jaw and stomped after her friend.

She didn't want to count. Counting was contagious, addictive. It was like an earworm, a song you couldn't get out of your head. But then, what was the alternative? Marching along through a featureless landscape, sweltering and airless, not a thing to distract her from the thoughts already circulating around in her head. If the alternative was seeing Tolks die again, or reliving the argument with Nana May, then maybe she should just blank it all out with mindless numbers. One...two...three...

...five thousand four...five thousand five... Claire stopped counting. That had to be about an hour, didn't it? More, if she added on the steps they had already taken before their last words. She looked again at Evie's shadow, then up at the sun. When they arrived the sun was mid-morning high, or late afternoon low. How come it hadn't moved?

"Are we getting anywhere?"

Evie stopped. Claire saw her shoulders lift in a silent sigh. "I told you; it's going to take time to get there."

"Time might be the problem."

"You've been out in the sun too long."

"Exactly."

Evie glowered at her over her shoulder. Claire pointed at the sun. Evie's gaze followed her finger, then her eyes widened for a moment. "Could be the days are longer here?" She didn't sound convinced.

"Are we any closer to those hills?" Claire asked. Evie held up her thumb and squinted at it. "Should have done this an hour ago," she admitted. "Grab the biggest stones you can lift and stack them in a tower. We need references. Everything is the same out here."

They built a pile of rocks. Clair fumed at the delay, and at the heat, and at the stones making tiny cuts on her hands. She dreaded starting the walk again, but at least then she could focus her mind on counting the steps. It was barely enough to keep her thoughts away from replaying all the stuff she had messed up. Evie took one last look at the cairn, slapped her on the shoulder, and set off again.

Claire kept her head down, looking at the floor. For one thing, it cut down on the glare from the odd sun. Better still, it stopped her constantly looking at the hills in front of them, trying to figure out if they looked any different. Only when Evie called a halt an hour later did she look up, then over her shoulder.

The cairn was out of sight. In front of them, things looked closer, and she held her breath, waiting for Evie's pronouncement. Were they making progress, or was some sick trick making them think they were walking?

"The hills are closer."

Claire breathed a short-lived sign of relief.

"But the sun is wrong," Evie added.

"How can the sun be wrong?" Clare regretted the bitchy tone as soon as the words left her mouth, especially as she had pointed it out first, but she couldn't call them back.

"Does that look like any sun you've ever seen? Anyway, its moved."

"It's supposed to."

"True, but it's not supposed to get bigger."

"What?"

"When I measured its width my thumb covered it. Now it comes past either side of my thumb. It's bigger." Evie frowned. "Or its closer."

They kept walking.

39

The jagged hills were a hundred feet tall, and curved away on either side of them. There was a fluidity to the walls, a glutinous upwards ripple that eventually tore into a serrated ridge at the top.

Claire shivered, partly because the air was much cooler now they were in shade, but also because the wall loomed over them, leaning outwards.

"Well we aren't getting over that," said Evie, turning away from the rippled face. "No way we can climb up an overhang."

"Left or right?"

Evie dug into a pocket and pulled out a poker chip. "Happy left, sad right". She flipped the chip into the air, caught it, and slapped it flat on the back of her hand. When she uncovered it, a smiley beamed up at them. "Left it is then."

It didn't take long for Claire's muscles to escalate their discontent to an aching grumble. She had become used to the furnace out on the plain, but now the relative chill of the shade was soaking into her, stiffening her legs and back. She pulled her duster closed around her, but it didn't help much.

As if the muscle aches had weakened her resolve, hunger began to gnaw in her gut and her tongue worked uselessly to moisten her parched mouth. She went back to counting steps, anything to divert herself from the increasing discomfort, but never made it beyond two thousand.

"Can we rest?"

Evie grimaced. "Not a good idea. Not much point either. Without food or water, we won't recover much."

Claire wanted to slap her, mainly for being right. She grunted and marched on.

She kept losing count. Even how far the shadow spread from

the wall never changed. Her world descended back into trudgery, one foot in front of the other, trying to ignore the pains in her belly, throat and mouth, and the blisters growing on her feet. When Evie thumped her on the arm, she carried on for several paces before she registered that Evie had been trying to talk to her. She half turned to look over her shoulder. Evie's lips were dry and cracked, but her eyes were bright.

"What?"

Evie pointed ahead of them. Claire turned forward again. Her eyes had been firmly on the floor, watching for small rocks that would turn her ankle. She peered. "What? I don't see anything."

"Look at the shadow. There's a notch, a bright spot where there shouldn't be."

"So?"

"The wall must have collapsed. It could be a way in."

"To what?"

Evie ignored her. Claire thought it was a question they should be asking themselves before they got much closer. Also, Evie's choice of words had sounded odd; why not "over" or 'through". She was already the better part of a hundred feet away and showed no signs of slowing or turning back. Claire set off, trying to jog but settling for a purposeful stride.

By the time Claire caught up, Evie had stopped at the side of a slope of loose rocks and rubble, and was edging from side to side peering up.

"What are we doing?" Claire asked.

"Waiting for you mainly, but looking for a safe way up too."

"Can't we scramble up like we were at the seaside?"

Evie withered her with a glance, then pointed. "Those boulders are too big. If we kick away too much shale, we could set off an avalanche."

Claire looked across the rockfall, but it all looked much the same to her. "So do we go on? See if there is another way in?"

Evie bit the side of her mouth and didn't answer directly. When she did, the first word drawled out. "No, this is too good a chance to pass up."

"Chance for what?"

"To see what's inside."

"Inside where? And what do you mean inside?" She had the grace to blush when Evie glared at her.

"This is the only thing we've seen bigger than a pebble since we got here, and a small sun is hanging over it. You really want to go past without looking?"

And Claire realised a part of her did. While she didn't know, while all around was nothing more than barren rock, there was nothing she could do. Nothing she had to do. No decisions she had to make. Nobody she had to hurt.

She was comfortable the way things were. She was even comfortable with Evie taking charge; it was like when they had first met, when she had been Evie's student. It took her back to letting someone else make the decisions, and make the mistakes. If Evie was making the choices, then nothing else could be her fault.

She noticed Evie was still looking at her, and offered a shrug. The lip-twisted scowl Evie shot back stung, then she turned away and climbed up between the edge of the rockfall and the jagged rim.

Evie picked her way up the edge of the shale, a steadying hand on the outward-leaning wall. Claire moved closer, but didn't start to climb. Dust and gravel rattled down the slope with every step Evie took, and it would be a bad idea to add her own disturbance to the mix.

As if her simple proximity had been a cue, a flurry of gravel slid out from under Evie's boots and she slid back ten feet, arms first flailing for balance, then content to simply keep her face out of the dirt. By the time she stopped, her DM's had sunk almost to the top lacing in the scree, and another avalanche ensued as she tried to dig herself out. Without another word, Evie slid to the bottom of the slope and walked around it.

Following a few steps behind, she wondered if she had gone too far. Evie was a good friend, but she had never been tolerant of anybody she thought wasn't worthy. Claire she had found suitable, after her almost accidental rescue, but Claire had never been sure she had been due the accolade. She certainly wasn't at that moment. She was sure Evie wouldn't throw her to the wolves, or whatever passed for the local apex predator, but her friend was losing interest — not in getting out, but in her. She scrambled along, trying to catch up in more ways than one.

The other side of the landslide was more jagged, boulders rather than scree. Evie scrambled up without conversation, and this time Claire followed, also without comment, ten feet behind.

It was easier than she thought it would be. The occasional rock wobbled, and there was a spray of dust every now and then as Evie scuffed above her. She watched where Evie put her feet, where she gripped with her hands, and tried to do the same to make use of the safe holds.

She stepped up onto a shallow ledge. Evie had stood here, then left foot to that ledge there and... Claire was shorter than Evie, or at least her legs were. To get her left foot up to the same point Evie had used, she had to push off with her right. A sort of one-legged bunny hop.

And that, of course, was the point where the ledge decided to give way. Before her left foot found the next ledge, her right foot was slipping away. Claire clawed her hands onto their holds and braced herself. Her body slammed into the rock with a breath-stealing thud. The hold under her right hand was not sound, and she scrabbled for somewhere safe to put her feet. As her right hand slipped free of its hold her right toe landed on something solid.

Grabbing the handhold again, Claire found somewhere safe for her other foot then leant against the warm rock and waited for her heart to stop hammering.

"Three points of contact." Evie spoke quietly, but clearly, and there was no edge to the words.

"Thanks," Claire muttered, sourly, and she heard a soft chuckle.

Her hands cramped and her leg muscles trembled. She had stopped looking to see how far ahead Evie was and was plodding upwards, picking her own path now.

Evie's foot appeared in front of her, startling her and making her miss a foothold. She looked up, and saw a hand making motions for her to stop and wait. They were a few yards from the top.

With waved gestures, Claire got the idea Evie wanted her to stay put. She raised her thumb, but thought it more than a little unfair to be left behind. Evie eased closer to the lip. The last boulder at the top was a slab. Evie pushed her weight against it first, then reached up to the top edge and pulled herself higher.

Claire distinctly heard a low "Wow" before the slab tilted forwards and slid over the edge.

40

Evie didn't scream. At least, Claire never heard her over the crash and rumble of the slab. She scrabbled up the last ten feet, hands and feet slipping in careless haste as she hauled herself to the edge and peered over. All she could see was a cloud of red dust, obscuring everything before and below her. The rumble went on and on, getting farther away but for a long time no less terrible.

There was no breeze to blow away the dust cloud, nor was there any point in calling out, now while the sound of the falling slab still rumbled like thunder. It seemed to go on for hours, but finally the grinding ceased.

Biting her bottom lip, Clare forced herself not to call out to Evie. If there was anybody, or anything, in this terrible place, her friend had sent up a huge flare announcing their presence. Landslides happened all the time, a least they did at home. If she screamed. If she did anything that made it anything other than a natural event, she might let others know she was there.

She ducked down behind the lip of the boulder she had been peering over and found somewhere she could rest without clinging on like a spider. It would take time for the dust cloud to settle, and there was no point tiring herself. She closed her eyes and counted heartbeats again.

Six hundred should have been ten minutes, but the way her pulse was hammering she admitted it was no more than eight, or even seven. Still, it was as long as she could go without looking again. She twisted round and raised her eyes over the edge of the boulder. The dust was settling quicker than she had expected, thinning visibly as she peered below.

She couldn't see as far as Evie, but she could see the rock wall beneath her and to either side. It looked like liquid mud that had splashed upwards and outwards, then frozen before it could fall back to the ground. She could also see the long scar Evie's slab had left; straight down and with a few gaps as it bounced away from the wall. There was no second track. Evie was either on the stone or under it, or was too soft to make any mark in the surface - which led to the terrible thought of what the surface might have done to her.

The rock she was leaning on shifted as she leant forward to get a better look and Claire eased her weight away from the edge. What worse epitaph for a Stone than to be killed by one. Her eyes lifted, and a shape began to form beyond the haze. She drew breath to blow the dust away, then rolled her eyes at what a stupid idea that was. In time, like a falling curtain of mist, the last of the dust floated downwards and the air cleared.

"Wow."

Her voice was no louder than Evie's had been, but now she understood how her fried had been so critically distracted. She was standing, figuratively, at the lip of a huge crater, and how far it stretched from side to side she couldn't even guess. That alone was sufficiently worthy of a "wow".

Added wow-ness faded in slowly, as artistic as a movie shot, revealing a bulk at the centre of the crater. At first no more than a shadow, the top of a tall finger of rock came into view. Directly above it hung the leprous sun. Claire could make a structure on or in its tip, then a thread winding up the outside of the pillar. Below that, a castle, and below that a citadel, all brooding red and black, with tiny pinpricks of windows, but no sign of lights. A third of the way farther round the curve was another notch in the crater wall, this one looking square and constructed, and a road of sorts ran from the citadel towards it, snaking up the rim in a series of switchbacks. No pennants or flags flew from the towers or walls, nor was there any breeze to make them flutter. The structure looked deserted.

Claire peered downwards over the lip again. There was still only one track scraped down the wall. The quickest way down, the quickest way to help Evie, would be for her to drop over the edge herself and slide down the wall. It sloped out gradually, and would catch her and slow her - a bit like the first drop of a roller coaster.

With a sigh and a frown she realised it wouldn't work. Her duster coat was strong, but the rock would chew through it, and then her clothes and then her. Also, if she bounced away from the wall or, worse, tumbled, it would break every bone in her arms and legs. She had no options; she had to make her way around to the road.

She had taken a few steps down — far more difficult than climbing up — when a bang echoed past her. Not the sound of rock on rock, or on the hard-packed earth. It sounded intentional, artificial. She hesitated. Had it been a gun? Was she about to hear the whoosh of a shell passing overhead, or just the explosion as it blew out more of the wall behind her? Was that what had caused this breech in the first place? She froze, clenching herself against the half-expected explosion, but nothing happened.

Cautiously unscrewing herself, Claire lifted her head cautiously over the top of the rock pile and looked down into the crater again. A plume of dust hung on the air, immediately in front of the citadel. Claire squinted, raised her hand to shield her eyes from the glare of the impossible red sun, and gasped. The dust was moving. The citadel wasn't deserted, and they had sent someone out to investigate the rockfall.

She scrambled down her pile of rubble a few seconds later, her lips pressed thinly together and her jaw clenched. She wanted to watch, to see if they found Evie and what they did, but she guessed it would take them more than an hour to get to the place the slab had come to rest. Whether they found Evie or not, whether she was alive or not, Claire still had to get down there. The only way she knew was to slog around the rim until she got to the road — and wasting hours watching a dust cloud wasn't going to help on that score.

Evie was gone, at least for the moment. There was nobody else to make the decisions. As she climbed down to the ground, Claire pushed aside the horrors of the past week. Once again, it was up to her.

Time had become meaningless. Claire had deliberately not counted heartbeats or steps. Her brain had tried to, but she had sung to herself, tried to remember entire books, anything to stop herself descending into a counting fugue. She knew if she did, she would start to worry, to panic. Whatever progress she was making would never be enough. She had set a steady, sustainable pace she could keep up for hours. If she went any faster, she would tire herself out and make things worse.

Not that things were that good. Even in the shadow of the rim wall, the air was still uncomfortably warm. Her tongue split and her lips cracked, and being hungry had evolved into a steady state pain in her gut. She couldn't ignore it, but the meditation skills she had picked up from Tolks helped her accept it and not let it control her. She flinched away from the thought of her teacher — and once friend — and nailed the lid firmly back down on all her emotions. Like it or not, she had to go back to what she had been when the white magic was controlling her; dispassionate and focused. She plodded on.

Despair welled up in her when she finally saw the break in the shadow. The soles of her feet stung like she was walking over toy plastic bricks and her tongue filling her mouth. Spit was a distant memory — and yet she still had to make it down from the rim to the crater floor, then across to the citadel. At a rough guess, she still had as far to go as she had already walked, and this time in the full glare of the sun.

She leant against the rock wall before she reached the gap, huddling in the last shade she would see for a while, then slid down until she was sitting. Another scuff and her feet sprawled out in front of her. She groaned and pushed her hands against the wall. She had to get up. If she didn't, what little strength was still in her would leak away.

It was too late. Her arms couldn't move her up by so much as an inch, and when she tried to pull her legs in to push herself up the wall, they refused to co-operate. Her shoulders slumped and her head fell softly to rock wall. Against her will, her eyes closed, and consciousness deserted her.

Claire didn't know if she had napped for five minutes or five hours. She didn't feel rested, but then her body had nothing it could use to repair her. She tried to open her eyes, but one was stuck firmly shut with dried rheum, concreted with dust from the air. She picked at it with a fingernail.

Leaning heavily against the wall she pulled her feet under her and levered herself upright. The pain teetered on the precipice of impossible, and she ground her teeth together. Every muscle protested, but the worst were her feet. They burned, like hot coals and acid. Her mind conjured up visions of blood and blisters, of split raw skin rubbing against the insides of her boots. She pushed the image back, feeling herself about to fall over the edge of the pain and onto to her knees.

Hand still on the wall, Claire shuffled to the gap in the crater wall. As she got closer she could see that the road was no more than a path cleared of gravel and small stones. There was no tarmac, or drainage, just a smoother space. At the edge of the gap she poked her head around the wall and looked out over the crater floor. A groan ripped through her throat. Miles and miles stretched out before her. She wanted to cry, but there was no moisture left in her to use. It would take her days to get there, if she could make it at all.

She sank to her knees. Had she made a terrible mistake? If she had stayed where Evie had fallen, she could have made more noise, or pushed over another rock. Whoever had come out to find Evie would have found her too. Even if they had been captured, it would have spared her the wasted walk to the road.

Or would it? Cursed again by her extensive imagination, an image of dragging along behind a horse at the end of a rope sprang into her mind, as did the consequences of losing her footing on this abrasive ground. She shook her head that her mind could come up with such an image in her current situation.

Now she had no choice. She had pushed herself as far as she could, but now had no way of letting anybody know she was there. She began a pocket inventory, and found a handkerchief, a non-functional mobile phone, a small charm she could not remember the purpose of, a bus ticket, and a handful of loose change. Not even a forgotten, fur-covered boiled sweet she could suck on and magically restore herself with; two teaspoons of sugar to moisten her mouth and spur her into action. She picked each up and put them away, wincing as the sun glinted off the phone's blank screen and into her eyes.

Her hand stopped, but she wasn't sure why. She turned the phone in her hand, her eyes twitching again as the sun reflected into them, the burn-mark on her retina almost obliterating the flicker of light on the crater rim. She frowned, knowing she wasn't thinking clearly. A black mirror?

Why not? She turned the screen towards the sun, then angled the phone until it cast a distorted shape of light onto the wall. It wasn't blindingly bright, but there was nothing else in this forsaken landscape that had ever sparkled or shone. It had to be worth a try.

There was no shining beam of light, no bright square

illuminating the citadel - at least as far as she could see. Still, Claire scanned the phone back and forth, up and down, trying for nothing more than a spark and hoping they had lookouts watching this way. It made sense they would. Who wouldn't want to watch the only road leading to them, and someone had seen Evie's rockfall.

She kept it up until her arms burned with exhausted muscle, then let her hands fall into her lap. It hadn't worked. She pulled a face. Be positive, she thought it hadn't worked yet. She may not have hit on the exact combination of angles that caught somebody's eye. She let her arms dangle, and shook her hands to encourage blood that was moving more like cool lava refresh her muscles, then she lifted the phone and tried again.

Less than a minute later a noise reverberated around the crater, subtly different to the one she had heard before abandoning Evie, but still like a huge door slamming closed. She looked expectantly towards the crater floor, and sobbed when a small cloud of dust marked a presence on the road, and heading towards her.

It meant an end, of one kind or another. Either whoever was coming towards her were saviours, or they were her executioners. But the pain would stop, and the responsibilities would be at an end. She would have done all that she could, and if that struggle ended here too, then so be it.

41

The wait was surprisingly short. First, four dots resolved out of the chaos of the cloud. A while later Claire thought they looked like horses, and a while after that, more like huge dogs or lions. Fear tried to sink its talons into her, but there was nothing left for it to grip. She had nowhere to hide, and no way to run. Even if she had brought her PPG, she doubted it would work.

When they reached the bottom of the ramp Claire could see that the shapes were indeed leonine, but with skins like lizards and crocodilian jaws. Tantalisingly familiar for a moment, her heart sank when she recognised them. She had seen them before, on the first day she had accidently fallen through into Underland. The one she met had been erect, and had possessed arms rather than forelegs, but she was in no doubt that these were Morphs. Her body sagged in final defeat, her eyes closing and her sighing outward breath seeming to never end.

A scaly appendage wrapped around her body and Claire steeled herself for some crushing contraction to squash the life from her. Instead, she felt herself lifted from the ground. It wasn't comfortable, but there was no brutality, and she opened her eyes as the tentacle unceremoniously plonked her on the back of one of the Morphs. Thick bands of flesh, if flesh they were, extruded from the creature's back and wrapped around her waist. She struggled, though with no effective strength, until she saw another extrusion in front of her, rising up between the creature's shoulders; a stick, with a bar at the top. A handle. At the same time blocks appeared under her feet. It was a saddle. Safety straps to stop her falling off. A tiny spark of hope kindled in her heart, and she struggled not to smother it with practicality as she admitted the straps were equally efficient restraints.

The beast's gait was smoother than a horse. She had tried riding once. They had pushed everybody up to a canter on the first lesson, and the potential for disaster had so disturbed Claire she had never been near a horse since. This was smoother, and lower to the ground, but she was glad she hadn't eaten. The subtle rocking back and forth was enough to encourage motion sickness - had she had anything with which to be sick.

There was also, of course, the distraction of the structure towards which they were making such good time. The closer they got the less sense it made. It wasn't that she hadn't been able to make out any windows, but that there were hollows, but no windows within. Then there were disturbing, semi-familiar features, like the seven levels of the outer citadel, and the widely-offset gates on each level. Nor could she see any sentries patrolling the battlements, or watching out from the tall towers set at intervals along the curtain wall. Yet someone had seen her signal, and sent out the Morphs to retrieve her.

In an impossibly short time the citadel wall was looming over them. The beasts showed no signs of slowing and Claire braced herself against the handle growing out of the creature's back. Directly ahead, an arc cut through the red stone of the wall, then a line split the shape in half. Two great doors opened outwards towards them moments before they would have crashed into the wall, and in an instant Claire transitioned from blinding heat to chill dark,

Shivering, she squeezed her eyes shut and willed them to adapt to the lower light level. The doors boomed closed behind her and Claire knew she ought to wonder why it had become so dark before the doors had closed. She opened her eyes but there was still nothing to see, not even the scales of the beast beneath her.

Her heart was in her mouth, her lungs apparently unable to find air to breathe. She trembled, partly from cold, partly from fear. Possibly, she finally considered, even a little from heatstroke.

243

The beast swung confidently left and right, showing no signs of slowing. Claire's hands grasped the handle as though her life depended on it, right up to the moment it dwindled away to nothing between her fingers and the harness around her waist fell away. A moment of nauseating deceleration, an uncomfortable slide down the beast's neck and over its head, and she hit the floor.

Claire tucked herself into a ball, hands locked across the back of her head and rolled. She tumbled sideways, forcing out a muffled cry as what air she had was knocked from her lungs. There was a scuffle-shuffle of feet, receding rapidly into the distance, but no sound of a closing door.

At least they weren't going to eat her. At least, not there and then. Every savage lair she had read about or seen in a movie sprang into her imagination, with half-eaten corpses and monsters waiting to pounce on a misplaced hand.

She pushed the nightmare aside and forced herself to sit up. Her hands found nothing but rough, dusty floor, and she conceded that no matter how much she ached, nothing was broken. Everything reported various levels of abuse, however, and her left leg and left hip warned that they would be paying her back for landing on them in due course.

Her feet were a different matter. They still burned despite their respite during the ride. Taking her shoes and socks off would let the air get to them and cool them, but she was afraid she would never get her boots back on. She ground her teeth together and tried to meditate the pain away

The scene flicked into life as if a switch had been thrown. Claire blinked. Her eyes didn't hurt, needed no time to adjust to the light, and yet nothing looked dim or indistinct.

The first thing she saw was Evie, strapped to a board tilted up about forty-five degrees. It looked deliberate, done to be sure she could see it was Evie and that she was helpless, or to make clear how badly she was hurt. Her eyes were closed. One puffed up in a purple bruise, and there was a deep cut across her right cheek. It might have been the way she was lying, but Claire thought Evie's left arm twisted too far, like it might be broken. Blood soaked the left leg of her camo pants from the knee down.

Behind Evie was Stuart, his wrists were chained to the wall above his head. At least he was standing on his own, but he looked furious and there were bruises down each side of his body.

At first Claire thought they had put tape over his mouth. She looked again, and her stomach heaved. It wasn't tape. Stuart had no mouth. Some foul magic had remade his face. She could see his jaw working, stretching and twisting the skin over where his lips should be. She turned her head to the side and puked a thin stream of dark vomit.

She lurched to her feet, ready to run to her friends, but staggered to a halt after a single step. What she had taken to be a change in the colour of the floor, in a circle around her, wasn't that at all. It was an absence of floor; a moat twenty feet wide. Much farther than she could jump, anyway. Her platform was ten feet from side to side. Claire eased cautiously closer to the edge and looked over. It wasn't a bottomless pit, but the floor was more than a hundred feet down and covered in sharp spikes.

So how had she got here? The Morph-beast hadn't jumped anything; she was sure she would have felt it. Nor was there any explanation what she had crashed into, nor why they would have taken so much effort to capture her only to put her in a position where she could have rolled over in her sleep and killed herself.

A presence behind her made her break off musing, coming into being as abruptly as the rest of the tableau. She wanted to turn so much it was a compulsion, but an equally opposite dread held her in place. As though an invisible hand had taken her shoulder, Claire twisted at her waist.

It sat on a throne carved from the ubiquitous red stone, leaning forward. Its elbows rested on its knees. One hand dangled, fingers twitching. The other stroked at the creature's chin as it stared with black, emotionless eyes. Claire flinched back. It was the Demon Lord who had come so close to killing her and her friends in Aslnaff's office, and she had nothing. No power, no weapons, no hope.

She turned fully to face the monster, and looked again. There were differences. It was wearing different clothes, richer somehow, and more ornate. It was, if anything, bigger than the one she had fought, and its reptilian face was subtly different. The muzzle was longer, thinner, and the ridges around the eyes less pronounced.

Perhaps she wasn't about to die. At least, not yet. She drew herself to her full height, squared her shoulders, and drew a breath.

"My name is—"

"You are Warrior Claire Stone." Its voice boomed around the room. Claire's mind threw up a memory of the Great and Powerful Oz, and a spark of life and defiance kindled in her heart.

"Yes, I am, and we have business to settle."

The creature let out a series of grunts, and it took Claire a moment to realise it was chuckling. "Indeed?"

"Yes." Claire faltered. She had no power, and her voice sounded so puny against the basso rumblings of the Morph Lord. "You have hurt my parents, taken their minds and their will from them. You must release them. And my friends."

The Morph Lord sat back in its throne, elbows on the arm rests, fingers steepled before it. Its eyes never left Claire. After a few seconds, the intensity of the scrutiny overwhelmed her and she looked away, hating herself for doing it. In Underland, it had been different. Here was the creature's own domain. Here it was very much in charge — and right now she had nothing to fight him with.

The chamber was dimensionless, the light sourceless, which was worse. There had to be walls somewhere, and not too far off judging by the echoes, and her eyes ached from trying to see them. Instead, she focused on the throne, set on a dais at least ten feet high. Eventually, there was nowhere else to look but the beast, or to watch the torment of her friends. It was as if it had been waiting for exactly that and, as soon as her attention returned, it spoke.

"I have no knowledge of what you speak."

The bottom fell out of Claire's world. She didn't for a moment think the beast might be lying. She knew, without knowing how, it had spoken the truth.

"Then who...?"

"We are many," it shrugged. "The point is not relevant."

Not relevant. Claire wanted to scream into the monster's face, to strike out at it. Had she been close enough, she would have flown at the beast with her fists; scratching, clawing, biting, and kicking. All she could do was clench her fists and wait to see what the next move would be.

"Where is the *Krezik Chet Knar?*"

Not unexpected. Claire lifted her chin. "Not here."

"Do not toy with me, human child. Your companions are weak, damaged. Give me the *Krezik Chet Knar*, or we will damage them further."

The threat was clumsy. Claire bit back on and instinctive shout of "No". There was something unexpected here.

"Why?"

"We want the *Krezik Chet Knar*. You will give it to us, or your friends will suffer."

"Why do you want it? Why do you hate humans so much?"

"Where is the *Krezik Chet Knar?* We know it is not about your person. We searched you. Where have you hidden it?"

Two lizard-soldiers appeared, one beside Evie, the other next to Stu. Claire blinked and stared. They hadn't been there a moment ago, and there were no shadows or walls they could have been hiding behind. One held a stick indistinguishable from a policeman's truncheon and the other a narrow-pointed javelin. Claire trembled. The weapons weren't to kill, they were to inflict pain, over and again.

"Why do you want the *Krezik Chet Knar?*" It was the only thing she could think of to delay the inevitable. "What can it do for you?"

The Morph Lord stared at her, eyes emotionless but head cocked to one side the barest amount. "We starve. The furnace is dying, and so are we."

"Who?"

"All."

Claire glanced at the soldiers. They weren't even looking at the Lord, just standing, weapon raised, attention focused on the exact point the blow would fall. They weren't even looking to him for permissions to strike.

As if her thought had been the cue, both struck; Stuart took a jab to the gut and Evie a spear-point deep in her thigh. Stuart grunted, but Evie screamed, and Claire screamed with her.

"No! Why would you do that?"

"Give us the *Krezik Chet Knar*. Then it stops."

"But why us?"

"You did it. You starve us."

Claire, on the edge of tears, felt her mental train switch tracks. They had? Which they? And how?

"How? I mean, what did we do? Or whoever did it. We're children. It can't have been us."

"But you hold the *Krezik Chet Knar*. You are tainted with the food from between the worlds." The beast shifted on its seat. "Enough talk."

Evie screamed again, and kept on screaming as her torturer first embedded the point of its spear into her arm, then twisted it

248

around. She watched the other soldier whack the truncheon into Stuart's rib's, and realised that the beatings she had received in the past were no more than a slap compared to this.

"Stop, please," she screamed again, but this time the Morph Lord said nothing, staring at her with emotionless, black eyes.

Claire's head exploded with each scream. She took half-steps in random directions, her hands clenching in front of her, then pounding her thighs, then her head as she tried to think of anything she could do. It was impossible. The sounds of the baton, the distinct crack as a rib snapped, the fresh screams as the soldier stuck his spear into a new part of Evie's body. All these things drove her wits from her. She had nothing; no local field, no *Krezik Chet Knar* to bargain with, not even access to the damned white magic that had brought her to this terrible point in time.

Her flailing hands thumped into her chest, just below her chin, and sharp point dug into her skin, hard enough to distract her from her whirlpool of hopelessness. She touched the spot again, and her eyes opened wide. She drew herself up to her full height and turned to face the Morph Lord.

"Stop!"

42

Her voice surprised even her. Not loud, but hard, implacable, and not to be ignored. The Morph Lord sat back in its throne and the two soldiers hesitated. Claire tuned out Evie's sobbing. She had control now. She reached inside her tee-shirt and lifted out the crystal Ostrenalia had given her. She had no idea how it could be here when she had lost everything else. Perhaps because the magic within was quiescent, unusable. Almost unusable.

"This is a storage crystal. It contains conventional and interstitial magic, super concentrated. Hundreds of times more powerful than a conventional magic-bomb. Send your soldiers away or I shall detonate it."

The Lord touched a hand to its chin. "You would not."

"What you are doing to my friends will kill them. I kill them without the pain and horror you would inflict on them, and deny you."

"You would also die."

"You have already taken my life from me. You have taken my mother and father from me. My good friend was taken from me, though not by you. I have no way to get home. What else do I have to lose?"

"I see no benefit to me."

Claire knew she hadn't kept the surprise off her face. Surely if she released so much magic he would have to be killed.

"You live?" Her words came out weak, and she knew she was losing control of the situation.

"We each die regardless."

"Why?"

"Stupid child. You force your way to this realm, yet you have no understanding of where you are. You think you see, but you perceive only what your mind creates to explain that which it doesn't understand. Tell me what you see."

Claire blinked, looking for the trap but seeing none — at least not yet. "A throne room. A pit to keep me standing here. You and your throne. Two soldiers with weapons hurting my friends."

"And before?"

"Outside? Bleak, barren. A castle, with a sun hanging over it, buried in a crater."

"Interesting." The Morph Lord appeared genuine. "The primitive mind is more creative than we would give credit. Everything bar what you term the 'sun" is unimportant, ephemeral, unreal. The 'sun' is our life source. Even your limited senses can perceive it is decrepit, failing. Since you sealed our boundary we have hoarded and husbanded what little remained. Now it is all but exhausted. We risked much of what was left to tunnel into the next realm, but their magic is of no use to us. The only strength we can draw into our world is from the realm beyond that. Your realm. It is fitting, no? That we survive on the crumbs from your table."

Claire didn't understand much of what the Morph Lord was saying, but she understood enough to realise they were talking about the possessions, and the red rain she saw falling through Underland.

"But you're stealing from us. You are hurting people, making them unhappy, stealing tears from their souls. You have no right."

"We have the right to survive, and if that means we take some minute measure back from our enemies, I see no injustice. Do we not have the right to live?"

Not at the expense of others.

The words stuck in her throat and Claire realised she had talked herself into a corner. The Morphs would not let her go. Even if she had brought the *Krezik Chet Knar* with her, they wouldn't do anything that might threaten their fragile world. She felt a bitter

251

sympathy for them, and a kinship. Was she any better? Wasn't she throwing her weight around in exactly the same way, trying to save her parents?

She knelt down. Stuart struggled hugely against the manacles holding him, muffled anguish mumbling past the ruin of his face. Claire had wondered if he had been able to see her, but he had been ignoring her, trying to distance them from each other's pain. Evie looked out of it, head lolling to one side, drool tricking down from her gaping mouth. At least she wasn't suffering any more.

At least none of them would be suffering any more.

One way or another.

Claire look the pendant and dangled it from her hand by the chain, looking at it. Weighing it.

The Morph Lord, voice concerned, leaned forward in his chair. "What are you—?"

Claire whipped the crystal around at the end of its chain and smashed it into the floor.

43

Magic exploded around her. Her skin burned away in an instant. Her lungs seared into ash as she drew a final breath, and her eyes boiled as she closed them one last time. She prepared herself for death.

She hoped it would be as quick for Evie, and for Stuart. She even hoped that the Morphs didn't suffer - at least not too long. Maybe a little bit. They deserved that.

She wondered if destroying the Morphs, at least the ones here, would release her parents. She hoped so, even though they would be sad that she had gone missing. How was Nana May going to explain that? She wished she could be there to hear that.

And then she finally got around to wondering why she was still wondering.

She opened her eyes, though they weren't eyes, and looked, though she couldn't see. Nothing made sense. Not true; she could see the billowing cloud that was the now slowly expanding explosion of white magic, riddled through with cooler spots where the conventional magic mingled in like chocolate syrup over ice cream.

She could, in a way, see herself, as a zephyr, whirling amongst the undefinable symbols and thoughts that reality had become. To her left, two more vortices marked the locations of Stuart and Evie. They weren't there at all. The minds were, or their souls, but they were not present in the flesh. Beside them were geometric shapes, simple constructs that had fulfilled the function of the soldier Morphs.

Hands that weren't there flexed, rubbing the concepts of thumbs against the notions of fingertips. Claire tested her control of the magic before her, borrowed a little, and used it to erect protections around her friends until she was sure what she was doing and knew what to do.

Everything had been a fiction. Unreal. Her mind, torn from what it understood, had struggled to make sense of the place into which it had been flung; "Beneath" had translated to Hell, and the citadel — not that she could think clearly about it — had been a composite, with parts borrowed from the White City or Gondor, Oz, Metropolis, and a dozen other films and books. Even the spear-lined pit had been a cliché from her own memories.

"Now you understand." The observation came from a shadow, some distance from her, on the other side of the explosion. The surface rippled in fractal confusion, looking chaotic, yet hinting at an order so complex it was beyond her.

"Some," she answered. "All this is in my head?"

There was no distinct answer, but a general sense of approval.

"You have made a decision. A commitment." Again, observations, not questions. Claire realised it was right.

"Yes."

"And you have accepted you cannot return."

Was it right again? Was she to die here? Or, at least, never leave this place? Rejection exploded in her as bright and as energetic as the magic in front of her, and that same magic wavered, its edges jittering, flexing. She reached out, through the barrier and out into the spaces between the realms. Her thoughts flew, but unbreakable bonds tethered her to this Beneath, to this event. She could not leave.

Well, what might be so for her would certainly not be the fate of her friends. She wrapped them in power, and gave it purpose — to leave this place, to find their bodies, and to re-join them. She sent them on their way. They would be safe now.

"You must release my parents too," she said to the Chaos. The surface shifted, scrolling and twisting around itself, and she faintly heard the massed minds of the host arguing, some for her, some saying she could not be trusted. An idea was born in her mind and, though still a babe, it showed her another truth. "I can take them if I must, but it will weaken us both."

Two pustules opened in the skin of chaos and each exuded another vortex of energy. They were deeply passive, almost inert, but they were whole and unharmed. As she had done for Evie and Stu, Claire wrapped each of her parents in a protective shell, filled with strength, suffused with all of her love, and sent them on their way. The Chaos squirmed. Voices within argued.

"She lies."

"It will deplete us."

"Restoration."

"Take what we want."

The surface settled, the voice of the Morph Lord again dominating.

"Your word?"

Claire nodded. She understood now. Beneath was not a place, not in the sense of there being anywhere to stand. It was energy, thought. Pure existence without substance. As, now, was she.

"I understand. Show me."

Voices rippled across the Chaos again.

"She will destroy us."

"Drain us"

"Deception."

"Death."

"Insufficient."

"Take it all."

"Destroy her."

"Will it suffice?"

"Show me," Claire repeated.

The Chaos parted. There was no distance, no dimension, but the dying heart of Beneath was gradually revealed to her. It was desperately weak, even more so than the leprous sun had made it look.

It wasn't just weak. It was diseased. The sustenance they had fed it, the tears from the souls of all the humans they had infected, had poisoned it even as they had kept it alive. She reached out to it, but drew back as parts of the Chaos darted to intercept her. It was, she decided, like a cat that wanted its belly rubbed, but couldn't overcome its nature to scratch. She waited for it to calm, then reached out again, feeling the heart of fire with her soul.

"What I have will suffice," she said. "But this must be the end. The souls you have stolen must return, and you must cease treating me and mine as food."

The Chaos moved back still further — angry, muttering, but in agreement. Claire turned her attention to the still exploding magical energy. She had to enfold it, control it, for the hour or microsecond it would take to do what needed to be done. Like never before, she needed to be the white magic.

She hesitated a moment longer, waiting to be sure she had control, easing the raw energy closer to the heart. As they touched, the white magic pulled back, refusing to touch the mottled surface, rejecting it.

Claire stopped, thinking. How was she supposed to merge the two energies? How could she bridge the gap between two such enemies? Then she realised she knew. She simply hadn't wanted to think about it.

She thinned herself, spreading outwards and inwards, soaking into the unwholesome cinder of the heart and the burning light of the white magic. She took one more moment, one more taste of her best memories, then she contracted, drawing everything into her soul, crushing it together until everything fused.

And Claire Stone dissolved upon the wave of light, and in her last thought she knew joy and tranquillity as the new heart spread its message of peace and its live-giving force through the new realm.

Epilogue

The chirping of a phone finally irritated Evie Jones enough that it was worse than being unconscious. She was lying face down across the airless remains of Claire Stone's bed, head thumping like the worst migraine ever. Each movement sent jagged spears of light across her eyes and into her brain.

The phone trilled again. She couldn't find it. A pair of jeans were in her way, the sound coming from beneath them. Now a phone was ringing downstairs, doing nothing to improve Evie's disposition. She tried hauling at the jeans, wondering at first why they were too heavy to move before realising someone was wearing them. Claire, to be precise.

Except her eyes were open and not blinking.

And her pupils were fixed and so dilated her eyes looked black.

And there was a dribble of blood out of her nose and across her lips, dry and crusty at the edges, but moist and glistening in the centre.

And there was a smear of blood down the wall behind her, also half crusty and half damp, not from the back of her head, but from the side where her hair matted to her scalp.

Evie's arms and legs were hooked up wrong. They certainly weren't capable of raising her to her feet. Her lungs, though, had no such problem. Nor did her mouth.

"Call an ambulance. Now."

It wasn't that they let her ride in with Nana May. It was simply that she climbed in behind them and sat on the floor, going limp whenever anybody tried to lift her. Finally, Claire's Nan had got feisty with the paramedics and they had set off. Evie liked Claire's Nan. She felt like family should.

At the hospital they took her straight into Resus. They pushed her and the old woman outside, into a dreary "Relatives Room". It stank of vomit and disinfectant, and of vain hope and stale coffee. She sat next to Nana May, who had shrunken into herself and looked like she should also be on a bed in a cubicle.

They had been there about an hour when the door burst open. A man with wild hair and a beard, wearing a hospital gown so loose that Evie saw many things she would need therapy for later. He stopped in the open doorway, looking in with crazy eyes that recognised neither of them. Then he blinked and it was as though he had put in anti-nutter contacts. His eyes focused on Claire's Nan.

"May?" The word was a croak, like he hadn't used his voice for way too long, then he was slumped on the chair next to her, his head buried in her shoulder as he sobbed. Evie stepped back. Too much family now, and she was a third wheel. She backed away farther, through the open door and out into the hall.

"Have you seen my daughter?"

Another crazy dragged a saline pouch along the floor, blood dripping from the cannula stuck into her arm. She pinned some porter against the wall with her other hand, peered into the porter's face for a moment, then abandoned him as useless. She staggering along the corridor again, while the porter went the other way, calling for security on a little radio.

Evie coughed loud enough to attract the woman's attention, and pointed into the room. The woman froze in the doorway, then Evie heard her gasp 'Mum?'.

The corridor was empty, but Evie could see the door they had trollied Claire through wasn't quite closed. She strode towards it, using the camouflage that people were less likely to challenge you if you acted like you were doing nothing wrong. She slipped through the door, and heard it clunk shut after her. There was a green button marked "Exit". Evie nodded. Always good to know your route out.

People bustled everywhere; nurse, porters, beds, wheelchairs, ringing phones, paramedics and, worst, cops. But around one curtain there was a wall of silence; no, of abandonment. There was definitely somebody in there, but nobody was bustling, as though there was no hope. Evie walked along the outside of the cubicles, giving the female PCSO a challenging raise of the eyebrows that the yellow-jacket chose to ignore.

Parting the curtain with her fingers, Evie peered in. Claire lay on the bed, bright orange blocks taped to either side of her head, a dozen ECG leads stretching off to a persistently beeping box. A cannula in the back of her hand for bloods leaked a trickle across her wrist. Another on her other arm hooked up to a saline bag. Tape held a tube in her throat and a valve in the side ticked softly as it breathed for her.

Claire's eyes were open. They stayed open, looking dull and dry. Evie stood behind Claire's head, leaned forward, and huffed moist breath. For an instant, the brief moisture made them look bright and alive again, then the faded back to death. She looked around, wanting to do more. A syringe of clear fluid rested in a cardboard kidney bowl, and looked like it might be the right thing, but Evie decided not to risk it. She leant forward again, kissed Claire's forehead, and jumped out.

Her hand reached out to the wall of Claire's temporary room. Bounce jumps into and out of Underland made her head swim, and she was out of practise. She set her feet, but kept her hand on the wall. She figured she would need the help getting back up.

It was the box. The damned box Claire had been going to smash against the wall before... She frowned. Every time she tried to remember what exactly had happened, it was slippery, like someone had been tampering with her memory again. She dropped to her knees, grabbed it, and hauled herself to her feet again.

The cube was warm. Not alive, but uncomfortably like it, and so subtle she was almost able to convince herself that she was imagining it.

A flicker of light, also on the floor, caught her eye and she saw the phone that had woken her. Seven missed calls, fifteen texts. All from Stuart. Perhaps the guy wasn't all bad. She pressed the button to redial.

"Claire? Where have you been?"

"Easy, lover boy."

"Evie?"

"Yeah. You should be sitting down for this."

She explained. The silence from the other end of the call was unnerving.

"Stu?"

There was a sigh, and a softly breathed word.

"Bugger."

"I don't feel dead."

"That's for you to decide."

"For me, or for you — whoever you are?" Claire could feel someone nearby, but the presence was indistinct, unfocused.

"You know who I am."

"I do?"

"If you think about it."

She thought.

"Are you the White Magic, cos that would be really lame if you were."

"Why?"

"Vast sentience giving me power, but doing the strong silent until it's all over. Weak."

A ghostly chuckle. "No. I am not the interstitial magic."

More thought. Suspicion, then realisation.

"Meldrin?"

"In a way. A memory of me, anyway."

"Is that all I am?"

"Isn't that all any of us are?"

"So you're a copy."

"Indeed. Or the original. It really makes no difference."

"And what does that make me?"

"You needed to go to a place and perform a task, from which it would not be possible to return."

"So I'm a copy?"

"If the copy is perfect, which is the copy and which the original?"

"It that all that fricking cube was? A memory stick for taking backups?"

Another chuckle. "Not quite. But certainly, a part of its purpose."

"I'm serious." If she had possessed a foot, she would have stamped it.

"And so am I."

"So can I go home?"

Stuart waited for her outside A&E. On the other side of the entrance an old man supped red wine from a bag-covered bottle with one hand while the other, wrapped in a bandage, held a cigarette. She led Stuart in, and played the "I belong here" game again. It was more difficult with the two of them, but the cubicle was still empty of staff — as if by design — when they returned to it. Stuart rushed to Claire's side, his hand fumbling for a way to hold hers without pulling out a drip, while another stroked at her hair. He muttered to her. His accent was impenetrable, but Evie caught a few words here and there. Enough, at least, to know that he was serious about her, at least for now.

The feeling of third wheel stole over her again. She threw

Claire a wry grin and patted her on the shoulder. "Can't help you here, kid. This you have to do on your own." Her eyes flicked towards Stuart. "Well, almost."

Muscles tensed to turn her away, but a weight in her pocket reminded her she still had that damned cube. She put her hand in the pocket. It felt warmer, buzzing against her fingers. Crazy metal was picking up her body heat or something. She took it out of her coat and stretched her arm out to put it on the table beside the bed. She stopped before it hit the metal surface. That felt wrong. Claire had spent so much time with the infernal thing that touching it might give her some comfort. She tucked it under Claire's free hand, then looked hard. Had she seen the fingers move? Clamping around the cube? Or was it a reflex clench, like a baby.

Stuart didn't notice. He wouldn't notice if she came in wearing a rah-rah skirt and playing the bagpipes. She patted Claire's arm one last time and stepped away from the bed.

Then Warrior Evie Jones jumped back into Underland.

If you enjoyed this book, and I sincerely hope that you did, I have a small favour to ask. Tiny little thing. Only take a minute or two of your time.

Please leave a review of this book on Amazon or Goodreads.

Not only do reviews feed writers — as it is always nice to know what readers think, both good and bad — but they also make an enormous difference when it comes to getting a book noticed.

Also, if you would like to sign up for my mailing list, or find out about my other books, go to www.metaphoric-media.co.uk

So, thank you in advance, and I look forward to meeting you again in another book.

Rob Harkess

UNDERLAND

Warrior Stone: Book 1

Underland is a twisted copy of our world and uses industrialised magic to power a weird mix of stolen technology and oddball inventions. It's just enough like home to make travellers overconfident – and get them into trouble.

Which is exactly what happened when Claire Stone accidentally falls through to Underland while rushing home one night.

Claire is offered a job as a Warrior, hunting down and destroying shape-shifting monsters. What adventure-hungry lover of fantasy stories could refuse? Everything seems great until a friend goes missing and the Warrior has to turn Hunter.

Visit www.metaphoric-media.co.uk for ordering information

WHITE MAGIC

Warrior Stone: Book 2

All is not well in Underland

Human Observers are being replaced by Grenlix, and humans are losing their memories.

Claire is being taught magic, which no human should be able to do. Somebody is not happy about this, and about Claire poking her nose into what's behind the missing memories

Things, nasty things, start to happen to Claire and to those around her.

Visit www.metaphoric-media.co.uk for ordering information

Aphrodite's Dawn

Garret's world is six floors tall by five hundred people wide, and when a voice in his head offers him and escape from his boring life, he has no idea how much being offered everything he could want is going to change him.

His universe is thrown into chaos when he discover he lives on an asteroid-sized sleeper-ship. The crew is missing, the computer has been damaged, and the only way they can reach their new home is if Garret takes a message to the other end of the world.

Visit www.metaphoric-media.co.uk for ordering information

Amunet

as Robert Harkess

(With Kristell Ink Books)

Amunet has a unique talent; she can talk to the dead. She has been told all her life that this is the key to rescuing her mother, who has been taken by mysterious and powerful forces. To unlock her mother's prison, all she has to do is find the Locksmith. Posing as a medium, she scours Europe for the one person who can help her.

Harry and his father are investigators, employed by the Church to hunt down mediums and hand them over to the mercies of the Inquisition. Harry has always believed he, and the Church, were doing the right thing. Until now.

Refusing to believe the Church claim that Amunet is evil, Harry risks his own life, and his relationship with his father, to free her from under the eyes of the Church. As Harry loses his heart to Amunet, she guides him on a journey to prevent a terrible evil being set loose in the world.

ISBN: 978-1-911497158 (hardback), 978-1-911497134 (paperback).
Kindle and EPUB formats available at all major online outlets.

MAVERICK

as Robert Harkess

They settled their world hundreds of years ago, turning their backs on technology, closing the Gate behind them. When their children began to develop impossible powers they rejoiced and called them Golden – until they took over. Now the Golden are feared.

Elanor comes to her powers not as a child, but as a young woman – a Maverick. The Golden are rumoured to do terrible things to Mavericks, so Elanor runs.

Anatol has travelled from the home world, decades of suspended animation, to stop the Gate malfunctioning and destroying both worlds.

He and Elanor collide, and form an uneasy truce of science and magic.

Visit www.metaphoric-media.co.uk for ordering information

A Meeting Of Minds

as Robert Harkess

Jaxon's world, our world, has been scorched by a solar flare. The Dagashi came in city-sized space ships to help, but all they do is use what is left of humanity to scavenge technology - and to get taken for 'rides' by youngsters with neural implants. Everybody thought the Dagashi could only use the interface to receive, to listen, watch, or feel - until one of them speaks to Jax.

On the other end of the link is a human girl, around his own age. Soon friends, when she tries to break off their contact because she is in danger, Jax offers to rescue her from the Dagashi ship. When he gets there, he not only discovers she is not what she led him to believe, but that the Dagashi aren't rescuers at all. Jax is torn, her betrayal ripping at his heart while he has to work with her to stop the Dagashi as they try to strip anything of value from the Earth before abandoning it.

Visit www.metaphoric-media.co.uk for ordering information

Proof

Made in the USA
Columbia, SC
18 September 2017